Steve,
Thanks for
Enjoy the b
-BK

HAJI DUTY

A SOLDIER'S PILGRIMAGE

BK Thomas

Haji Duty

ISBN 978-0-9854442-0-4

Contents

1
WELCOME TO THE STAN

High above the Afghan valley, a plane, full of eager soldiers, started its approach toward the air base below. The descent was well underway. Like a hawk circling its prey, the plane picked up speed as it rolled into a dive.

Everyone in the crammed C-17 started to prepare for the landing. They packed up their DVD players and put away their music. Craig Steele's heart beat faster with each turn the plane made in the dive to the runway.

"This is kind of crazy, huh?" Conner, a soldier from his unit, leaned back into the seat as his face went flat. He felt his chest without looking till he found the gold cross hanging from its chain. He kissed it and tucked it back in his shirt.

"Didn't know these big planes could move like this." Steele rubbed his hand down his pant leg.

The plane banked close to a ninety degree angle and jerked hard like a roller coaster. Craig's stomach pulled down and made him feel queasy. He had never experienced this sensation in a plane before.

His eyes opened wide as he looked out of the window across the aisle.

The Afghan countryside passed by like he was on a New York subway. Irrigated farms and green land near the air base made an oasis in an otherwise bleak landscape. The plane continued its steep bank and his stomach tightened.

He could have been on a ride at Six Flags, except for the Apache helicopter chained down next to him. The palletized equipment, attached to the floor, shuddered and the chains moaned as the plane maneuvered into position. The ground was getting closer and the speed of the descent made his body sink even deeper into the seat.

Mud homes flickered by outside the window. The wing was so close to the ground that he thought it would clip a roof any second. The plane leveled suddenly, surprising him.

It felt like the pilot hit the brakes as Craig lurched forward. He gripped the web seat and prepared for a hard jolt, as the C17 slammed onto the tarmac. Looks of disbelief were painted across the soldiers' faces as a collective sigh of relief went up and the plane rumbled to a stop.

The tailgate lowered and a ray of sun pierced the darkness of the fuselage. The engine whine grew louder as the tailgate opened like a doorway to a new world. The air filled with the flavor of oil and jet fumes. The soldiers were hit with a gust of hot, dry, dusty air.

Craig looked out the open bay and soaked it all in. The heat waves rising off the pavement gave the landscape a mirage like quality. Apache helicopters, like the one he sat next to on the plane, lined the tarmac. Further down in the distance were Blackhawk helicopters, gray A-10 Thunderbolts and Harrier jets. Beyond the flight line were gray wall-like barriers. Just above them, he could see the tops of tents next to ragged mud buildings. Engulfing it all was a mountain range that rose to the sky where snowcapped mountains disappeared into the clouds. He was finally there.

The heat filled the cabin and they grew restless. The moment of stillness was broken when the NCOs erupted. "Get your gear!" "Assemble outside!" "C'mon get movin!"

Craig grabbed his weapon, threw his ruck over his shoulder and made his way down the ramp. The group assembled in the grass next to the runway. They sat on their duffle bags with their rucks on their backs or in their laps. They waited for the next block of instructions.

Craig spotted a forklift lumbering toward them as he surveyed the tarmac. The airman driving the forklift wore a white t-shirt. It made him stand out against the military hardware behind him in the distance. He was yelling something, but Craig couldn't tell what it was over the engines of the C-17. A husky NCO near the plane chatted with the air crew and either didn't notice or didn't pay any attention to the approaching driver.

The forklift closed the distance and the airman continued to yell, but he was still too far away to be understood over the roar of the plane. The veins in the airman's neck bulged and his wide-eyed look caused Craig's muscles to tense. The airman continued yelling as he pulled up.

Over the roar of the engine, Craig couldn't quite make out what he was saying. Craig leaned his six foot one frame forward and strained to hear. It came in waves over the roar as the airman got closer.

"...mines."

"Get out..."

"That area hasn't been...mines! ...of there!" The airman was almost audible now.

"What? What'd he say?" Someone asked as they caught some of the words washing in.

"That area hasn't been cleared. Get out of there!" The airman's voice rose above the noise.

"Did he say mines?" Another asked confused by the idea.

"MINES?"

Craig froze in stunned silence. Adrenaline rushed through his veins. He struggled for a moment to catch his breath. His senses absorbed the scene. The grass waved back and forth in the breeze. Helicopter blades thumped slowly in the distance.

Panicked looks began to spread across the group. Heads turned and looked at the ground to check if they could see something, anything that didn't look right. One soldier made eye contact with Craig then took off in a sprint for the pavement, leaving his gear behind.

"Everyone stop!" An NCO yelled above the noise.

Fear rippled through the grass and soldiers fought their instincts to run from the danger.

"I said stop!" The NCO yelled again as he watched the lone soldier run to the tarmac.

He took charge without skipping a beat and continued, "No one move or I'll kill you myself!" He commanded. His eyes narrowed and his brow furrowed as he looked at everyone in the grass.

"I'm going to take my gear and walk to the tarmac. If you have gear on the ground, leave it there. Get everything else and follow me, single file."

Other NCOs joined in.

"Grab your bags and get them on the tarmac!"

"Move!"

Craig could see the engines turning, but he couldn't hear them anymore. The airman stood up in his forklift and stared at the scene. A make-shift single file line formed as they followed the Sergeant back to the tarmac.

The NCOs in the rear urged them on. "Nobody's dying on the runway. Get movin!"

The flight was exciting, but Craig could feel the blood pumping in his veins now. His legs shook as he shifted his bag on his shoulder and followed orders. The idea that he could set off a land mine any minute roared in his mind as he picked his steps carefully through the grass.

"What the hell were you guys doing in the grass?" The forklift driver demanded as they walked up.

"At ease airman," a gruff NCO snapped. "You think we would have been out there if we knew it wasn't cleared?"

"Maybe you fly boys should get a better handle on your area of operations." Another NCO snapped back and pointed at the airman.

"I swear with so many different air crews flying in here someone's going to get killed," the airman complained to no one in particular as he ignored the NCO's comments. He turned and pointed to the forklift. "Throw your equipment on the pallet and follow me to the gate."

"You heard the man. Get your gear on the pallet and let's get movin'," An NCO snarled. Everyone felt relieved to be back on the runway. Not five minutes in country and nervous looks of wonder spread across the group.

Another NCO grabbed the soldier that ran out of the grass, "Parade rest, Private!" The soldier snapped his arms behind his back and stared ahead. "Just what the hell do you think you were doing out there?" He continued without giving the soldier a chance to answer. "You disobey orders. You hit the panic button and out here it will get you killed! Even worse, you can get other people killed! I tell you to do something, you better do it. You understand me?"

"Yes, Sergeant." The private's voiced cracked in response.

"Now, get in formation and leave your bag in the grass."

"Yes, Sergeant." The private hung his head and made his way to the group by the pallet.

"Newbies acting like they are on a field trip, like they've never been across the pond...," the driver murmured as he climbed back on his forklift.

The group of soldiers followed him past the rows of aircraft to the edge of the tarmac. Their pallet was placed at the edge of the pavement where tire tracks crossed onto a dirt road. The road led out of the flight area past a gate and continued into the heart of the base. The soldiers grabbed their bags and equipment from the pallet as they were met by cadre from their units.

"You Steele and Conner?" A short, stocky NCO from Craig's section called to them as he met them by the pallet.

"Yes, Sergeant." Steele was relieved to find someone that knew what was going on.

SGT Ensly flashed a big smile back showing tobacco between his teeth. "About time you boys showed up. Hope your flight wasn't too rough." He let out a harsh laugh and spit tobacco juice at their feet. Steele's smile faded.

The NCO showed his teeth again. "Welcome to the Stan boys."

2
A RELIGIOUS MAN

Steele grabbed his gear from the pallet, "Glad to finally be here," he forced a laugh and looked at SGT Ensly.

"You can't be nearly as glad as I am. I've been here for two miserable months already." They followed Ensly to a Hummer parked inside the gate. Ensly's gaze drifted to the planes in the distance as he looked past them. "Every time I see one of your ugly faces, it means I'm one step closer to home." His shoulders dropped as he let out a sigh.

"Alright, load your bags into the Humvee and I'll have the guys drop them off in the tent. You boys have a mandatory welcome-to-Bagram briefing to attend, so enjoy it. In an hour, I'll be back to take you to your new home. Head on over to the tent behind you and let them give their speech. Any questions?"

"Nothing yet, Sergeant." Steele stared at all the activity around him.

"Good, get moving then and I will see you boys later."

Steele took his Kevlar off as he entered the processing tent. On his right, just past the entrance, was a table with some pamphlets. The subjects ranged from cultural topics to disease prevention and the local languages. Steele browsed through them and flipped the pages for a moment. Not really interested, he looked around the rest of the tent. It was almost empty except for the rows of folding metal chairs. Other newcomers drifted in and the chairs started to fill up. A podium stood in the front flanked by an easel that held a map of the base.

An Airman met them as they walked past the table. "We will start the briefing in a few minutes. We have one more flight we're still waiting on," he explained. "Go ahead and sign in, then take a seat."

Sweat rolled down Steele's forehead. Conner sat down beside him.

"Didn't realize it was so hot." Steele wiped his head with his sleeve.

"Speaking of hot, what did you think about that thing on the tarmac?"

"What? The mines?" Steele sat his kevlar on his knee. "That was something, wasn't it?"

"That's an understatement," Conner scoffed. "Makes you wonder though. What kind of circus is this? I mean, you'd think the air crew would let us know about the mines or something. If they didn't know it makes me wonder even more about who knows what the hell's going on out here. I was thinking, shit! I don't want to die when I just get off the plane! Man. That was intense."

Steele laughed nervously, "Yeah I know what you mean. My heart just about jumped out of my chest. No glory in dying like that. We'd be just some news flash back home. Some poor suckers who had an accident. That would be messed up."

"Man, just think about it though. That could have been all she wrote back there." Conner reached in his shirt to find his cross again and kissed it before tucking it back in.

"Yeah, that was pretty crazy, but nothing happened. So don't sweat it." Steele tried to brush off Conner's concerns till he noticed Conner staring off into nothing.

"That really shook you up, huh, Conner?"

"Got that right. All I could think about was my little girl. She's four, you know." Tears swelled up in his eyes and one rolled down his cheek.

"Yeah, I know, it's about all you talk about."

"Of course. You wait till you have one. She lives with her mom now. You know, I'd never see her again. The thought just tears me up." He smiled big fighting through the sadness and wiped his cheek.

"You'll be okay. I hear this place is easy, like being home practically. I bet you probably won't be that close to anything dangerous the rest of the time you're here. I heard we work in the same tent as the commanding general, so nothing is going to happen to us here."

"Yeah, I guess you're right. I sure hope so."

"It'll be fine. Trust me."

"What's with that NCO? Spitting at us when we meet him? What's that about?"

"I don't know what to tell you about that. Caught me a little off guard. Guess he's hard-core or something."

"I guess. If that's what you call it. This kind of stuff will make you a religious man."

"Oh so you're going to church now?" Steele goaded.

"You have to keep the man happy. Besides, after today I think I need it, how about you?"

"I don't know if I'd go that far." Steele paused, "I guess there's a God, but I don't think I believe in all that church stuff."

"Yeah, sometimes I don't know about all that church stuff either. It wouldn't be so bad if it wasn't for some of the people."

"You got that right. Religion can be a dangerous place. It's no place for rookies."

Conner's brow furrowed, "What, you some sort of pro?"

"Ha!" Steele slapped his knee. "Nah, I'm just saying. I'm just not into all that God stuff. It takes a certain type of person to do that and it's not me. Don't sweat it here, man. I've got your back. I'll keep an eye out for you."

"That's great and all, but who's looking out for you?" He slapped Craig's shoulder as he shook his head.

The people from the other flights trickled in. The briefer walked past the map and up to the podium after a few minutes. He cleared his throat and started.

"Welcome to Bagram Airfield. I am going to cover some things that you need to know for the time that you are going to be here. This briefing will tell you what you need to watch out for and the areas to avoid. When we're finished, if you have any questions then I will answer them or I will point you in the right direction. Alright, let's get started. Bagram Air Base is approximately two miles long." The briefer pointed to the map. "The first thing you need to be aware of is unexploded ordinance.

It's literally all over the place. We find Soviet made land mines, grenades and other leftovers every day around here. The red lines on this map mark areas that have not been cleared of mines and other ordinance. Plenty of areas still need to be cleared, even on the runway."

Now you tell us! Steele looked at Conner who shook his head and frowned.

"Most danger areas are marked off with tape or wire. For your own safety do not go into those areas. If you find an area that has not been cleared for mines, stay out of it until someone can check it out. We see local casualties all the time that have set off mines and we don't want to see our personnel losing limbs or life, so stay alert." He paused for effect then continued.

"Other dangers here range from malaria to vipers. Most of these things are rare and if you pay attention and just take your medicine you won't have any issues. We receive incoming frequently and you'll find shelters throughout the base. You get two hot chows here a day, breakfast and supper. You're on your own for lunch, but your units will provide MREs if you want them. Waste services are provided through contracts with locals..."

The briefing started to cover the mundane. The heat made it hard to concentrate. Steele felt his t-shirt stick to his chest as he sat back in his seat. Steele drifted off into thoughts of home.

He had just quit college before he joined the army. The Army had been the adventure he had been looking for. First stop was basic training where he learned to be a soldier. He was surprised at the amount of classroom time. There were more rules to being a soldier than he had imagined. The endless duties such as cleaning the barracks, the yards, and gear weren't very fun, but the field time made it all worth it. Whether it was basic rifle marksmanship, bayonet training, hand to hand combat or the ruck marches, he enjoyed it all.

Next he was off to Advanced Individual Training or AIT as it was called. It was all class room this time around, but they kept him busy, so he didn't have much time to get bored. He learned a new skill set that consisted of communications, computers and security. The only field time was the daily physical training. The classroom training was interesting but he missed the physical challenges of basic as the classroom time wore on. When he finally graduated training he was sent to his first post, Fort Bragg, North Carolina.

The history of his new home and the great soldiers of the past that had flowed through it gave him a sense of awe. Oral histories were passed down through song in choruses of battles and bravery. The warriors from the past called to them and challenged them to do better. The soldiers sang these histories on their morning runs through the post. He was inspired running down the fabled streets listening to the units defy each other in cadence. Units passed each other on opposite sides of the road and their volume grew as they drew close. The desire to fight was tangible. The Army had turned on an aggressive instinct. It was indulged and fed on a daily basis. He was hungry for adventure and it was just the beginning.

His next stop brought him across the world to a place he knew very little about. He heard the Soviets had invaded years ago and it became their Vietnam. His father feared Craig would end up in his own Vietnam, but Craig assured him things were different.

The anticipation of getting into the action was all he could think about at first. The moment they had stepped on board the plane for deployment, the excitement began to build. The flight had been electric with nervous energy. The long flight and the four day layover took its toll as they sat around. The excitement gave way to frustration and impatience as they waited. Reality had started to sink in now that he was finally in country. The adrenaline rush from the tarmac was gone. He couldn't help but wonder what other dangers might lay ahead, even though he had tried hard to reassure Conner. The whole experience had been a roller coaster of highs and lows so far. He shifted uncomfortably in the metal chair. For the first time he really felt alone and thousands of miles away from everyone that mattered anything to him.

The still moments unsettled him. All the activity usually didn't leave much time to think about where he was going and what dangers might lay ahead. When he didn't have something pressing to do, his father's voice would echo in his mind.

Steele noticed the monotone voice pick up speed and snapped his attention back to the briefing. He could tell it had started to wrap up, "Remember tuberculosis is rampant here. Don't eat food with the locals or drink their water. Take your mefloquine malaria pills. You don't need to take malaria home with you. Make sure you signed in so you don't have to sit through this again. That's it for this briefing. You can leave if you don't have any questions."

SGT Ensly waited for them outside the processing tent. "So, you ready for Bagram now?" He sent another round of tobacco juice at their feet.

"Its official now, Sergeant, we signed the paper." Steele moved his foot to miss the splash and Conner nodded in agreement as he ducked his head in the wind.

"Good. Don't worry, soldier, ducking your head won't help. Dust gets in everywhere out here. It's what the locals call the one hundred twenty days of wind. You're gonna love it. This lasts from June through September and since it's the end of July, you're in time to enjoy it. We have a lot of work to do right now. A Special Forces unit got into some trouble up in the hills and lost some crypto. We'll be lean the next couple of days so we'll probably have to send one of you out."

"You can send me anywhere, Sergeant," Steele offered.

"That right? Didn't realize they sent me a hero on special order." He snorted in contempt.

"No hero, Sergeant. I just want to get out and see what it's all about."

"Plenty of action out here, Hero. You'll find out soon enough and we'll see how much you like it."

3

PHONE HOME

Ensly walked them down the dirt road from the briefing tent along a wall to an opening where some MPs stood guard. "We have to make a stop in here. SSG Hallis wanted to meet you guys." He motioned them to the table where the MPs stood. The MPs checked their ID cards then SGT Ensly signed them in to the compound. "We'll get you added to the list today so you don't need an escort. You'll have to show them papers every time you leave or come back with your computers or other crypto," he instructed as they walked into the command tent.

Few places were more secure than the tent where the commanding general worked and their cryptography assignment demanded a secure area. They made their way into the large tent where their eyes took a moment to adjust to the subdued lighting. The room was full of activity as they made their way to the commo section.

"SSG Hallis, the new guys are here."

"Steele and Conner? C'mon in. Good to have you guys join us." He welcomed them and shook their hands.

"We have some things to cover so you guys can get your bearings."

They gawked at the activity around them as they entered the commo area. Rows of officers hovered in front of their laptops preparing for their morning presentations. Some stood around talking while others banged away making last minute adjustments to their briefings. The voices of Allied officers could be heard distinctly in the mob of American noise. The uniforms looked so different, it was hard to tell where some came from.

The morning briefing was displayed on a large screen near the back. Overhead projectors filled the large screen with a slide indicating the time of the next briefing. A timer on the screen counted down the minutes. The screen was flanked by large flat panel monitors. The monitors showed various satellite feeds and supplemental intel. He could only imagine the things he would see and hear. This was better than watching CNN. This was where it all happened.

"The coalition officers brief the general here. It's quite a scene, isn't it?" Hallis glanced around with a grin.

"Sure is. I wasn't expecting to be here on the floor like this." Steele looked over the display wide eyed.

"Yeah, I love it. You ever see anything like this? We're living history. I guarantee you this beats sitting in some cube farm back home." Hallis smiled pleased with himself and continued.

"Roger that, Sergeant," they parroted as they nodded in unison.

"Good deal, you boys take a seat." He pointed to the rear of their section to chairs by the familiar concrete gray Comsec safes. He sat on the table in front of them. "Look, here's the deal. The OIC in all his wisdom decided to split us up into two twelve hour shifts. The shifts are rotated each month. Everyone pretty much likes working nights. They're not as busy and you can email and call home without any grief. Don't get stupid with calling home and talking all night to your girlfriend or something though. Keep it reasonable. If the Colonel gets any heat about the calls back home I will put your ass on guard duty till you leave. You won't like it when we get back if I have to tell my wife one of you soldiers got my phone taken away. You understand?"

"Yes, Sergeant."

"Alright, anyway, there's a catch to working the night shift. The days are hot. Real hot. Like Robin Williams said, 'Africa hot'. Trying to sleep during the day is like taking a nap in an oven. You won't get much sleep when you're working nights. So make the most of your time when you're on the road to catch up on it."

"Conner, you will start out on the day shift and Steele will work the night shift. Any questions so far?"

They shook their heads no.

"Alright fellas, that's the fun stuff. I know you had your first briefing already but this is the one that matters. This is my Welcome-to-Bagram briefing so listen up." He leaned forward on the table till it squeaked under his weight. "The mission here is not like the one at home. Here it's crypto key anywhere, anytime. It's not like the gig at home where everyone comes to get it from us. We pick it up, we deliver it, we secure it, we destroy it. This is the real deal. You lose key out here and people can die. You make mistakes and it affects soldiers throughout a number of countries, and exposes them to potential compromise. It also increases our time on the road and makes our lives more miserable. So don't make our lives miserable. Some people get nervous about getting out of the wire so they don't travel too much. That being said, everyone travels. Some places you go will be nicer than it is here, but plenty of places you visit you'll be glad you're just passing through. If at any time, you ever feel your mission is compromised, destroy the key! Got it? Destroy the key!" He looked at them for a moment as they nodded.

"Now it's time for the Hallis ten commandments. Break these and you'll find out what the wrath of God is all about.

One, do what you're told.

Two, Drink plenty of water. The heat here will kill you. You have to drink constantly because you will end up dehydrated quickly if you don't. We sweat all day long. If you are thirsty, drink something, if you're not, drink something. Get some kool aid to add to your water if you don't like how the water tastes. Just make sure you keep drinking day and night.

Three, don't sleep on duty. It's against regs and besides it'll make the Colonel look bad. If he looks bad, my life gets bad and it rolls downhill.

Four, don't eat Haji food. Really shouldn't have to tell you that. When you see how nasty these people can be, you'll understand. There's always one of you guys that won't listen, but you've been warned.

Five, don't mess with the women. You get caught with a woman in a tent, the can, or a shower and you'll find yourself losing rank and money.

Six, don't be late for guard duty. They come looking for me because you're not where you're supposed to be and you'll get plenty of practice showing up on time with all the extra duty you'll get.

Seven, don't sleep on guard duty. Ever seen Platoon? Don't be that guy. Someone gets through the wire and it'll hit the fan. Duty will be the least of your worries if that happens.

Eight, when we have incoming, get to a bunker. If you're not smart enough to do that then I guess it's natural selection, but don't push it. I hate paperwork.

Nine, don't eat too many MREs--or you'll regret it.

Ten, do what you're told.

That clear enough?"

They nodded

"Alright boys, you will be making courier runs all over the Combined Joint Operations Area so I hope you like to fly. That's probably enough for now. Conner, you go finish getting settled, eat something, then get back here and finish out the shift. Steele, you go back and get some sleep and be here tonight to pull your shift."

"Thanks, Sergeant." They stood and SGT Ensly escorted them back out past an intersection where Land Rovers and Humvees kicked up dust. Past the intersection he noted the concrete, box-like structures rising out of the dirt and pointed at them, "You see those bunkers over there? It's simple, get in them when we receive mortars and rockets."

Doesn't look like much to me. Steele squinted in the wind as he looked them over.

"Wait." Conner stopped and held up his hand. "I thought we wouldn't be seeing much action here. This is a safe place since the general is here, right?" He turned to Steele with his mouth agape.

"Sure, being around the general makes it safer than other places, but we still take fire here. This is a war zone, if you didn't hear. Now as I was saying," SGT Ensly rolled his eyes and continued, "if you hear any incoming you make a beeline for these things. You understand? Don't let me catch you lying in your bunk when they hit either. Don't screw my tour up by getting killed and getting me in trouble."

"Good to know you care, Sergeant."

Ensly turned to look Steele in the eyes. "Do what you're supposed to out here or that incoming will be the least of your worries. You read me, Steele?" He spit another round at Steele's feet and looked him in the eyes.

"Loud and clear, Sergeant." Steele stood up straighter. He stared back, and smiled.

Ensly finally broke his stare and continued to walk. Steele shot a glance at Conner and shrugged his shoulders as they followed Ensly. Steele looked at the small city of brown tents ahead with interest as they cleared the bunkers. He could see a guard tower in the distance standing watch over a large wall. His heart beat faster when he saw the shadowy silhouettes of the soldiers manning the tower. He felt like he was walking through a movie that he had seen before.

Ensly followed Steele's eyes, "Take a good look. That's the guard tower you'll be pulling duty in. You'll have plenty of time to get acquainted. Screw up out here and you'll be watching shadows in the dark or guarding some concentration-camp-looking local your whole time here." Ensly puffed his chest out with the last few words.

Steele and Conner nodded uncomfortably as they made their way to a large tent. The tents stood next to a building with a Red Cross sign.

"This is the morale tent. We're going to stop here for a moment so you guys can phone home and tell someone you've made it."

The desk at the front was empty and no one was in the tent. Metal chairs faced a blank white screen in the middle of the tent. Ping pong tables filled the leftover space. A refrigerator in the corner had a sign that stated, *Water/ Gatorade 1 BOTTLE PER person*. Ensly checked the fridge for Gatorade and took three. "One for now, two for later." He snorted as he turned to them. "Don't pay attention to that sign. These things never last. Maybe once a week Gatorade will show up in here, so if you see some grab it, if nothing else, get me some." He snickered.

He pointed Steele and Conner to the phones.

"Tell someone you're here, that you'll write in a few days. We have to get to the chow line." He patted his belly that puffed out his BDU top and smiled.

"Roger that, SGT." Steele and Conner made their way to the phones that sat on a long wooden makeshift table. A plywood divider rose up about two feet in the air between each phone to create three booth-like stalls. This offered the soldiers no real privacy, but it assured them a halfhearted effort was made. Steele dialed home. After some static and a slight delay, it started to ring.

"Hello?"

"Hey Dad, it's me, Craig."

"Oh, hey Craig."

"Is Mom around?"

"No, she ran to the store."

"You sound funny. You still ticked at me, Dad?"

"You caught me off guard. That's all."

"I thought you'd be happy to hear from me at least."

"I am. You just took me by surprise."

"Really? Sounds you're still mad about me joining."

"You didn't listen to me when you were here. Why should we talk about it now?"

"I know, Dad. But give me a break. It's too late now."

"You're right about that."

"C'mon Dad it's what I always wanted to do. Besides, you did it."

"Look, I'm not going to talk about his again. That was different. I had too. You didn't."

"I know, but..."

"So, you want me to tell your mother something?"

"Sure, tell her I'm here and I'm ok."

"Ok, I'll tell her. Sounds like you made it in good shape. You ok?"

"Yeah, I'm fine."

"Well, keep your head down and don't volunteer for anything."

"Ok Dad, thanks-"

"Wait, your mom just pulled up. Let me go get her."

He stared at the phone. He heard Conner still on the phone talking with his parents. He looked over his shoulder and saw Ensly looking at a paper on the cork board.

"Craig! Are you okay?"

"I'm fine, Mom."

"How long have you been there?"

"We just got here today. Not much happening here so far. Just getting the this-is-your-life-tour.

"What's it like?"

"It's hot. Real hot. They briefed us and warned us about land mines and the local food. Just the basics. Nothing you wouldn't know if you watched the news."

"Land mines? Could you end up where there are land mines?"

"No, we won't have anything to worry about here. Like I told Conner, we'll be working in a safe area, nothing to worry about."

"Why was he worried?"

"Oh, he was shook up after the landing. It was a little exciting."

"Were they shooting at you? Was something wrong?"

"Nah, someone said they call it some kind of combat landing. It's pretty crazy. Makes you think everyone is going to die. They do things in these planes you wouldn't think was possible. Hardest landing I've ever had in a plane that's for sure. Then when we landed some guy drove up yelling at us saying we got off plane in the wrong place. It shook Conner up a little that's all."

"I wish you hadn't joined the military. Land mines and combat landings!"

"I know, but this is something I had to do."

"I still don't understand it, I told you not to do it!"

"Look, I got enough of that from Dad already, could you lay off?"

"You don't understand. You get to run off and have your adventure and I'm stuck here worried about you. I didn't want you to go..." she breathed deeply. "Ok, look, I'm sorry. I'm glad you're okay really. I've just been so worried about you. The news just talks about people getting killed all the time..."

"Don't worry about me, Mom. I can take care of myself."

"I know, but I just don't want anything to happen to you."

"I'll be fine."

SGT Ensly coughed nonchalantly and pointed to his watch.

"Hey, I don't have much time, this is supposed to be just a quick call home, but I'll call you later. I just wanted you to know I'm okay and I miss you guys. Look Mom, I have to go. I'll talk to you soon."

"Okay, bye. I love you. Take care of yourself."

"I love you too, Mom. Bye."

Steele hung up and let out a sigh.

"There'll be plenty of time for that later. Let's go get some chow," SGT Ensly intruded.

By the time they reached the line, the wind had picked up to a howl. It blew without mercy at the hundred plus people standing there. Steele thought he knew all about dust storms. He was from West Texas and had even seen it rain mud, but he hadn't seen anything like this before. The dust was fine like powdered sugar. It settled around their feet like snow. It stirred in the wind, gathering in drifts inches deep.

The entire time they moved through the line, more people kept coming. The line consisted of everything from soldiers and airmen to Brown and Root contractors. Everyone dealt with the wind their own way. Some wore goggles; some wore wraparound sunglasses or even the old standard, the bandana. There wasn't much conversation. Heads were down as the wind howled at them. They shuffled a step or two at a time in the brown blizzard. He caught a glimpse of the food every time the flaps on the chow tent blew open. The aroma of hot food and dust swirled around them, riding the wind and dancing off into the valley. It wasn't very enticing, but it was all they had.

Finally inside, they moved along the buffet-style layout and told the server what they wanted. Behind the Plexiglas, the server with a hair net and gloves dumped their selection on a paper tray and handed it to the next server down the line.

They each took their tray and walked out of the chow tent back into the blowing wind. The next tent held the picnic tables where they could eat. Nothing connected the two tents. It was an exercise in futility as they tried to cover the food to keep the dirt out.

A soldier ahead of them tried to cover his tray with one hand and hold it with the other. The cheap tray buckled under the weight and the hot food disappeared into the blanket of dust. He looked down then shot a glance back at the growing line. He shook his head and left defeated.

Steele could feel his heart sink. He looked at the dust wrap around the soldier as he walked away. Steele wondered if everyone else was right about him joining the Army. Just when he thought he had done the right thing his mind swirled with doubt as he wondered what kind of circus it really was.

4
TRUITT'S BRIEFING

Steele settled into the routine of the night shift in a couple of days, but as the weeks passed he struggled with the lack of rest. Working twelve hours shifts every day made them feel even longer. The action happened as the soldiers came onto shift. Briefings, daily reports, and instructions for the night were given. The night died down after all the commotion and there was a long lull. The taxing part was to stay awake after not really sleeping all day.

"Man, I'm tired," Steele sighed as he collapsed on his cot.

"Getting used to night shift is going to take a little while, rookie. Nah, you never get used to it you're just tired all the time. That's one of the good things about the courier runs. You can finally get some sleep." Charlie took off his boots and lay down on his cot.

"That sucks."

"Welcome to the Stan man, welcome to the Stan," Charlie murmured as he crawled into his summer sleeping bag to get some rest.

Steele woke up soaked. *What in the...* He decided to sleep in a t-shirt and shorts. It was cool early in the morning but now it was hot. It was zero eight hundred hours and he was cooking. He took off his shirt and lay on top of the sleeping bag.

The guys had already opened the flaps on the tent to let in a little breeze. It didn't matter much. He almost wished the wind was blowing, but the dust wasn't worth it. The heat felt like a weight on him squeezing out his resistance to the misery.

He finally drifted off to sleep again. All he could dream about was planes. They were always taking off and landing. The two parts he hated about flying. He woke up again in a pool of sweat. His cot was drenched. It would be a long morning.

The sweat rolled once again as he lay on his bunk. It didn't matter if he was in his underwear or not. It was just hot. He drifted in and out of sleep as the sun grew hotter and the tent filled with stagnant air.

"Steele, SSG Hallis wants to see you." Robinson stood over him and shook him.

"All right, be there in a minute." Steele groggily pushed him away. He got dressed in his BDU's and walked to the command center.

Steele ran through the things he had done since he arrived. He couldn't help but wonder why he would get called to see SSG Hallis right after working the night shift. The MP's at the gate checked his badge and let him into the command center. There were a handful of people working and milling around. He approached the communications area when SSG Hallis saw him.

"Hey Steele, got a question for you."

"Okay."

"You ready to get in the game and go to Kabul tomorrow?"

"Just tell me where to be and I'm there." Steele's heartbeat was a little quicker and butterflies filled his stomach.

"Alright then, you're up. You'll work your shift till midnight then go get some sleep and head out at zero seven hundred hours in the morning. The job is like being stateside except you will have a loaded weapon at all times. If anything happens, ANYTHING, destroy that material ASAP! Understood?"

"Roger that."

"Okay, today at thirteen hundred hours you need to see SSG Truitt for the mission briefing come back here ten till and I'll let you know where to meet him. In the meantime, go get some sleep, but get back for that briefing."

"Roger that." He turned and walked with a quick step out of the command tent. He did a fist pump, almost giddy at the prospect of finally getting out of the compound after a couple of weeks.

A tree outside the Red Cross building provided good shade as SSG Truitt leaned against it. He held a Gatorade in one hand and a cigarette in the other.

"You Steele?" Truitt let out a trail of smoke with his question as Steele walked up.

"Yes, Sergeant."

"Hey there, Lewis. I know you've heard this briefing before, but you can hear it again anyway." Lewis nodded as he walked up.

"Listen up, Steele. I know my way around this area. I've been here for half a year and go to Kabul nearly every week. They have designated me the unofficial "tour guide" of Kabul. Anytime anyone needs to go to town, I lead the expedition. It can be fun, but this stuff is no joke. When we first get off the compound we will dismount from the vehicles, chamber rounds and roll out. After that we'll haul ass between here and Kabul. You will need to keep up with me because there are a couple of choke points along the way. If someone shoots at us, keep driving. If you get knocked off the road, check to see where you are because there are mines everywhere out here. The rocks on the sides of the roads are painted to let you know where they are because they have so many. If the rocks are white and you end up off the road, you can follow your tracks back to the road. If the rocks are red stay where you are or exit at your own risk because you will be in a mine field. If we are taking fire then it's up to you to decide. We will have MRE's and water in the truck, so if we do have contact and a vehicle is disabled, we'll call it in. Just stay put. Wait for the cavalry to arrive. Again, we will be driving at a high rate of speed, so stay with me. Don't stop for anything, and don't get separated in the city. You get lost in Kabul and it might not be a fun detour. These people tolerate us, but they don't like us. You get lost in the wrong area, you might just find out how much some of them don't like us. Don't get out of your vehicle unless I do and don't stop for anything. Any questions?"

"Are we the only ones going?" Steele inquired.

"No there will be some others, but don't worry about them. We will get you where you need to go to do your job and then we will take care of them. They're the tourists."

"Where are we going to meet?"

"Oh yeah, anytime we go to Kabul we'll meet here. I'll bring the vehicles. You just show up ready to go, any other questions?"

"No, I'm good, how 'bout you, Lewis?"

"Nothing here."

"Alright gentlemen, see you in the morning at zero six forty five."

Lewis went back to the command center. Steele headed to the tent to get some more sleep. He was finally going to be doing something! He stripped down and laid on his cot thinking about his first trip off the compound. Road trip to Kabul. Sounded like a movie. It was hard to relax and the heat didn't help. The briefing was a wakeup call. So far it seemed like this place was like life back home except no ac and bad food. This brought everything into focus. There was a reason they lugged M-16s around everywhere they went, dinner, the shower, the can, etc... He was in a combat zone. It didn't seem like it so far, but that was about to change. The briefings that he overheard in the command tent described contact with the enemy in remote locations, but nothing close by. It didn't seem very real yet. He might as well have been watching the news at home, because everything sounded so far off. Now things were different. He was about to go live.

5
LOCK AND LOAD

Steele tossed, turned and tried to get some sleep. It was too hot to sleep and he was hungry. He decided to get up when he heard Mike and Charlie making noise.

"What'd you have to go back to the command center for this morning?" Mike grabbed his Camelbak for some water.

"SSG Hallis said I get to go to Kabul tomorrow."

"Oh yeah? You'll like it. That's a fun trip to make."

"I don't know, that briefing that SSG Truitt gave made me think I was driving into the teeth of combat."

Charlie stretched and joined in. "Yeah, he gives an intense briefing, but don't sweat it. Someone will shoot at vehicles on that road once in a while, but that's no big deal. First time was a little nerve racking for me, but you'll see for yourself. We haven't had any problems on that route. Just don't let your weapons out of your sight though. A couple of guys were on a 'sightseeing' tour in Kabul last month and put their weapons in the back seat while they drove around. When they got stuck in traffic someone came up, opened the back door and stole an M-16!"

"Yeah, the other day there were some Special Forces soldiers in Kabul and they shot a guy." Mike was excited to tell.

"Really? Why?"

"Some Haji got cocky with them. Standard rules of engagement, if someone raises a weapon at you out here and you feel threatened, they're fair game. There were four SF guys and they lit the dude up. Guess the guy didn't realize who he was pointing at. But don't get trigger happy out there, because you're not SF. It won't go good for you if you shoot some Haji. Don't sweat it, you'll have a good time."

Craig was thirsty for adventure. This is why he joined the Army. He was restless all day. He pulled half a shift and headed back to the tent about midnight. He didn't even change since he would be up in six hours. He would sweat all day on his trip to Kabul anyway. Tomorrow it was go time.

Steele crawled off his cot at zero six thirty hours to get some chow. A quick breakfast was a must since he would be gone all day. He didn't know what to expect and wasn't sure when or if they would eat that day. He saw Lewis at a table and sat next to him.

"You ready to go today?"

"Yeah, I can't wait. I was beginning to wonder about this deployment. I was starting to think it was going to really suck. Getting out of here will be good."

"Yeah, it's good to get out of here now and then." They ate in relative silence until they finished.

It was zero seven forty-five when they showed up in front of the Red Cross building. SSG Truitt was already there with the Land Rovers.

"Morning, Gentlemen. You ready?"

"Can't wait to get going." Steele smiled like a kid on Christmas morning.

"Good, there are three officers going with us. They will be here around zero eight hundred hours. One is Colonel McNeme. He's an old warrior. He won't say much. Just don't bug him. They will probably ride with me, so you guys will have your own vehicle. Which one of you wants to drive?"

"I will!" Lewis volunteered.

"Works for me, I'd rather ride shotgun anyway."

"Fine, just make sure you don't stop for anything unless I do and stick close. You know that I drive fast, so keep up."

SSG Truitt finished his cigarette and double-checked the MRE's and water. The Colonel showed up while SSG Truitt rummaged in one of the Land Rovers.

"Good morning, Men."

"Morning, Sir."

"It's a good day for a drive into town." They nodded in agreement. The Colonel had an air of confidence. He had the presence of an experienced man. The other two officers, a major and a captain showed up a few minutes later. Quick introductions were made by SSG Truitt.

"Okay Gentlemen, here's a quick brief of today's events. We have two soldiers here who have work to do in Kabul. We will make two stops before we head to Chicken Street. First stop is at a special unit in Kabul. The next stop is the embassy where Colonel McNeme has some business to tend to while the soldiers take care of theirs. After the work is done we will head to the market. Any questions?"

They shook their heads no.

"Okay, let's go."

Steele was surprised they had Land Rovers. He expected to take humvees. The vehicles had thick coats of dust, decorated with some miscellaneous bullet holes on the sides. The windows were rolled down, if there were any. *When in Rome.* They drove slowly down the long main road of the compound while Steele gazed at the surroundings. He noticed the black, red, and gold flag of Germany. The blue, yellow, and red flag of Romania and others snapped in the breeze as they passed. The hescos, topped with razor wire, glistened in the sun, separating the edge of the compound from the wild. They pulled up to the gate and the MP's chatted with SSG Truitt and waved them through.

Locals lingered just outside. They smoked cigarettes and talked. Some made their way to get in line for the daily work crew.

SSG Truitt pulled over and the Land Rover emptied. Lewis pulled over too. Everyone got out with their weapons.

The officers pulled their pistols from their shoulder holsters. Slides were pulled back and released. Officers chambered a round in their pistols as the distinct snap penetrated the cool air. Steele and Lewis followed suit.

Steele was suddenly aware this was the first time he ever loaded a weapon where the object was to kill someone if necessary. The blank looks on the locals, standing around watching them, made the whole moment surreal. *I wonder if they gave the same looks to the Russians.* SSG Truitt came over, "Lock and load Gentlemen, and stay close."

6
ROAD TRIP TO KABUL

Steele's heart raced as they pulled away from the gate. Trembling from the excitement, he brushed his hands down his pant legs to settle himself. They drove slowly till they cleared the locals then pressed the gas to the floor and bolted into the valley.

They left Bagram behind and Steele was confronted with the reality that the trip could get dicey. He felt his stomach get a little queasy and a light sweat broke out across his shoulders. His field of vision narrowed as the adrenaline rushed through his body. He felt a little light headed as he looked around. Traveling at speeds over a hundred miles an hour, they raced down the road to Kabul.

"Yee haw!"

Steele cracked a smile at the heart attack Lewis just about gave him. He wiped his mouth and brushed his hand down his pant leg once again. He watched the countryside rush by as he stared out of the window.

"You can't beat this," Lewis continued. "I've never driven one of these Land Rovers, heck, I've never even been in one. Who'd believe that I'd go join the Army and blaze a trail through the Stan in one of these high dollar rigs?" He bragged with a big grin.

"I've never driven around the countryside with a loaded weapon wondering if someone was going to try to shoot me, much less in a Land Rover." Steele grinned back.

"So, what do you think of all this beautiful countryside?"

"It reminds me a lot of West Texas. Dry and desolate. I'm just wondering where the oil wells are. Probably not much different out here than back home. People trying to make the best of where they are. Carving a life out of the earth."

"I guess, except these people are carrying AK-47s and would really like to take a shot at you if they could."

"I guess there are some of those too."

Homesteads like little oasis were sprinkled along the route. Some were half hidden by medium sized walls that surrounded the homes. A few had patches of green and a handful of trees, while others were just a mud hut with nothing nearby. Once in a while they would see a home in the distance where someone outside paused as they drove by. Even in the early morning there wasn't much activity they could see.

"Up ahead on the left is a little guard post. Sometimes we see a guard at these and sometimes we don't."

A uniformed guard stood alone with an AK-47. Steele watched him closely with his weapon ready. He didn't care if they had uniforms or not.

They passed the post and Steele relaxed his grip on his weapon. "Wonder what that dude thinks of all of this?"

"Man, just another day at the office for them. They've been doing this all their lives."

"You're probably right, but what a life. Living in a mud hut. Scrambling for survival every day. I like to travel and all, but places like this are not really what I had in mind."

"Yeah, glad I'm just visiting. We're coming up on one of the choke points. We'll have to slow down here so keep your eyes open." Lewis leaned over the steering wheel as they came up on the S curve in the road. He looked for anything out of place.

Steele's heart beat faster, his eyes scanned the hills as they slowed to make the sharp turns. Every rock and shadow looked like someone hiding. His uniform was damp from sweat already and they were just fifteen minutes into the drive. Steele felt his palms slip on the rifle as he moved it around. Lewis punched the gas once again as they came out of the narrow pass.

"Well, that was uneventful, huh?"

"Yeah, nothing that time," Steele replied trying to sound less shaky than he felt.

They raced off through the countryside as they exited the pass. The wind offered no relief since it was already heating up.

"There they are!"

"Who?" Steele raised his weapon and looked around frantically.

"Those painted rocks that SSG Truitt was talking about."

"Oh yeah," Steele exhaled as he lowered his weapon. "Yeah, I see them."

"I swear, with so many mines around here you'd have to take off the top six inches of the entire country to make this place worth keeping. It's a shame what the Russians and the local warlords have done to this place."

"Yeah, I sure would like to go skiing in those snow covered mountains back there," Steele said.

"Man, I can't think of a reason I would ever want to come to this place. Much less to ski. I can go skiing at home just fine."

"Sure you can, but you wouldn't be able to say you did it in the Stan."

"Like I care. I want to go skiing then go back to the lodge and warm up with some Jack and Coke and a ski bunny. Can't do either one here. You'd probably be lucky to get a tent in this third world dive."

"You got a point there."

When they came to the outskirts of the city they slowed as they approached a T in the road. An Afghan guard with an AK-47 stood on the side of the road and stared at them as they made their ninety degree turn to head downtown.

"Okay, so we keep seeing these guys everywhere with AKs. The question is do they know how to use them?"

"Not likely."

"My point exactly, they might as well be statues. It's not like they've had any real training around here."

"Then again, they have been doing this stuff for decades, so they may be alright. Probably a roll of the dice either way. Let's not find out today."

"Not in my plans."

The mystery of this new place deepened as they entered the city. He felt like they stepped back into the past as he looked at the buildings. The architecture was an eclectic mixture of third world mud buildings and left over Soviet era creations. Many buildings on the streets looked similar to storage units back home but with the fronts painted in greens and yellows. The colorful Afghan buildings stood out in contrast to the dull Soviet structures in gray and white. Vendors outside the small buildings sold meats hung from hooks in front of their stores. Some cooked food to sell while others offered bread. People everywhere walked, talked, and shopped. People rode bikes and darted in and out of the cars while music from radios echoed down the street.

They followed the lead vehicle more closely now as they weaved through the congested city streets.

"Watch out!" Steele yelled as the Land Rover was nearly sideswiped by an oncoming bus.

"These guys need to take driver's ed," Lewis cringed as he pulled the Land Rover away from the traffic.

"No negotiation on these streets. Looks like it's winner takes all. Narrow streets and no traffic rules. This trip could be crazier than I thought."

After a couple more close calls, they made their way to the first destination. He was told it was a typical Afghan city building. It looked like it was made of mud and painted bright yellow. A high wall hid much of the building. A small gate provided entrance from the street. They slowed down and the air became hot and stuffy. They drove down the narrow street and stopped by the gate. As they pulled up they were met by a bearded man wearing a ball cap and an M-4 slung across his chest. An Afghan with an AK-47 stood by his side.

"Morning, Truitt."

"Morning, have some guys here for a special delivery."

"Yeah, no problem, come on in." The man waved to someone behind the gate. The gate opened slowly and a barrier forced them to turn into a make-shift parking area away from the building.

Lewis met Truitt by the door. "Back in a minute, Sergeant."

"Come with me, I know where their commo guy works." Lewis waved and led Steele into the building. It looked like an Adobe building from New Mexico with its grainy texture. The blue and yellow walls reminded Steele of a beach house, just no beach. They followed a hall to the rear of the building. Steele saw another bearded man walking out of a room as they neared the back.

"Hey Lewis, how's the general?" The man stopped in the doorway to speak with him.

"He's great. Though he wants to know why you guys haven't finished killing all these Taliban yet."

"Well, must be because we have too many soldiers sitting on a strip of dirt near some planes not doing anything."

"Hey now, someone has to watch all those Armed Forces Network broadcasts. Besides, we can't all be hardcore like you. Then it wouldn't be so special."

"Oh, you are special Lewis, trust me." The man pushed his Florida Gator ball cap back and laughed.

"This is Craig, he just got in."

"Good to know you, Craig. I'm Tim. You need anything when you're out here, you let me know."

"I told you we're not hard core like you, Tim. We don't need anything unless you can get me some backstage passes to a USO show or something."

"I might arrange that sometime just to see your reaction. But I'm more interested in seeing which one of you guys might have what it takes to walk on the wild side. One of you guys might turn out to be a hard charger too."

"What's this wild side talk? This doesn't look much like the wild side to me." Craig looked around the room with a grin.

"You've got a quick one here, Lewis. Looks can be deceiving, Craig. We run missions here just like we do out in the boonies. We do a lot of intel gathering and some other things. But sometimes we'll run a direct action mission where we get to hit the bad guys when they come into town."

"Direct action, you mean kicking down doors and taking out bad guys?"

"Yeah, we don't get as much of that here like in other places, but we still get a call once in a while."

"Now that sounds more like the kind of stuff I want to do."

"Hear that, Lewis? Sounds like we might have a winner. Someone that wants to see what the wild is all about."

"If this was the wild like back home, I would be a hard charger, but this is nothing like it."

"Lewis, you'll find out more about yourself out there than you ever did back home."

"I've only found out one thing here. That's how much I miss the clubs and dancing with women all night."

"Well, like I said, you're special Lewis, but there's hope for the other guys. It's a matter of time before you boys see some action out here. When you do, you'll see what I'm talking about."

7

AFGHAN STRIP MALL

"Speaking of action, one of your compadres lost some gear in the mountains, so we had to come by and give you some new crypto. That happens out in the wild. It can get sloppy when things get busy sometimes," Lewis chimed with a smile.

They made their way back to Tim's work area. A desk in the corner was crowded with papers, sports magazines and surrounded by communications equipment. Around the room were enough weapons to field a small army. There was a Florida Gator helmet on the desk and a football poster hanging on the wall behind it.

"A bit of a football fan, are you?" Craig noted as he scanned the room.

"Put it this way, if I'm breathing I'm thinking about one of three things. My girls back home, football, and how long till the season starts."

"That's pretty intense, Tim."

"Yeah, I played in school. My daddy was a coach, so it's in the blood. I made it to the University of Florida and played for two years. I got mono from a cheerleader and ended up dropping out of school. Go figure, right? I never got back on track and ended up in the Army. Now I'm teaching Afghan kids how to play the best game in the world and in my spare time dealing with jokers like you guys."

"Is that right? So what were you, a safety?"

"Linebacker."

"I could see that. Sounds like you could be a coach."

"I have to finish my twenty first, but that's what I'll be doing as soon as I'm done."

"Hate to break up the meet and greet social fellas, but we have work to do." Lewis pointed to his watch. "I mean you southern boys talk about football like I do women. Don't you know there are better things to spend your time on?"

"Alright, let me get my computer out." Tim moved some equipment off his desk that looked to be in the middle of repair.

Steele pulled his computer from his bag and powered it up. "What do guys like the SF do here anyway?"

"Could tell you but we'd have to kill you"

"Fair enough." Steele laughed. "What's it like living in a city like this?"

"Pretty good. We have real bathrooms, running water, and electricity. It's more than I can say for most deployments I've been on. Of course we can't drink the water, but we do have real showers. We're in the lap of luxury here in the big city."

"What about the locals? They give you any trouble?"

"Not really since we have some natives pulling guard here, besides we hang with the locals, so they put up with us. You have to watch everybody all the time anyway, but you get used to it. You just can't trust anyone. The bad guys don't wear uniforms around here. They like to hit the embassy every now and then to make a statement, but no one messes with us. Just don't let down your guard. Those smiles don't mean they like you. They'd just as soon kill you as they did the Russians."

"I'll keep that in mind." Steele disconnected the cable from the computer and slid his computer back into his bag.

"Nice chatting with you boys. You come by anytime and I'll tell you some stories about the interception I got in the SEC championship."

"On that note, we'll be seeing you, Tim. When you get back stateside, look me up and I'll show you what the real wild is all about." Lewis laughed and patted him on the back. Tim shook his head and waved as they left.

The transaction was complete, so they hopped back in the Land Rovers. They weaved their way through side streets to the US Embassy. They turned onto an empty street and spotted the Embassy. The tires on the pavement made the only sound on the street as they slowed and made their way down it. The lack of people unnerved Steele as he scanned the street.

"Feel like we are driving up to the OK corral." He looked around constantly. "But it looks like they are ready for business." He motioned to the Marines on guard.

The Embassy compound was surrounded by walls topped with razor wire. The walls were peppered with bullet holes from attacks. The Marines greeted them with cautious looks and weapons at the ready. Two more Marines overlooked the guards on the ground from an elevated position. The position was surrounded by sandbags. A Marine manned an M-60 with a belt of rounds hanging from its side. The other stood ready to feed the weapon rounds from a nearby ammo can. The Marines spoke with SSG Truitt for a minute, then waved them in. They crept into the compound and dismounted from the vehicles.

"These guys are alright, but instead of football they'll talk your ear off about weapons. Typical Marines just want to kill something. Come to think of it, you'll probably fit right in here too."

They stepped into the commo SGT's office and were met by a blast of cold air from the swamp cooler hung on the wall.

"A guy could go into shock stepping into a place this cold," Steele noted as the sweat on his body chilled him.

"Yeah, got that a while back just in time for winter. Making up for lost time with it now."

"I hear that you guys see some action here once in a while." Steele made small talk as he passed the crypto to the Marine's computer.

"Yeah, we see a little. We just got hit a few days ago. They like to keep us on our toes. They pop us with some shots here and there, mostly small arms fire. Once in a while they'll change it up, but they don't really do anything all out."

"Why not?"

"They don't have the muscle to pull a big attack around here. We hit back hard anyway, so they don't want any of this."

"So, what's this place good for?"

"Nothing good here except the food. We have an occasional beer with the Aussies and everything, but the food is great. They don't feed us that field slop they feed you guys. I mean we get five star meals here."

"No kidding? What do you get here that's so great?"

"Man, we have a real chef that cooks for the compound and it's good. I never knew how good food could be. But it's good here. Rich people good. I mean, it's better food than I had at home."

"I may have to check that out."

"Unless they have some hot waitresses around here, I'd just as soon roll on. I haven't seen any around here, so let's go see if those officers are ready to leave." Lewis pushed, bored with the conversation.

Steele shook his head as they walked out. They found the officers shooting the breeze at a table in the courtyard. An Australian officer held up a six pack of cold, sweating Fosters. "You mates need a brew to cool off?"

Steele noticed none of the officers had one. "Love one, but we're on duty. Maybe next time."

He hated to say it. Lewis didn't say anything. It was just too painful. They waited on the officers to finish shooting the breeze then SSG Truitt told them the plans for the rest of the day.

"You're in luck, Boys. Colonel McNeme is meeting with the ambassador. We're going to eat lunch here in an hour. After we're finished we'll go drive around a little to see some spots the Colonel wants to see, then we will head to Chicken Street to do some shopping. After that, it's home sweet home. Any objections?"

"Sounds good, Sergeant."

"Alright, be back here in an hour for lunch."

"Let's go find a place to crash." Steele slapped Lewis on the back.

The Marines lived in empty converted shipping containers called con-ex boxes. They were air conditioned so the guys found some floor space and slept till chow.

The alarm on his watch was sounding off as Steele slept on the floor. It blared without success till a Marine nudged him with a boot. "You gotta be somewhere?"

"Oh yeah, thanks." He rubbed his face and shook his head, looking around. He let out a content sigh. "You guys have it good."

"Sure, it's great to be stuck in this building all the time," The Marine countered flatly.

Steele shrugged and went to get Lewis. They made their way to the courtyard to find Truitt.

"You guys look like you got some shut eye," SSG Truitt remarked as he met them in the courtyard.

"It was good, pretty cold with that air conditioning. Felt good."

"Colonel got us a table for lunch, so let's go get some grub."

They sat down to a shade-covered table behind the Embassy. A white table cloth spread out before them with a proper setting. Beads of sweat trickled down the tea glasses as they glistened in the heat. The food was brought out on china plates.

"Sirs, today we are having steak with garlic mashed potatoes, green beans, salad and tea, followed by a chocolate mousse for dessert," the embassy wait person said as he delivered the first round of plates. As the meal progressed, they relaxed and enjoyed themselves. It was almost easy to forget that it was one hundred degrees.

"If an Army traveled on its belly and they ate this good, they wouldn't get very far," SSG Truitt observed sitting back in his chair with a satisfied grin.

"I could get used to this," Lewis chimed.

"No complaints here either," Steele agreed.

They sat in silence and enjoyed the dessert and the full bellies. SSG Truitt was the first to stir. "Alright, Gentlemen," he started with a look at the Colonel. The Colonel nodded and Truitt continued, "We had a good meal and you got some rest, but now it's time to move on. So stay alert and don't fall behind." They made their way to the vehicles and were off once again.

"So what's this Chicken Street thing?"

"It's the Afghan version of a strip mall, just dirtier." Lewis let out a laugh at the confused look on Steele's face.

They weaved in and out of the narrow streets. They finally pulled over and everyone unloaded as SSG Truitt motioned for them to get out.

"Welcome to Chicken Street, Gentlemen. Don't let the kids bug you too much and have some fun," Colonel McNeme advised as they were surrounded by kids asking for money.

"Dollar, mister?" A blue-eyed boy in front of Steele pleaded.

8
POPCORN

A merchant nearby hurried over and started to yell at the child. The child took another look at Steele then turned and ran away. The man apologized with his native accent then he tried to direct Steele into his shop. Steele smiled, shook his head no and started to walk down the street.

He browsed from the sidewalk as the merchants greeted him and tried to maneuver him into their stores. Most spoke in a broken English, "Mister, please come. I have..."

He was nervous because Afghans were everywhere. He didn't know much about these people but knew enough to know the bad guys mingled among them. They all dressed alike. There were no uniforms to separate them. Steele walked around with his weapon at the ready. Locals going about their business walked right next to him. Some stared absently, others smiled. He shifted his weapon as one passed by and brushed him. To his surprise he noticed that the officers never unholstered their pistols. He didn't find that comforting at all. The Afghans were selling jewelry, chess sets, rugs, antique guns, and more. You name it they were ready to negotiate for it. Steele walked in a store with chess sets and the owner greeted him.

"What do you need my friend? I have beautiful pieces."

The owner laid some sets out before him and watched closely to see the reaction on Steele's face. There was little reaction to the plain chess sets so he pulled out more sets with pieces carved with added intricate detail.

"How much?" Steele picked up a rook from a marble set with inlaid squares before him.

"For you, $25"

"I'll think about it." He sat the rook back down and began to walk out.

"Mister, you won't find better sets on this street. I will give you this set for $20."

"Okay, but I still want to think about it."

"Okay Mister, I will give it to you for $15."

"I still have to go look and see what everybody else has first. If I don't find anything I like, I'll come back and buy this one for $15, okay?"

"You are welcome." The shop owner resigned himself to losing the sale as he watched Steele walk away.

Steele made his way down the street and haggled with a couple of shop owners about vases and other trinkets then returned to the first shop owner after he walked the entire street.

"Welcome back, Mister, here are the chess sets." The owner eagerly pulled the sets out again for Steele. Steele was impressed with the attention to detail when the store owner remembered which sets he displayed earlier. Steele bought two sets, excited about the price. He also bought a couple vases to send home to family. He didn't know much about rugs or jewelry, so browsing those shops didn't spark much interest.

It was early evening when they had finished browsing the shops and decided to load up. They took off again and worked their way through the city and headed back to Bagram. There wasn't much to look at now the sun was down. The night air was cool so they rolled up the windows. The two vehicles raced through the lonely night and followed the path to the coalition compound.

"What do you know about Colonel McNeme?" Steele looked at Lewis then back into the dark.

"Not much, but I heard he was here helping the Mujahedin back when they were fighting the Soviets. He's supposed to be real hardcore.

Nobody messes with him. I think he worked with the CIA back then or something. He's laid back. Seems pretty cool too."

"He seems like he's at home here that's for sure."

"Guess that's what a life like this will do for you. Hard to imagine"

"Intense that's for sure," Steele nodded in agreement.

Steele didn't think much about the future before entering the Army. Now that he thought about it he was sure he could do thirty years of a life of adventure in foreign countries. He would enjoy setting out to see new places and meeting people of different cultures. The only hitch was being away from home. The hardest thing about being deployed was being away from the ones he cared about.

Deployment to a combat zone hadn't amounted to much so far except for the mine field. It was office work at the big tent since he arrived. Today's trip finally made it start to seem real for him. His mom kept telling him the only thing the news showed back home was everything bad that happened. It drove her crazy with worry. She had developed a love hate relationship with the news but still tuned in to hear what was happening anyway. The deployment wasn't any easier hearing how the people back home were worried. He took comfort knowing that at least this was something worthwhile. *This isn't a deployment in some part of the world our country has no business being in. Those planes didn't fly themselves into the Twin Towers. Those people murdered thousands of people. Who knows what they will do. My family could be next. We have to be here. They hit us first, we have to finish it.*

His thoughts merged with the rumble of the road. The dark surroundings eased his eyes shut. His shoulder slumped into the door. His M-16 pinched his leg, his head snapped up and he looked around startled. He sat up rubbed his face and shook his head.

"Don't sweat it. Go ahead and get some sleep." Lewis laughed at him. "There's nothing out here. You couldn't see anything out there if you stayed awake, anyway."

Looking out his window into the pitch black night, Steele couldn't see a thing. "That's true. I don't think I'll get any sleep but I think I'll get comfortable just the same."

Steele shifted his weapon and found a more comfortable spot. His muscles loosened as he began to relax. The heat had sapped his energy, as usual. The vibration of the road and the sound of the rushing wind was soothing. The darkness wrapped him like a blanket and his fatigue grew heavy as he settled into it. His mind and body were exhausted after the full day of adrenaline and excitement. His eyes stared into the night and became heavy once again. The rush of the shadows became a blur as his eyes fought instinctively to stay open. He was losing the battle when he saw a light turn on beyond the road in the dark.

In the back of his mind the sight seemed odd. For some reason he couldn't put his finger on what bugged him about it. He stared for a moment. The light in the distance flipped on and off.

"Hey, I think I just saw someone turn on a light." He started to sit up. "I didn't think..."

POP! POP! POP!

He looked back in the SUV and could see dust kicking up and sparks fly as pop after pop sounded inside. He could hear the rounds pop in one side and slam into the far side of the vehicle.

"Holy! Someone's shooting at us!" He yelled in disbelief.

"Some dirt farmer on hash with an AK probably!" Lewis yelled back wide eyed. He looked back over his shoulder then at the taillights of the lead vehicle ahead.

The rear passenger side window exploded. Pieces of shattered glass flew into the cab. Lewis tried to dodge the rounds as he jerked the vehicle to the left. He slammed the brakes as fragments rained down on them. The tires screeched as the vehicle lurched forward holding to the road for life.

"GO, GO, don't stop!" Steele looked around searching the night for the rounds that might find them again.

The radio crackled. "You guys alright back there? Saw your headlights jerk what's going on?"

"Someone's taking shots at us!" Steele's voice was pitched with fear and excitement.

"Did you guys stop?"

"Yeah, bullets were hitting the back and ..."

"Well, keep going. Don't stop. Everyone alright?"

Lewis punched the gas once more. The vehicle jerked to the left. He straightened it and they gained speed once again.

"We're good, truck's got some new tattoos, but we're good."

Steele had finally raised his weapon to return fire but the flicker in the distance had stopped. He looked around with his mouth agape.

"Keep the pedal down. It's mostly a straight shot back from here. We'll call in the action. Don't stop again." SSG Truitt ordered.

"Roger that. Out."

"Whoo hoo! Better than a movie, huh Steele?"

"I guess so, you crazy bastard." He looked back at the glass sparkling in the floor behind them and laughed.

He was wide awake for the rest of the drive as they raced back to the base. They laughed some more at the pure insanity of driving through the countryside at night getting shot at. When they arrived at the base, once again they stopped at the gate. Truitt assessed the damage in the cool night air while the MPs cleared them to get back onto the base.

"Looks like someone was having some late night fun at your expense. That happens once in a while at night. They'll send someone out to take a look but that guy is long gone or back in his house with his weapon stashed somewhere." SSG Truitt ran his hand over the bullet holes.

"It was weird. I saw a light flashing off the road and couldn't make sense of it till our cab sounded like a popcorn maker."

"Guess you guys are real combat veterans now," Truitt stated.

"Didn't feel much like combat. More like ducks in a shooting gallery," Steele argued.

"It's like that sometimes, eh Colonel?" Truitt smiled at the Colonel.

"More often than not. Glad you boys didn't catch one."

"Yes, Sir."

"I'm sure you boys are ready for some sleep after all that excitement. Let's get inside so we can call it a day. I'm tired."

"Roger that, Sir."

They entered the gates and stopped the vehicles to clear their weapons once they were back inside. Without any rounds chambered they continued into the base. They parked the Land Rovers where they had picked them up and Lewis and Steele headed to the tent with their gear and new trophies.

"That makes for a memorable trip, huh? You think you're up for it again?" Lewis put away his souvenirs and looked at Steele.

"Definitely. Being a sitting duck isn't exactly my idea of a good time, but it was still fun. I have to find more excuses to get out. It was worth it to do something besides sit in that circus tent all day."

"That was the first time getting shot at for me, but it's usually fun to get out of here." Lewis lay down on his cot and turned the light by his cot out. "See you tomorrow, Steele."

Craig sat on his cot and shook his head. The adventure was starting to unfold and it was nothing like he expected. He turned off his light and lay down on his cot. He could finally fall asleep. It was the deepest sleep he had since he arrived. It was sweeter because he knew that more adventures lay ahead.

9
TOWER TOUR

September came before he knew it. A Special Forces unit in the mountains lost some gear in a flash flood. A vehicle washed into a ravine and the equipment couldn't be recovered. All the units throughout AOR had to be issued new crypto. There were a lot of flights. The soldiers left behind had to take up the slack and the everyday duties became more frequent.

"You and Grant have tower duty tonight at zero hundred hours," Sergeant Hallis informed Craig as he walked back in the work area after lunch.

"Haven't pulled that duty before. What do I do?"

"Mike can take you over there and show you around. You guys go eat lunch then show him around okay, Mike?"

"Right on, Sergeant."

Mike and Craig went to the tent to grab something to eat. Craig grabbed an MRE and tore it open. He ate the crackers and peanut butter then scarfed down the M&Ms.

"You better take it easy with those things. They'll catch up." Mike's eyes widened as he patted his belly. "You got to get to the PX and get some real food."

"These MREs aren't so bad."

"You gotta have some standards."

"I've got standards. I think I lowered them when I didn't join the infantry. That's where the action is."

"Action? What are you loco, dude? You want some action? Should've gone infantry then."

"Nah, not yet. Told my dad I'd do a commo job so I wouldn't be on the front lines. It was the only way I could keep him from practically disowning me."

"Those shots you guys took the other night didn't make an impression on you?"

"They did but that wasn't exactly what I'm talking about."

"What? Do you like this kinda stuff or something? "

"This is what I have wanted to do since I was a kid."

"You are loco."

"Maybe, too many war movies as a kid, I guess. Not to mention the epic battles in my room with all my plastic army men. Besides, this is a family tradition. My family has always been in the military."

"Figures. But this isn't pretend. Those are real bullets and people try to kill you out here."

"What made you join then?"

"Dude, I want to go to college. I didn't have any money so I joined the Army to let them pay for it."

"So, here you are traveling the world and living large."

"You got it. You wait till we get back. I'll head home to Cali and then I'll really be living large. Speaking of living large let me show you what this duty is all about. You may change your mind about the Army after you pull some of the duties we get stuck on." They exited the tent and made their way through the maze of tents in the direction of the tower.

"We'll swing by the 82nd tents and I'll show you where you go if you need anything when you're on duty. If anything happens we call them to report it and if something crazy goes down, they will send out a quick reaction force to check things out."

Mike pointed to a tent on their right. It sat in the middle of a row not far from the tower. "Here we are."

The smell of gun oil and sweat drifted out of the tent as they entered. A soldier near the entrance sat reading a comic book next to a radio. He looked up at them then turned back to his comic.

"You really don't come here unless the radio dies and you need to swap it out. It's good to remember where this place is though. When it's dark, it can be hard to find. Let's go take a look at the tower, just so you know what to expect."

They made their way back through the maze of tents toward the perimeter wall. The hescos were stacked two high. The tower overlooked them and rows of razor wire glistened in the sun on top of them. The engineers had welded a tower platform together along with some stairs to reach it. The metal tower box stood slightly above the hescos. It was surrounded by sandbags on each side with more piled on the roof for good measure against incoming rounds. Craig noticed the stairs were steep and narrow as they climbed up to take a look around. Nodding at the soldiers on guard, Mike continued his tour as they stood on the landing outside the guard box.

"Not much to see, really. That shelled out building in front of us is used by the locals to take a leak, sometimes. They'll also dig around these burnt-out, rusted trucks for who knows what. Probably getting parts to make bombs or something, who knows? Past those trucks on the left is the village itself. That road from the village leads to a spot down the perimeter line where they're making a gate for traffic to pass through. It'll give the quick reaction force a better sprint into the area when someone lobs a rocket or something. We don't do much at this tower. Down by the airstrip is where they usually take fire. You usually hear about it in the shift briefings, but we hear it live on the radio once in a while. It's kinda cool."

Steele surveyed the area for a moment. He noted the rusted tangle that he could tell used to be a truck. Islands of grass led to the building in front of them. The roof was gone and the mud structure was crumbling. There were large holes all through it and what looked like fifty caliber holes climbing up the wall facing them. It looked odd with half the pieces of the building gone but the window sill still intact.

"Someone must have been holed up in the building once, huh? Looks like they lost that fight."

"What? Oh yeah, sure." Mike pulled out a cigarette with little interest in the surroundings.

Behind the building was a field of grass at least three feet high. A meager stream could be seen at the wide spots where it turned. The field ended at a row of trees in front of the village buildings.

"Wonder why they didn't clear all this area out?"

"They cleared the first twenty feet from the tower all the way around the post. Don't guess it was a priority for them at the time."

"Seems a little risky to have that building right there. Good cover if someone wanted to try something."

"No one's trying anything here. The warlord of this area doesn't want any trouble. He won't let anything serious happen here. I heard they are paying him pretty good, so he keeps things mostly quiet. So any questions about the duty?"

"For starters, how long is the duty?"

"Oh yeah, two hours."

"So, we just sit here and what? Do we get night vision goggles or something?"

"Nah, they don't give us those. I guess since we don't see much action here they don't waste them on us."

"What if we do get some action?"

"I guess you'd better get on the radio fast and let the eighty second come save the day."

"That's a crock. What kind of duty is this? Pulling night guard at zero hundred hours with no night vision."

"You think that's bad? Sometimes you can't see your hand in front of your face. If there is cloud cover it's just a waste of time but hey, I just do what they tell me. I'm just here for the education. Don't sweat it, you're the man of steel."

"If you're following orders blindly like this, you do need an education."

"Talk it up, Steele. The longer you are out here the less gung-ho you're gonna be."

"Oh yeah? So you were gung-ho when you got here?"

"I never was a hard charging idealist like you. I'm just saying I've seen it happen to guys just like you. You guys are ready to charge the hill and save the world when you get here. Then reality kicks in and you see that there's so much BS that it's just not worth it."

"Humph," Steele looked back at the village.

"That's about it for the duty. Come by the tent and wake Grant up about fifteen till. Sound good?"

"Works for me. This doesn't seem so bad really."

"You haven't been sitting on a two mile strip of dirt for six months waiting to leave yet either."

10
TP

Craig headed to the tent to grab a snack and wake up Grant at twenty three thirty hundred hours. He entered the dark tent and turned on his mag light. The red lens shot a beam of light through the tent.

"Grant," Craig shook him a little. "Grant, get up it's time to pull duty."

"Huh?" Grant managed. He lay there waiting for his brain to catch up. Sitting up he shook his head to clear his mind. "Man, I was back home at a pool party with some friends. We had this barbecue going and music playing. The drinks were cold, the women were hot, everything was going great. Then the music stops and a voice came over the radio calling me. There was this one female in a blue bikini. Man, she liked me too. All my friends looked at me and started to say goodbye and turn around and leave. Then the chick in the blue bikini said it was time for duty."

"Sorry, man."

He let out a sigh, "Ah, don't worry, it only gets worse. Let's go."

The base was like a big city. The obvious difference was the lack of street lights. The noise never stopped. Generators chattered throughout the night. The airfield was busy as usual. The only light was the moon and the stars. Craig couldn't help but glance around at the sky as he made his way to the tower. There were more stars in the sky than he had seen since he was a boy. He used to see nights like this at his granddad's place in the country, but it had been a long time. *Too much time in the concrete jungle. It's good to be out.* They made their way through the shadowy tents and climbed the metal stairs.

"Anything going on?" Grant asked the soldiers on shift as he and Craig walked in.

"Nothing, another quiet night." One handed Grant the radio and the two disappeared down the stairs. Grant was in the tower first and took up a position on the right side. Steele followed and took the left.

Grant called in, "Cherokee this is tower 5. Grant and Steele are on duty over."

"Copy that tower 5."

They didn't think this thing through. Craig complained to himself.

What business do we have in a guard tower next to an afghan village with no night vision? This isn't Vietnam. They have night vision on police cars back home, so why don't we have any here for crying out loud? We're a pretty good target silhouetted up off the ground against the night sky.

Not something he wanted to be in a country where the people didn't necessarily like them. He couldn't see ground beyond the buildings. He looked out into the night. The landscape just disappeared into blackness.

There wasn't much to talk about at zero hundred hours. They would both rather be doing just about anything other than sitting in a guard tower locked and loaded, staring into darkness. An hour rolled by and they called in their status.

"I'm going to take a nap, wake me up when it's time to go."

Grant left his weapon on the sand bags lining the window. He lowered himself into the corner on the tower floor.

"No problem. Get some rest." Craig scanned the darkness. *Maybe he was right. This could get old quick.*

It didn't take long before a slight snore came from the lump of clothes in the shadow. Steele looked out in the darkness to find anything unusual to occupy his time. Lights flickered in the windows of some of the buildings in the village. *A late night fire to stay warm I guess.* There were fires on the mountainside directly in front of them. He couldn't make out where they were, but they had to be pretty big. The fires were high up on the mountain. There was so much he didn't know about these people. He couldn't imagine the lives they led war after war. Even if there wasn't a war, land mines were always blowing away someone's foot or leg, or worse. *A miserable little existence.*

What was that? Something moved ahead of him and to the left. Or did it? He couldn't really tell. Maybe his mind was just playing tricks on him.

It's late after all. There was some motion again! His heart started to beat quicker.

His senses sharpened. He could hear the slight wind moving the grass. He still couldn't see anything.

He looked down at Grant who was still snoring, then back at the landscape. He eased back into the shadow of the tower. He waited.

Left of the building in front of him, a figure darted out from the weeds to the rusted truck in front of them. Steele leaned forward and zeroed his weapon on the figure as it disappeared next to the hunk of metal. He gripped the stock of his weapon with his shoulder. His trigger finger rested on the cold steel above the trigger. Steele kept his eyes scanning from the pile to the building and nudged Grant with his foot.

"Wake up," he squeezed the words out in a whisper.

"What, time to go?" Grant questioned loudly half asleep.

"Shhh! Someone is out there by the truck." Craig strained to see where the person was. "I couldn't tell at first, but he came from the left side of the building."

Grant scrambled up to his feet and grabbed his weapon.

"Don't think I've ever seen anyone out here at night."

"What the heck is he doing?"

"Maybe he came to take a dump," Grant snickered.

"Hope so."

"Could be some kid screwing around, you know."

"Should we call it in?"

"Nothing to call in yet. You might have seen a goat or something."

"It wasn't a goat, it was a person." The defiance grew in Craig's voice.

"Well just the same, we should wait 'til we have something to report."

They both stared out into the darkness. Steele could hardly breathe. The figure reappeared and ran to the building. Steele and Connor followed him with their weapons as he made his way back to the grass and disappeared.

"That was weird," Grant stated blankly.

"Sure was. We better call that in. The guy could have been doing something."

"I guess. Couldn't hurt to let them know someone was out there. They'll probably send the quick reaction force, but that guy'll be long gone. At least they'll have fun though getting all hyped up to grab someone. I'll call it in."

"Tower five to Cherokee."

"Tower five to Cherokee."

"Yeah tower five, what's up?"

"We just had a local come nosing around our area. Was running around in the weeds trying to stay out of sight. He got about fifteen feet from us in a covered position. Stayed for a while, and then took off. Over."

"Okay, tower five I'll pass it along."

"Roger that. Out."

"That was intense. If the guy wasn't doing anything, he shouldn't have been sneaking around like that. Doesn't he know he could get shot?"

"He probably knows he won't. Damn Hajis. Irritate the hell out of me."

"Cherokee to tower five."

"Tower five, go ahead Cherokee."

"LT wanted to know if the guy had toilet paper stuck to his shoe when he was running off. Over."

Grant cursed again.

"Tell the LT that we didn't see any but he can come up here and take a look for himself if he'd like. Over."

"LT says he'll leave those important things to you. Cherokee out."

"What'd I tell you?" Grant slammed the radio down annoyed.

They stared out into the darkness in silence. There was no more sleeping now. The excitement faded into boredom as the night wore on. They finally heard footsteps as their replacements made their way up the tower stairs.

"We've got it from here, guys."

"Later, enjoy your watch."

Craig and Grant made their way down the stairs back into the maze of tents.

"Glad that's over."

"Yeah, now I can get some real sleep."

"So explain this to me. When we work the day shift most of the time we pull night duty. When we work the night shift we end up doing commo runs half the time."

"Man, that's the Army way. If it makes sense, don't do it, or at least do the opposite."

Steele heard something like a whistle faintly over the noise of the generator and turned to look.

"Did you hear...?" He couldn't finish the sentence. Both ducked on instinct.

An explosion, so loud the heater couldn't silence it, ripped through the night and the ground shook from the impact. A flash at the tower lit the area for a moment.

Steele couldn't believe his eyes, looking at the cloud of smoke over the tower. Soldiers began pouring out of the tents scrambling for bunkers.

His chest began pounding. The adrenaline made his body tremble from the rush. He looked around taking in the scene.

"Where are you going?" Steele yelled when he noticed Grant on a dead run to the bunkers.

"Going to get some cover!" Grant yelled looking back over his shoulder.

Steele looked at the stream of soldiers headed in the opposite direction of the tower and back at Grant already on his way to join them.

"Grant, get over here. We have to check on those soldiers in the tower!"

"What?! You check. I'm outta here."

Steele shook his head in disbelief then ran to the tower.

"You guys alright?" He yelled as he climbed the stairs.

"Yeah, about pissed myself though," one yelled and laughed.

Steele entered the tower. Dirt was everywhere. Dust still filled the air from the explosion. All he could smell was sand and gun powder. He half expected something else.

"What did they say on the radio?"

"They're sending out the QRF to see if they can find the launch site."

"Good sized hole over there," Steele noted as he looked to the right of the tower.

"Yeah, glad that missed us. We'd have been toast."

"Alright, you guys keep your heads down."

"Hate it when that happens," one laughed.

"Yeah, see ya."

Grant was climbing the stairs as Steele came out.

"Everyone okay?"

"Change of heart?"

"I felt kind of bad," Grant replied sheepishly.

"Yeah, it hit about twenty feet out. Want to come take a look?"

"Hell no! I want to get to a bunker in case there's another one. Not go and take pictures like a tourist. Let's go."

"On the way."

"You're crazy, man. Don't you know when we have incoming fire you're supposed to head to the bunker?"

"C'mon man, we had to go check on them. They might have been hit. What if it had been you?"

"Whatever, you're crazy, dude."

Equipment rattled as soldiers in full battle rattle brushed passed them and headed to the tower.

"Guess the eighty second is on the way to check things out. That was intense." Steele watched the heavy laden soldiers pass in disbelief.

The soldiers in the compound were already leaving the bunkers as Craig and Grant made their way back to their tent.

"Yeah, it was intense. Don't need to be taking any chances out here, man. I'm trying to get home in one piece alright. Next time I won't go back with you to check." Grant threatened Craig halfheartedly.

"We'll see."

"Hey, check out that." Grant pointed with a laugh.

"Hey, Charlie! Your mom would be proud." Steele joined Grant in his laughter.

"Not the best way to pick up chicks, man."

"Hey, if she doesn't like me all nat-u-ral we're going to have some problems anyway. Might as well get started off on the right foot." In the rush to get out of the tent Mike had grabbed his weapon but that was it. Charlie smiled big and looked around proud of himself.

"You're not getting anywhere if she sees you like that."

"You kidding me? I'm in all my God-given glory. There's nothing to hide here."

"You need some help. I'll see you guys later. I'm headed back to the circus tent where it's safe."

"Later, Steele."

The guys made their way back to the tent, giving Charlie a hard time. Steele made his way back to the circus tent. The MP's cleared him and he sat down in a chair. The adrenaline wore off and he was exhausted. There was always something happening to keep him on his toes.

Not much happens here, right.

11

STEAK NIGHT

He lay on his bunk and thought about being in class back home getting ready for Thanksgiving. It didn't seem much like November.

"Morning, Hero." Ensly walked in the tent with a smirk.

Craig stretched and replied indifferently. "That it is, SGT."

Ensly kept on talking. "Looks like we're going to send you to some nice locations down south. How does Kandahar sound?"

"Sounds good. I'm not going with you am I, SGT?"

"Laugh it up." Ensly shot him an angry look. "You don't run anything around here."

"Am I flying out anytime soon?"

"Hallis has you out on a flight in a couple of days."

"Great, I knew I could count on you, SGT Ensly. Thanks."

SGT Ensly huffed and turned on his TV. He popped in a DVD, put on some headphones and grabbed a bag of chips.

Craig glanced over his shoulder and laughed as he dressed. He made his way to the circus tent and Hallis met him as Craig entered the commo section.

"You'll be heading out again tomorrow with Flores. I'm sending you down to Kandahar. There's handful of units down there you'll need to see."

"Be glad to go. Being on the move is the best thing about this job."

"Tell me about it. I hardly ever get to leave so don't rub it in or I'll throw you back on some sorry duty." He slapped Craig on the shoulder.

The flight to Kandahar was uneventful. The airport was a throwback to the seventies.

"That's a sweet look" Craig noted the wave of arches that spanned the entrance to the airport.

"Guess we don't get to go check out the scenery." Flores observed as the group ahead of them walked off the tarmac to a little wooden shack near the corner of the airstrip.

"Can you tell me where the 5th Special Forces group is located around here?" Craig asked an Airman at the counter.

"About a quarter of a mile down the main road, on the left. You can't miss them."

Kandahar had been a Taliban stronghold and was still a hot spot for a lot of activity. The Taliban enjoyed a lot of loyalty from the locals so the coalition forces took fire more often than Bagram.

There was more ground activity here with vehicles headed up and down the main street. A steady stream of contractors from the states were working almost everywhere they looked. The Special Forces location was non-descript. The tip off was all the soldiers walking around in half uniforms or whatever attire they chose.

"Can I help you guys?" A bearded man met them as they entered the compound.

"Looking for SFC Blackburn."

"He's over in that building if he's not already eating. They fired up some steaks on the grill if you boys are hungry." He motioned them in and walked off to a little hut next to the entrance. Craig and Flores looked at each other in disbelief.

"This is my kind of deployment." Craig motioned Flores toward the building.

"You guys looking for someone?" A man with a mustache and ballcap offered to help as they roamed the hallway of the building.

"SFC Blackburn"

"He's in there." The man pointed over his left shoulder to an open doorway. "Hey Jesse! You've got some visitors."

Jesse met them at the doorway. "Hey you my crypto kings from Bagram?"

"Roger that, Sergeant."

"You guys haven't been around here before have you? Just call me Jesse. We use first names around here."

"Alright then, I'm Craig." He smiled and shook Jesse's hand.

"Mike," added Flores.

"Welcome to my humble abode boys. We'll get you settled outside in a tent in a minue, but first, let me get off the phone with my lady and I'll give you guys the tour." He stepped back to the desk and chatted for a moment then hung up the phone. "Alright where were we? Oh yeah the tour. It's pretty simple. Commo shop is right here. Up this ladder is a loft that we have turned into a movie room. We have a projector hooked up to a laptop and show movies every night. Whatever's playing in the states is playing here every night. Your tents are back outside the way you came. You probably saw the grill pad on the way in."

"They were grilling steaks when we came in."

"I forgot its steak night. We better get out there and get some. They don't last long. They are good, some nice New York strips done right on the grill. You can't beat them. Tim is from Nashville and he cooks them like one of those high dollar places. Drop your bags and c'mon." He walked out of the doorway and they dropped their bags and followed. Jesse shook hands with a couple of men along the way then got in the line.

"Like I said this will make your whole trip worth it." The smoke rising from the grill and the smell of the steaks was intoxicating. "I can't believe you have a steak night." Craig shook his head.

"Better believe it. We have better food than I get at home, and my wife is a good cook."

"Smells better than the food we have in Bagram," Mike agreed.

"Of course it is, you kidding me?"

After the steak they took their servings of corn and potatoes and made their way to the picnic benches.

"So how do you boys like that Army chow?" Jesse teased.

"It's okay." Mike answered.

"Welcome to excellent then. You boys need to decide if you want okay or great!"

"I have to tell you this is the best chow I've had since I've been here."

"No kidding," Jesse exclaimed feigning insult. "You boys must not get out much," he mocked.

"Guess not," they mumbled through stuffed mouths.

"I tell you what. Let's get you settled in your tent and we'll take care of the crypto tomorrow. You boys need a rest. Even better. We'll catch a movie after chow and call it a night. Sound good?"

"Sure." Craig wasn't sure what to think of the difference in lifestyle. Other soldiers sat down at the tables spread around the yard. Craig observed the lack of conformity. There was no standard dress code other than anything goes. From ball caps to jungle hats to t-shirts and cargo pants. He could tell the point of the clothes had more to do with practical utility mixed with personal preference than anything. Some guys went with lighter pants that breathed while others chose heavier ones that would stand some rough wear while outside the wire. The variety of weapons matched the clothes. Personal preference abound. The weapons were not straight issue concerned with the lowest bidder and the simplest grunt to be able to use them. Weapons were customized and higher end. It was a gun lover's fantasy. H&Ks to MP5s and everything in between. Some hummers in the yard had .50 calibers mounted on top. This scene was enough to convince a person that these guys were ready to inflict some damage when called upon.

"If you boys have had enough to eat let's get you to your tent." Jesse got them up from the table to throw away their plates. They picked their gear up from Jesse's office and he showed them the visitor tents. Mike took off to the can and Craig took their bags in. Another person was in the tent as Craig entered. He sat on the edge of a bunk with his weapon laid across the black duffle bag in his lap. He opened his eyes as he looked up at Craig. Wrinkles marked his weathered face. Gray hairs speckled his hair.

"How's it going?" Craig offered as he threw the bags on the cots.

"Pretty good." The man looked tired.

"You staying here?"

"Just passing through."

"You look like you're SF. I'd have thought you'd have a room in one of the buildings." Craig opened his bag and rolled his sleeping bag down the cot he had picked.

"I'm just waiting on my team leader so we can get back to our FOB."

"You guys come to town often?"

"Not really. We we're here just picking up some cash. We got that." He patted the duffle bag. "I wanted to get some sleep while he was taking care of other business."

"Sorry for interrupting."

"It's okay. I never get much sleep anyway. The body gets used to it."

"Cash? What do you guys need cash for out in the middle of nowhere?"

"It's the only way we get anything done out there. We get most of our stuff from the locals. Fuel and stuff we just pay them cash for. It helps build cooperation. They don't like seeing their cash cow disappear either so they're pretty helpful when it comes to finding the bad guys."

"Really? Wow. So what's life like out there?"

The man smiled and sat up straighter. "Time goes by fast. We stay busy all the time. You can work twenty four hours straight without realizing it, there's so much to do."

"You serious? What are you guys so busy doing?"

"Well, for starters we get hit with incoming or small arms fire just about every night. Our twelve man team is split up with half working during the day and the other half working at night. Since we take fire so much we don't get a lot of sleep. The day shift doubles as the quick reaction force so when anything happens we have to go check things out. We rarely find anything. The bad guys have fired and taken off most of the time, but we still have to go check it out. Then if we pull a night mission you miss part of your sleep again."

"It goes on like that the whole time?"

"Most of the time. We have some Ranger platoons rotate through sometimes and they pull some of those duties for us and it helps but it's still hard to sleep when someone is throwing a rocket at you."

"So what are you doing during the day?"

"During the day, it's constant work too. We're always improving the position, cleaning weapons, training locals, patrols, you name it there's always something to do."

"You guys even work with the locals?"

"Sure, that gives us something else to do."

"Yeah, like what?"

"Watch them and try to figure out who is legit and who's not."

"How long have you been doing this?"

"Longer than you've been around probably."

"You have to love it to be doing it this long."

"Something like that. I've got a couple of ex-wives and child support so I have to do something to keep the money coming in." His teeth glowed in the early evening light.

"I've thought about going Special Forces but wasn't sure what you guys did."

"We do a little bit of everything. Depends on where we are. We do a lot of combat missions and social work out here. Some places it's more helping the locals with medical and dental missions, some it's training militias how to fight, others it's pure combat and hunting the bad guys. I can tell you this much, if you join you won't get bored. There's no time to. We don't keep guys around doing nothing. If we're not on missions or training we'll send you home to relax. None of that keeping guys around just to have them around. That regular army crap used to kill me. I couldn't take it now at my age. If you want some adventure get out of the Army and join the Special Forces." He smiled again. "It's been good talking with you, Son, but I'm going to get some more sleep before I head out."

"Sure, good luck."

"Thanks."

Craig shifted his sleeping bag and lay on top of it. Staring at the tent fabric, ideas of the front lines in the war on terror raced through his mind. He imagined what kind of man it took to do such a hard job. He realized he had butterflies in his stomach as he lay there thinking about the idea. Smiling to himself he laughed, *get out of the Army and join the Special Forces!*

The man was long gone when they woke up in the morning. They saw Jesse first and then were off to other units they had to see. They found a Marine unit on the outskirts of the base and an Air Force unit by the tarmac. It felt like they had walked miles with their full BDUs, rucks and weapons as they made their way back to the SF compound. In the commo room they found Jesse on his laptop chatting with his lady back home.

"You boys get it all done?" He waved them to some seats.

"That we did." Craig inclined his head as he sat down. "Jesse what made you join Special Forces?"

"Well, just seemed like the thing to do. Best decision I ever made. Why? You thinking about joining?"

"Thinking about it. Thinking about a lot of things but it's one of them."

"It's a great life that's for sure."

"It is for you. I met a guy working out of an FOB who made it sound like life was pretty hard where he was."

"It all depends. Just like any job in the Army there are tradeoffs. In SF you have plenty of things to do and the best equipment and people to do them with. Can you say that about what you've seen in the Army so far?"

"A good point, but I don't know."

"What's her name?"

"Huh?"

"Your girl back home. What's her name?"

"Oh, Melissa." He smiled sheepishly.

"That's the one thing that'll keep a guy out of the Special Forces. You have to make that choice but I tell you it'll change your life and you won't want out when you get in. Melissas will come and go but you can only be in the Army for a little while."

"That's what they tell me but I keep seeing old men like you running around and it gives me hope."

"Hey Cap," Jesse called out.

"What's up Jesse?"

"This young man will be headed back to Bagram tomorrow and is thinking about getting out of the army any words of wisdom?"

"Leaving the army will be the best decision of your life. You come and run with us and you'll have the best time of your life. There's nothing happening up there in Bagram but that three ring circus they call a command center. You should get out in the wild country and see how the other half lives."

"I've seen some of the wild country, Sir."

"Name's Eddy." The captain walked over and extended his hand.

"Craig."

"Well Craig, it's nothing but wild country out here. When we leave the comforts of the big base we make peace with the people we can and kill or capture the ones that have other ideas. It'll change your life."

"I'm thinking about it Sir, but I only have a year in right now."

"You have any college?"

"I have two years."

"Oh really? And you've got a clearance?"

"Top Secret."

"How long is your tour?"

"Looks like it'll be a full nine."

"You give me a call if you decide to join and I can get you in the Q course at Bragg by the time you're heading home if you get serious."

"Alight, I'll keep that in mind."

"Don't do it because you're bored. Do it if you want a real challenge. If you're not ready and mentally tough you'll never make it." He disappeared down the hall with a wave.

"See boys. If you want some real adventure, take the next step."

"The next step huh? I don't see a lot of chicks around here and the next step I take will be in their direction." Mike huffed.

"What do you think Craig?"

"I think I have a couple months to figure things out."

"Sure, Special Forces isn't going anywhere but you don't want to miss where it can take you. That, I can guarantee."

12
TURKISH NIGHTS

Winter snuck up on them. Snow crept down from the peaks and into the villages. The strong winds had long died down and the cold December nights in the valley left behind a frost in the air. The ground had turned into mud and stagnant pools of cold, dirty water.

"This shuttling between tents is getting to be a real pain."

"At least those one hundred twenty degree days are gone."

"Wonder how long before we get heaters?"

"Bet it doesn't take long, too much brass around here not to get them."

"Speak of the devil, check it out." Charlie pointed at the commercial grade heaters that lined the tent rows.

Between the tents stood heaters that were four foot high and chugging away. The air reeked with diesel fumes. Not exactly up to military specifications with their yellow and black paint, but they would do the trick. Collapsible vents ran from each generator to multiple tents. They marveled as they passed the heaters. They reached their tent and hot air blasted them as they walked in.

"What the..."

"They're not kidding about these heaters."

The guys were lying on their bunks with no covers.

"It's like summertime in here now. Yesterday you nearly had to have your jacket on, but now it won't be long and we'll be sweating again."

"Keep that flap open a little to let some of this heat out." Mike croaked.

"We'll have to see if we can adjust the temperature on those things or not."

"Didn't dehydrate with the summer heat, but I just might in this," laughed Charlie.

They settled in for another night of popcorn and the "Sopranos" on DVD. Grant came in the middle of the first episode.

"Come to get a nap?"

"I wish. Someone lost some crypto in the field and the chief wants you to head up to Uzbekistan with Conner, Craig. You up for it?"

"Heck yeah, I'd love to go somewhere."

"Alright, get your stuff together for a trip. The guys are getting the crypto ready so you can check it when you pick it up."

"You mean right now?"

"There are a couple of stops on this trip so chief wants to get it out right away. You're headed out ASAP."

"Sweet!, Tell him I'm packing up."

"It'll be good, dude. They have some pretty good food and Air Force chicks up there. They wear civilian clothes too. Miss that. Not to mention the perfume."

"Ok, ok. Do you need to hit the shower or something?"

"Laugh it up, Steele. When you're here six months you'll be doing the same thing. You'll miss that stuff."

"What are you talking about? Six months? I think you were missing that back home." The guys joined in laughing.

They packed up their rucks and made their way to the big circus tent.

"You guys going somewhere?" the MP at the gate asked.

"Yep, hot women in civies and good food!"

"Take me with you. I haven't seen or smelled either since I got here. It's been five months." The MP pleaded with his eyes as he looked up at them from digging through their rucks following the security procedure.

"Tell me about it. Feel sorry for you guys. You got the wrong job!"

"Seems like it now. Rather be flying to some spot with clean women than talking to you guys, that's for sure. Alright, you guys are good." The MP gave them back their bags and sent them in.

They made their way back to the office and picked up their crypto, then made their way to the flight line. They waited an hour then they heard their names called.

"Steele, Conner," the Airman called motioning them to the counter.

"You guys are up."

They made their way to a C-130 with engines running in the pitch black night. The air was a mixture of JP8 fuel and oil. The winds billowed in hot gusts from the engine, mingled with the cold night air. The plane had touched down unloaded, reloaded and was ready to go. The two of them threw their gear on the floor and strapped in.

"It's lights out on this flight. If you need some light, make sure its red lensed." The load master yelled to them over the noise of the engines.

Nodding, they strapped in. The plane lurched forward then clawed its way up out of the valley into the pitch dark sky. The pallets on the floor shifted as the plane took flight upward. The chains caught and snapped tight in the red glow. The force of the lift made it hard to relax until they left the valley. When they reached their flight altitude and leveled off, they unbuckled and stretched their legs. The hum of the engines and the darkness made a perfect combination for catching some sleep.

The sound of pants shuffling woke Craig. Glancing up he saw the load master looking out of the window over the wing. Shining a flashlight and talking into his mic, he moved around trying to get a good look at something. The load master kept talking. Pressing the Indiglo on his watch to see how long he'd been asleep, Craig noticed it had only been an hour. The load master went to the other side of the plane. He looked out the window at the other wing. Craig realized something was wrong and sat up. He looked around and saw the others were awake and paying attention now too. The load master stopped talking into his mic and the plane banked to the left. The load master noticed his passengers were awake and made his way over to them.

"We have to go back. We have some ice starting to form on the wings. We didn't get de-iced in Bagram, so we have to turn this bird around. We'll be fine heading back but we can't make it all the way to Uzbekistan like this." He grinned at the nervous faces in the red light.

They looked at each other in the dim red light as the load master went back to his station.

It wasn't easy to sleep with the thought of icy wings rolling around in the back of their minds. Anxiously they sat in the darkness waiting to be back on solid ground.

Three hours later they were back in the air on a C-17. Practically a luxury liner compared to the C-130, the power of the C-17's lift was much stronger and they leveled off quickly. The smooth, quiet ride made him think they'd be rolling out the snack cart any minute. He smiled at the thought and drifted off to sleep. They made it to Uzbekistan and were met with more weather. The plane descended and everyone started getting ready to unload but it never touched down. The new load master was nodding and talking on his mic as they descended and rose for a second time. Craig sat up concerned again. The load master made his way over and explained.

"The pilot can't see the runway. There's too much snow. We're going to fly on to Turkey. You guys will have to get another flight when we get there."

"You been to Turkey before?"

"No, but I like this trip already." Steele settled back for the long flight ahead.

They arrived in the early morning.

"This way, gentlemen." An airman greeted them as they unloaded. "You guys here for some R&R or going home?"

"Our flight was rerouted. We'll be here till we get another flight back to K2," Conner answered.

"Sorry to hear that. This place is nice though. You guys can have a pretty good time while you're here."

"Plan to. Any chance of getting off post and into town?"

"Sure, just make your way to the gate in the morning and request a pass. It's easy. First we have to check you guys in though. We'll need your weapons and all your rounds."

They followed her into a concrete bunker. An armed airman stood at the counter waiting for them to check in.

"I'll need you to fill out these forms." The airman slid the paperwork across the counter at the soldiers.

"You'll need to write down each weapons type, serial number, enter the amount of magazines, and any ordinance you have, we will count your rounds and you'll get a receipt when it's all done."

"We have some crypto that we need to store with you guys too. You guys hold Comsec here or do we need to see someone else for that?"

"Pete here can take you to our communications people and they can hook you up after we're finished with the weapons."

"Yeah, and I'll take you to the bus that'll get you to your housing after you guys finish up," the female Airman offered.

"I'll start with you, Conner. One rifle, two magazines, twenty four rounds each. Anything else?"

"No, that's it. We travel light."

"Ok, sign this paperwork. Here is your copy."

"Steele?"

"The same. One rifle, two mags and forty eight rounds."

"Ok, you? Last name?"

"Winter, One rifle, eight mags, one hundred ninety two rounds, one pistol, six mags, fifty-four rounds, two grenades."

"Ok guys, you're set. I'll see you guys when it's time to go."

"Gents, you can follow me and we'll go drop off your commo gear and get you settled."

"So what's with all the hardware, Winter? Who are you, the lone ranger?" Conner joked.

"Counter intelligence division. We go to a lot of hot areas and have to be ready to roll. What are you doing running around with forty eight rounds in this AOR anyway? You guys aren't going to be worth much good if anything hits the fan."

"It doesn't hit the fan in the places we go. What kind of hot areas do you go to anyway? Forward operating bases?" Steele joined.

"Yeah, I go to FOBs all the time. I spend most of my time with the Special Forces. Those guys like to requisition things that are destined for other units. I go investigate the missing equipment then bang out reports all about it."

"You kidding me? The SF is stealing from the other units and you're typing reports on it?"

"Happens all the time. Not just them. Everyone is short of something out here. Someone is always taking something that belongs to someone else. The SF are just the best at it. No one really likes to go out to the FOBs to check things either. I'm the new guy, so I get tasked with it most of the time."

"So what happens when your reports go out?"

"Not much really, they get a slap on the wrist but their brass doesn't really care. They care more about results so they could give a shit. The regular units have a different perspective and take it a little more personally, so we get some results with them."

"That's got to be weird going out to an FOB to track down stuff they've taken. How do they handle you coming around asking questions?"

"They don't care. The treat me like one of them. They just think it's funny. They're out hunting and killing bad guys and the government is looking for missing steaks. They just fire them up on the grill and cook dinner then throw a plate in front of you. What do you do?" He smiled with a shrug.

"Man SF lives the life," Steele admired.

"Those guys live a hard life but they're the kings out in the wild that's for sure."

"That's what I want to be someday. The king of the wild."

13
AREA 51

The cold rooms and soft linen on the beds kept them asleep till lunch.

"Hey Winter, been up long?"

"Hey guys. I made my way to the flight line, no flights today."

"Sounds like we're headed off post then." Conner rubbed his hands together. "Let's go get that pass."

"Easy, Conner. We might not get a pass. I'm hungry anyway, let's go eat first."

"Alright, but we head straight to the gate after we eat. I want to see some concrete and local beauties. You in, Winter?"

"I've been around nothing but stink'in dudes for the past couple weeks. I haven't been here before either so it sounds like a winner to me."

The whole event reminded Steele of being in school. It was like getting a permission slip to go to the bathroom. A little piece of paper saying "yes", they were allowed to roam the halls during the afternoon. Their papers were stamped and they were on their way.

"Took long enough. With the runaround I thought we'd never leave!" Conner exclaimed.

"So, which way?"

"Looks like everything is that way." Winter pointed to the right where they could see some shop signs.

It was still early in the day, but the aromas of meat and bread cooking filled the air. The fragrances, mixed with the sweet smell of alcohol, enticed them down the road. The sun heated the pavement in the cool, morning light reminding Steele of the short summer-like bursts during winter in Texas.

"Can't beat this. No snow and you don't even need a jacket." Conner basked in the balmy afternoon.

"I remember one Christmas back home when I went fishing in December. Nothing but jeans and a t-shirt."

"Man, Steele, you gotta get out more. You don't go fishing when it's like this outside. You hit the town and find some ladies."

"Ok Conner, lead the way."

"Hey, let's go check out the goods." Conner motioned them into a store.

"They have everything. Nike, Timberland, and Adidas." Steele flipped through the jackets on a rack.

"But they're all knockoffs." Winter dismissed them with a wave of his hand.

"Yeah, but who cares? Besides, it's not like you can tell they're not the real thing. They're made pretty good."

The shops had everything from music, movies, to jewelry and furs. The hours passed as they browsed the local goods.

"They don't jump at the chance to make a sale here do they?" Steele observed as they walked out of a failed negotiation as they left a leather shop.

"I think the base gives them steady business. They probably don't sweat it much," Winter suggested.

"True."

"Man, you guys sound like a couple of old men on a park bench somewhere talking about the weather or something. What I want to talk about is the women. Where are they?"

"Easy, Conner. It's still early. I bet they'll start hitting the clubs when it gets dark," Steele reassured him.

"You guys ready for some dinner?" Winter patted his stomach and looked around.

"I've been having so much fun I hadn't noticed. Let's grab something local," Steele responded.

"Easy with that local food. Let's go back to the base, get some chow, then come back to drink," Conner contested.

"What? And miss this local food? No way," Winter continued. "I thought you were into the local scene with the women and all."

"Women and drinks, yes. Food, no."

"Look, you have to broaden your horizons. What if you fell for one of these local Turkish women and all she cooked was kabobs and stuff? What would you do then?"

"Ka-what? She'd have to learn how to cook and eat American food. Pizza, hamburgers and hot dogs. Besides, you must have me confused with someone else." He smiled and looked around. "I'm not trying to get married. I'm just looking for a little fun."

"Talking about getting out. Conner, you need some exposure to the real world."

"Man, I'm here, right? That's all the exposure I need. Pulling guard duty in the Stan is more exposure than I want. I'll take a honey in the city any day."

"All right, but we're eating here. Not back on post. You have to deal with it."

"Fine, we leave when I want to though. Deal?"

"Deal, let's go eat."

They walked down the street they were told was the "Incirlik alley" and saw a corner restaurant with a sign painted red and white.

"Kelebek. Don't have any idea what that means, but it smells good," Steele observed as he led the way.

The door opened to a dark room. A plump, balding man greeted them from the bar, squinting as they walked in.

"Welcome, welcome, my friends." The man greeted them in heavily accented English. "Will you be eating, drinking, smoking?"

"Eating and drinking for now. Are you open?"

"Always open. Come in, welcome." The host led them past the simple chairs and tables at the bar. He took them through a doorway with beaded curtains. The guys looked at each other as they followed, not knowing what to expect. The room was a scene straight from a seventies movie. It was covered in red felt. The familiar smell of cheap cigarette smoke combined with spices and filled the room. The host pointed to some cushions on the ground. The cushions were scattered around a knee high table and had bare spots from years of use.

"Please, sit down here, relax." He invited them and motioned for them to take a seat. He clapped his hands three times as he turned to leave.

They each took a spot around the table. The table had a large platter in the middle that spun around. The table was well worn around the edges where countless meals were shared and toasts given by patrons. They settled in and got comfortable then a waitress appeared with tea.

"Good evening, gentlemen."

The dark-haired angel placed the tea in front of them.

"Good evening, indeed," Conner replied glancing at the guys with a smile.

She smiled back. "Would you like sugar for your tea?"

The scent of the black tea was strong. "That's a good start." Conner sipped his tea with a pleased look on his face.

Her scent was alluring as she danced between them delivering tea and sugar. She disappeared through the curtains as they all watched her disappear.

"Now, that's what I'm talking about." Conner leaned back acknowledging the beauty.

"Easy killer, it's probably his daughter or something," Winter cautioned.

"What?"

"She's just dropped off the tea, relax."

"She looked good, that's all I'm saying."

The angel reappeared shortly with a plate full of food. She set out before them a colorful picture of reds and yellows, mixed with browns and greens. The fresh sautéed vegetables topped brown rice and accented a luscious display of meats and kebabs. Two plates of pita wraps were tucked in next to the local masterpiece.

"Alright, I have to give it to you guys. This beats McDonalds."

"McDonald's? You kidding me? This is real food!" Winter argued as he grabbed a wrap and piled on the food.

"So tell me, Winter. What's it like to work with those SF guys?" Steele asked between bites.

"They're cool cats. They live by one of those, whatever it takes to get the job done, mottos."

"Then you show up when getting the job done interferes with the Army's rules."

"Exactly. It's a bit absurd, I know. I chase down the stuff they take to get the job done. Feels like Keystone Cops sometimes. I don't really do anything about it. I just write it up. The commands always come up with a reason to let it slide."

"Sounds like you'll be in business for a while."

"No kidding. As long as there is a war around they'll be able to do what they want. Don't blame them though. If it was me out there all the time, I'd be doing the same thing."

"You think so?"

"Oh yeah, if I was out there beyond the front lines. I would expect a certain amount of freedom."

"I guess, with so much on the line."

"With it all on the line, who really cares? If it was my last days out in some God-forsaken patch of dust, I'd want whatever I needed to get out of it. Screw the Army's rules."

"Ever see any cool places?"

"Not really. If I have to go looking for someone most of the time it's not a nice place. Most people I have to track down don't really want to be wherever they are, much less me. This is the best place I've been since I got deployed." He sat back on the pillows with a hand on his belly and a smile on his face.

"Well, if everyone is done stuffing your faces, we have more of this place to see. Let's head to the club already," Conner encouraged them.

The green neon sign flickered "Area 51" overhead as they walked up to the club door. The smell of urine, smoke and stale beer floated around them in the breeze as the doorman took their money so they could go inside. Past the doors and down the hall they made their way to a table near the dance floor. A belly dancer on the floor glided back and forth teasing them with a sultry smile.

"Jackpot!" Conner exclaimed.

"Conner, man, it's like you've never seen a woman before."

"I've seen women. I just appreciate each and every one of them, that's all." He smiled as his head swayed back and forth with the dancer.

"The man does have a point. She does look good," Winter conceded.

"Thank you, brother Winter. It's hard to be patient with you guys, but I knew if I just waited long enough you would come around."

"May I get you something?" A waitress flirted with them leaning over the table slightly. Her denim shirt had knot in the front revealing just enough skin to tease them as she asked for their order.

"Absolutely! Shots all around. And the best local beer you have." Conner undressed the waitress with each word.

"You better take it easy, Conner," Winter raised his eyebrows and his forehead wrinkled as he spoke. "These Turks can be real protective. Don't mess with the local women. Stick to the Air Force babes, they're a lot safer."

"Why? You think they're too much for me?"

"From what I hear, you don't want their families after you. I've heard that if you tick them off, you'll get the whole group after you, from brothers to cousins to friends from the neighborhood. You can get a real beating if you don't watch out. I just wouldn't mess around with these women. That's all."

The waitress returned with a round of shots and glasses filled with a dark local beer.

"What time do you get off?" Conner slammed a shot ignoring Winter's advice.

"Early morning, soldier," she replied brushing him off.

"What?"

"Conner. I mean really. Do you have to ask? Lay off man. You're not going to get any tonight, so just relax."

"You relax. I'm just having fun out here. Besides, you never know what might happen. Besides, I may never get back here again anyway. I've got nothing to lose."

"Yeah, but you mess with the wrong woman out here and she may be the last one that you ever mess with. I'm telling you man, it can be a powder keg here messing with the locals. I know these women look good and all, but the families here take this stuff serious. You make the wrong girl mad and it could turn into Mogadishu trying to get back to the base."

"Alright, I'll try to take it easy. No promises, but I'll try." Conner held his hand up trying to appease him.

The dance floor opened as the belly dancer in her shiny outfit swayed back and forth shimming in the lights.

"Yeah, I'll try." He eyed the swaying hips before him.

"Boys, I have to admit it. This is what I call a cultural exchange," Steele confessed.

"You got that right! Now this is my idea of winning the hearts and minds. You boys just sit back. Watch and learn." He grabbed Winter's shot and downed it as he stood up from the table. "I think I'll go learn a little about the culture myself." He gave them a wink as he turned to the floor.

Steele and Winter glanced at each other as Conner headed to the dance floor. He swayed side to side, looked back at them and laughed.

"You think he's going to do anything stupid?" Steele wondered aloud.

"Is that really a question?" Winters replied.

"He's a little crazy. But he's not dumb. He's definitely crazy," Craig admitted.

Conner worked his way to a dark haired girl swaying by herself on the floor. "Hi!"

She smiled seductively at him.

"Do you speak English?" He yelled above the music.

She smiled again. He swayed with her and smiled back.

"Looks like your boy has found a friend," Winters observed.

"Let's just hope her family is not here too."

"You ever dance with an American Soldier?"

She continued to sway but nodded.

"Okay. Now we're getting somewhere. Do you work here or do you just like the club?"

"My brother works here. I come to dance and meet my friends."

"Can I get you a drink?"

"Yes, soldier." She offered another smile.

They left the dance floor and made their way to the bar. He looked back at the table of guys and gave a thumbs up.

Winter shook his head, "Drink up this could be a long night."

14
PURE ENJOYMENT

"So what's your name?" Conner yelled over the pounding bass and dance music.

"Asya" She leaned into his ear.

"That's a pretty name. What does it mean?"

"I am named after my land Asia, vast, beautiful, and full of riches." Her green eyes flickered with the pulsing light.

"That's the most beautiful name I've ever heard." Entranced by her eyes Conner moved closer.

She laughed lightly throwing her head back sweeping the air with her long black hair.

"Where are you from American?"

"New York, home of the Yankees, the Giants and the hottest nights on the planet."

"You are an American man, for sure. Sports and parties. That's what I always hear from you Americans. You always have the best."

"Except, it's true about New York. Why don't I buy you that drink and we can talk some more about it."

"Yes, we can."

Conner moved in next to her. She looked up at him and smiled. He put his arm around her pleased with himself. He felt a sudden weight on his shoulder and looked to his left to see what it was. A tanned, dark-haired man smiled at him.

"She's not for you, soldier." The condescending tone annoyed Conner.

Conner looked at Asya. "Are you with this guy?"

"No, but maybe you should..." Her eyes darted from Conner then to the man interrupting them.

"Don't worry about it, American. She's not with you. You should go back to your base." He pointed behind him.

Winter finished his beer and started to get up from the table. "Looks like things are going to get lively. Pay attention."

"Sounds like you are in the wrong place, my friend. She's with me right now, so go find someone else." Conner popped off.

The Turk shook his head in disgust. "You Americans think you can take whatever you want."

"What? What are you talking about? Look dude, I'm just hanging out with my lady friend here. You got a problem with that?"

"Yes, I have a problem with that, American. I am telling you to go back to your base and leave our women alone." The Turk stared down at him.

Conner took a look around and noticed a small crowd starting to gather.

"Dude." Conner shook his head and leaned back.

An uppercut connected with the jaw and dropped the Turk to the ground. He never saw it coming as Conner struck first.

The place erupted. A few men, gathered nearby, lunged for Conner. The wave of heat and force was overwhelming. Conner could hardly breathe as the mob grabbed him.

A fist struck him on the cheek. Another in the forehead. He fell back into Asya.

His head grazed the bar on his way down. Steele raced forward, catching Conner as he fell.

Winter rushed in between Steele and the crowd.

Winter dropped a guy with a left cross, but then took a fist on the right side of the face. He bobbed back and forth to miss the incoming punches. He covered himself, dazed for a moment then gathered himself and struck back at the crowd pressing in.

Steele grabbed Conner, sat him on a stool and yelled at Asya. "Hang onto him!" Wide eyed with fear, she took hold of him.

Steele entered the fray. Fists and blood flew as Winter and Steele stood their ground. Some locals jumped in on the side of the Americans as the room erupted in violence.

Men hit each other for no reason other than pure enjoyment. The pain of bone on bone shook the room in waves. Jolts of pain pulsed with the music until it stopped.

A voice roared above the crowd. The large bartender yelled at everyone to stop fighting as the lights came up. The men paused to absorb the command.

The club's security made their way over to stop the fight. The sides were separated as they pushed their way into the crowd. The bartender made his way to Conner, who was still groggy.

"You must go now."

"What? Why? He started the whole thing," Conner contested, still woozy.

"The United States will make my bar off limits. You must go. These people will not follow you. I will keep them here, but you must go," the bartender insisted firmly.

"I'm not going anywhere," Conner argued defiantly as his eyes began to focus.

"C'mon Conner we're out of here." Steele grabbed him by the shoulder steered him toward the stairs.

"What?" He said with a half-aware smile. "Hey! Where are we going?"

They walked toward the stairs with Winter bringing up the rear. He watched to make sure no one changed their mind and followed.

"You crazy..." Steele half carried him and half pulled him down the hall.

"What were you thinking?" Winter looked over his shoulder relieved no one was following.

"What do you mean? The dude was going to kiss me if he got any closer. I had to do something, besides I was starting to look like an idiot."

"Starting to?"

"Shut up. At least I had the balls to do something out there."

"Tell you what Conner. You keep it up and since they obviously didn't knock some sense into you I just might." Craig shoved him down the hall.

"I didn't ask for you guys to help."

"You didn't need to. If we didn't jump in, there might not have been anything left of you. You forget we're just passing through. I don't want to find out what Hallis would do if we got arrested in a riot out here."

"If it wasn't for that guy, I would have had her. Did you get a whiff of her? Man, she smelled like heaven."

"I'm sure she tasted like it too, but we're done for the night."

"You guys should've let me have at him. I could've taken him."

"What were you going to do with his ten friends?"

"Ah, you guys gotta lighten up. That's how I do it. I'm not scared of anyone. Besides, she was into me."

"Shut up and get out the door before I finish what those Turks started."

"Alright, alright. But I know you boys can't pull anything that nice at home. It's okay though. I could hook you up." He teased them and laughed as they made their way onto the street. "C'mon guys let's head to the club Eiffel or whatever it's called."

"What? You gotta be kidding. You didn't have that much to drink."

"I didn't have enough that's for sure, let's go!"

"We're going back to the base and you're hitting the rack."

"C'mon guys. When are you going to get a chance to see ladies dance like that again?"

They corralled Conner back to his room on the base and called it a night.

Steele was up early and headed to check the flight schedule.

"Trying to get an early flight out, Steele?" Winter chided seeing him there.

"After last night, I'm ready to get back to the Stan, so I don't get beat to a pulp trying to take care of Conner."

"I hear you. That guy is trouble."

"Nah, he's harmless. He's just trying to have fun. He's a good guy, but yeah I'll be glad to get him back to lock down so I don't have to deal with him. It's like watching my five year old cousin or something."

"I hear you. Looks like we're in luck though. We have a flight to Uzbekistan at fourteen hundred hours. I talked to the airman about the weather. The flight path is clear. We'll have a quick flight if you guys make it."

"It'd take an act of God to keep me off that plane."

15
SPRITE

The Uzbekistan base was small. It was a mixed population of Air Force and Army personnel spread across abandoned Soviet bunkers that once housed Soviet planes. Just beyond the bunkers tents littered the area. After making the rounds to deliver crypto Craig left Conner to hunt women and made his way to headquarters to see about getting a pass off the base. He still wanted to get out and mix with the locals but knew it would be less drama without Conner.

"Excuse me."

The clerk looked up from his magazine.

"Can I help you, Specialist?"

"Can you tell me how to get a pass off base?"

"Fill out these papers." The clerk handed him a two sheet questionnaire and returned to his magazine.

He filled out the forms and was approved for the pass. The pass wasn't valid until the next day so he had a whole day to sit around. He decided to make his way through the compound to check out the area. He found an Uzbek shop and money changing store that was just outside the airstrip but still inside the base.

"Hello," the tall bleach-blonde shopkeeper greeted him in her strong slavic accent. "Can I help you find something?"

"I'm just looking." Craig browsed the local quilt-like coats, t-shirts, and the variety of Soviet leftover relics and knockoffs. There was everything from lapel pins with Stalin's picture to flasks with the Soviet hammer and sickle emblems in bright red against silver and gold.

"What do Uzbek men wear?"

"Uzbek men?" The bleach blonde smiled at him. "They wear these caps." She pointed to what looked like skull caps in blacks, reds, whites and a variety of other colors.

"And these." This time she pointed at the quilt like coats. He tried one on. It covered the length of his arms and his legs down to his ankles.

"Svetlana!" A brunette burst out with a giggle as she entered the room. She was followed by two squared-jawed Uzbeks in full length leather coats.

"Oy," she exclaimed when she saw Craig. She put her hand to her mouth and looked apologetic.

"It's okay I was getting ready to leave." He waved as he began to take off the coat. He laid the coat down on the table and started for the door.

"Allo, Svetlana." The taller of the two men looked softly at her.

"Allo, Dmitry."

"American soldier!" The other noted loudly.

"Allo," Craig replied half laughing.

"You speak Russian, American?"

"A little. *Min ya zavoot* Craig."

"Craig!" The dark haired man exclaimed. He reached out to shake his hand and slapped Craig on the back. "I am Alex!" Craig could smell the Vodka as the man breathed heavily in his face. "Where are you from my American friend?"

"Texas."

"Texas! A cowboy! Do you have a horse? Dmitry, did you hear that, he's a cowboy!" Alex pretended to ride a horse and waved his arm around his head. Acting like he had a rope he smiled and laughed.

Craig shook his head no, but smiled at their enthusiasm.

"No horse?" Alex looked slightly disappointed as he slowed his ride down.

"That's alright, did you know we were also soldiers, Craig?"

"In the Uzbek Army?"

"In the Russian Army, Uzbekistan Army, doesn't matter we were soldiers. Now we are capitalist soldiers!" He smiled at his companion. "Right Dmitry?"

"Yes, we are businessmen and you are drinking too much," Dmitry answered with a laugh and shook his head.

"Yes, I drink too much, who cares? Do you jump out of planes, Craig?"

"Not yet."

"Oh, but you will. Yes you will." He looked him over.

"You are a young, strong American. You will do well. We jumped out of planes and helicopters, too. Didn't we, Dmitry?"

"Yes, Alex." Dmitry waved him off and smiled at Natasha.

"We were Russian Special Forces. Have you heard of us?" Alex inquired eagerly.

"Spetsnaz?"

"Yes! Spetsnaz! We jumped right outside of this building for practice."

"Alex, let the man finish his shopping and leave him alone," Natasha chided.

"I'm not interrupting. I am talking with a new friend," He retorted and waved her off with his hand.

"Alex, don't you want to eat?" The girl's face flushed as she grabbed his arm.

"Eat? Yes let's eat! Craig, you must join us."

"Well, I uh..." Craig stammered as he looked around.

"Yes! We will have lunch. Svetlana, go get the food out of the car. Dmitry, go help."

Svetlana rolled her eyes and left. Dmitry laughed as he walked out. Natasha cleared off some counter space.

"Ah, Craig! Have you ever eaten Uzbek food?"

"No, can't say I have."

"I have eaten Texas barbeque! Ha! I beat you." Alex roared making Steele laugh along.

"Ah, here it is. Uzbek lunch."

Svetlana walked in with a large platter and a covered bowl. Dmitry followed with another covered bowl and some white ceramic cups decorated with a bright pattern of yellow, blue, and red.

"Oy," Svetlana let out as she sat the platter down. She quickly opened the bowl of rice and emptied its contents onto the platter. Taking Dmitry's bowl she poured grilled meat with sautéed vegetables on the rice. Natasha handed everyone a spoon.

Craig looked around and wondered where the plates were. Svetlana closed the door to the shop and flipped the sign to "Closed". Natasha filled the small cups and passed them around with the first going to Craig.

"Craig! Welcome to Uzbekistan. Let's eat." Alex watched as Craig hesitantly reached with the spoon and ate. They all smiled and looked at each other, laughing, and joined Craig eating. Craig grabbed his cup to wash down a bite and his eyebrows shot up with surprise.

He expected Sprite seeing the clear liquid, but it warmed his throat and stomach on its way down. A flush of warmth washed his body. Alex slapped him on the back and refilled his cup, and laughed.

"What do you think, Craig?" His voice was full of pride.

"It's great! I have tied you now since I have had Uzbek food!"

Alex's eyes grew big as a smile stretched across his face. "Ha! You have tied me now, Craig!" He roared with a loud laugh. "You must come to town with us this evening."

"I can't. I have to stay on base till I get a pass."

"Pass? You don't need a pass. You will come with us."

"The guards won't let me off base without a pass."

"I will talk to them. They will let you out. I know them."

"I don't have any clothes." Craig gripped his cup and downed another mouthful, stroking his chin thoughtfully.

"We can get you clothes."

"I tell you what. We'll play cards to decide."

"Hmm, we don't have any cards. How about chess?"

"Sure, I'll take that bet."

"Ok, we will go next door after we eat. They have tables and chairs. We will settle the matter there."

They took their time with the meal eating, drinking and laughing about things they didn't quite understand about each other. Craig was impressed with the flavor. The buzz from the vodka didn't hurt the experience, either. They left the shop and walked across the courtyard to an unmarked building. They walked past the heavy wood doors into a dark room. A guard met them and greeted them casually.

"Good day, Alex. What can I do for you?" The Uzbek Air Force guard pulled a drag on his cigarette.

"We need a table, chairs and the chessboard."

"I will bring the chess. Help yourself to a table."

They sat and poured more vodka. "You know how to play, yes?"

"Yes, I'll do my best."

An hour passed. The room had grown quiet. Alex's brow furrowed. "You have set a trap for my queen, Craig. You have played very well. Now you must come to town with us. My friends will never believe I could lose to an American." Alex smiled as he lay his king down.

"I guess I'll be a legend here then, because I have a plane to catch tomorrow and can't visit tonight."

"You must come with me. My friends will never believe it. I will get you back in the morning."

"I really can't. I'm in uniform. I can't walk off base. I'd get in big trouble."

"I can get you off base with no problem."

"I really can't. Maybe next time."

"That's fine, but when you come back I will take you on a tour of my town. We will go to the theater, listen to music, dance, and we will eat at my place. Natasha will cook us a feast. It will be a great evening."

"I'll take you up on that. But now I've gotta go. If I stay here much longer I won't be able to walk."

"You are a good American, Craig. I have trained many soldiers. I think you will be a good soldier like us," he assured him.

"Time will tell. I'll see you next time I come through and we'll have to hit the town."

"Hit the town?" He stood for a moment trying to comprehend the slang. "Yes, we will do that. One more drink before you go."

"Last one."

"To Craig. Another great soldier like Alex and Dmitry. Health and prosperity."

They raised their glasses to the toast. Craig's body received the drink and it warmed him from head to toe. He smiled and thanked them. They exchanged pats on the back and toasted a final drink to the victory in the chess match.

Craig began the walk back to the tent holding the things he bought from the store with a smile on his face. His legs were numb. Each step was like a dream as he walked back to the tent. Conner wasn't there and he was thankful. He was having enough trouble getting into bed without having to explain what happened.

As he crawled into his bunk he noticed he still had a hat on and pulled it off. He laughed when he realized he had a black skull cap on. He and Alex had traded hats earlier and he forgot he was wearing it when he left. He had walked through the entire base with the cap on with the rest of his uniform. This trip was off to a good start. He was in bar fights, breaking regulations and losing pieces of his uniform. He laughed as he curled up and wondered what the rest of the trip would have in store.

16
IN THE STICKS

The landing at Mazar-i-Sharif reminded him of his first one in country, except for the white blanket covering everything. They dove from the ceiling of clouds around the mountains to land quickly on a short air strip. The tail lowered in the early evening light. Craig could see a soldier at the ready manning a fifty caliber machine gun on a jeep at the end of the runway, to his surprise.

"You boys have fifteen minutes to do your stuff. When we get our pallets unloaded and pick up whatever they have for us, we are outta here. With or without you. There won't be another plane through here for a week or two. Clear?" The load master yelled the instructions over the roar of the engines.

"Clear!"

The familiar smell of dust and fuel engulfed him as they made their way past the wash of the C-130 engines still running. "Looks like we're the only ones here." Craig yelled to Conner as they left the airstrip noting there were no other planes.

"Yeah, not even any hangers. Looks like we're in the sticks."

A lone, light blue adobe building stood to the side of the airstrip in the twilight. A light snow was falling as they made their way to the door. They were met by a soldier in BDU pants and a puffy black jacket. He was unshaven and sported a ball cap. "You guys the commo crew from Bagram?"

"That's us, you have your equipment?"

"Nah, it's in my hooch. We'll have to go get it. I'm Tim." He extended his hand.

"I'm Craig and this is Conner. No offense but we only have fifteen minutes, so let's do this fast. We don't really want to be hanging out here for the next couple of weeks, though I'm sure it's a great place."

"Don't sweat it, everything's close out here. The jeep is out back." He motioned them to follow.

"You gotta be kidding me." Conner's eyes opened wide.

"It's a beauty isn't it? This is World War Two stock, the real thing. Don't know where they got it, but we bought it off some of the locals here. They've probably been selling that jeep to every army that's been through here for the past fifty years."

"Does it work?"

"Of course it does."

They jumped in the beat-up green Army jeep and bounced their way through a maze of barriers and razor wire. The jeep hit a top speed of forty miles an hour on the straight away, leaving clouds of dust in their wake.

"What are you guys doing out here anyway?" Craig asked as they pulled out their computers and began transferring data.

"Winning the hearts and minds of the locals."

"You're not SF though, are you? So what are you?"

"No, we're civil affairs. We work with the SF guys all the time, though. We connect with people and bring along the Army's money to help the locals. We help build schools, roads, water wells or whatever they need."

"No kidding, you guys are out here doing Peace Corps work?"

"Pretty much. Except we carry guns, grenades and whatever else we need. I don't think the Peace Corp rocks it quite like we do." The crypto transfer completed on the computer. "Looks like we're good here. Do you want to take the tour or you in a hurry to catch the plane?"

"I think we'll catch the tour next time."

They left Tim's hooch and climbed back in the jeep. The jeep roared, then sputtered and shook violently, then went quiet.

"We have a problem?" Conner's face told it all.

"She does this some times. Sometimes she can be a bit crabby. She just needs a little more attention I guess. It can take a couple of tries, but she won't fail us." Tim cranked it again without a care.

It roared again. It coughed a little smoke out, then shuddered and almost started. He tried again with the same result. "Well boys, you may have to walk back. She may not be interested in going out tonight."

"Walk? We'll never make it back in time. You gotta try her again, man. I'm not trying to hang out here," Conner insisted from the back.

"Ok, ok, it's not so bad out here, though." Tim cranked the engine one last time and it responded with another roar, some coughing, a brief shudder, and then the engine began to hum.

"She must like you. I told you she wouldn't fail us."

"At least they haven't left yet," Craig observed as they barreled back down the road to the airport.

"Man, I can't see a thing," Conner complained.

"Yeah, but I can hear the engines."

"I told you we had plenty of time," Tim reminded them.

The light from the building made the muddy path look like a side-walk that led to the back door. Walking into the hallway Craig was blinded by the light. He looked out the front door into the darkness and his heart rate spiked. His steps shortened as he sped up to get outside.

He could hear the plane engines whining and growing louder. He knew what it meant but couldn't make out where the plane was on the tarmac. The combat zone light discipline made sure there were not any exterior or interior lights which made the plane hard to pinpoint. Still running in the light of the building he couldn't see anything twenty feet outside. The sound of the engines grew distant as he stood staring into the blackness.

"Damn, Craig!"

"You can say that again. I can't believe we missed that flight. Those guys must have been in a real hurry."

"Well fellas, looks like you'll be around for that tour after all." Tim leaned on the door frame as they walked back into the building.

"Not cool." Conner's voice cracked, making Craig laugh.

"It'll be ok. Don't sweat it. We'll pitch in around here till we leave and we'll get to see what they do out here. It'll be fun."

"Fun? Fun? You think being out here in the middle of nowhere is fun?"

"Conner, you'd be surprised at the fun we have out here. We mix with the local population and they're pretty cool, once you get to know them," Tim interjected.

"Maybe if we're smoking some hash with them," Conner whined as he shook his head.

Craig and Tim laughed.

"You'll see tomorrow. I'll take you out to meet some of the locals. You'll be surprised. It's actually more fun than you'd think. We can do just about anything out here. It's like the wild west."

"Where are we going to crash around here?"

"There's some room in my hooch. You can crash there."

The night was calm and quiet compared to Bagram. There were no flights at the airstrip. Nothing disturbed the silence as the night grew deeper. The small outpost was far from the political center of the country. They didn't have the luxury of generators to run all night creating the racket they had become accustomed to back in Bagram. Craig crawled into his bag and fell fast asleep in the quiet of the night.

"That's some of the best sleep I've had since I've been in country." Craig stretched as he stood up.

"It's one of the bonuses about working out here. I've been to Bagram. It's like Los Angeles with all the lights and noise."

Conner stirred. "That's probably the only good thing about being out here. If you like that sort of thing. I prefer the noise."

"Where are you from, Conner? With that accent I'd say New York?"

"Brooklyn."

"Just wait. You'll see. It's pretty interesting out here. There's a lot more going on out here than you think. You guys want some coffee?

We're headed to the hills today. You might want a little kick start." Tim held the pot out to them.

"We taking the jeep?"

"Nah, we'll use something a little faster and more reliable. That jeep is like our golf cart out here. Gets us back and forth but not something we take outside the wire."

"That's comforting. Sounds like a plan. Let's do it," Steele urged as they finished their coffee.

They loaded up into three humvees with a couple of other civil affairs soldiers from Tim's unit. The drive led from the somewhat-barren snow covered area they were in to a very desolate area east of the compound. A southerly turn led to the steps of a mountain range.

"We'll take this road that leads up into the hills and see where it takes us," Tim yelled at them over the noise of the vehicles.

They scanned the hills looking for the signs of life, but didn't see anything and kept climbing higher. A couple of men and a boy, in traditional Afghan clothing, stepped out from behind some rocks as they turned a corner and the convoy halted. Tim jumped out with the some team members and a translator to chat with the men. The Afghans stood expressionless except for the one doing the talking. He pointed up the road and watched blankly as they drove on.

"He said the village is up ahead. He's got some goats roaming around here somewhere he says," Tim informed them as the convoy trudged on. "He was curious to know who we were. I doubt they get a lot of Americans up here."

The vehicles lumbered up the steep road. They watched an occasional rock roll off the edge of the road out of sight and it made their chests pound with excitement.

"You guys are getting to see parts of this country not many people in the world have seen," Tim reminded them.

"I think there's a reason for that," Conner noted. He was compelled to look out the window yet scooted away at the same time.

"I normally don't agree with you Conner, but this time you may have a point," Craig agreed as viewed the vast nothingness of mountain terrain.

"What do you boys think? Left, or right?" Tim looked at them pointing to the fork in the road.

"What do you mean, don't you know where you're going?" Conner looked at Craig and back at Tim as his voice creaked.

"We didn't exactly have a formal plan as we headed out this morning. We kind of played it by ear. We knew the general area we wanted to hit today. It's good operational security out here anyway. The bad guys never know where to hit us."

"Didn't that guy back there tell you there was a village up here?" Conner wiped the sweat off his forehead.

"He did, but he didn't say that the road forked. So what do you say left or right?"

"I thought Craig was a little crazy, but man, he's got nothing on you. Right, man. Let's roll to the right."

"Right it is." Tim smiled and they drove roughshod over the Afghan trail, higher into the mountains.

"Looks like we'll visit a new village today," Tim informed them.

"New village?" Conner inquired. "I thought you guys had this area scoped out?"

"We have a general idea of what's up here, but we just kind of head off in a new direction sometimes. When we make contact, if haven't met them before, we see if they're friendly and do what we can."

"What the hell are you guys really doing out here?" Conner demanded exasperated.

Tim sat up stiffly, "Well, we are the extension of the Army that meets the needs of the locals while accomplishing the mission of the Army," he stated formally, then laughed and continued. "Aside from that, we're just out having fun roaming the hills. We help the people we can and shoot the bad guys if we get the chance."

"You guys are crazy if you ask me," Conner concluded then he looked out the window.

They headed up the dirt road and the grade became steeper as they climbed further into the mountain. There were many small trails leading off the main road. They kept passing them by until they were high into the mountainside.

"You see those two trails, Conner?"

"Yeah, so what?"

"Which one do you want to take this time?"

"Dude, you are crazy. Let's go left for my man, Craig."

"Left it is," Tim agreed as they turned left upward, steeper into the mountainside. The Hummer slowed as it adjusted to the steep climb. Craig began to look around nervously as the Hummer slowed to a snail's pace. Conner looked around with a concerned look.

"Don't worry, fellas. If there was anyone here who wanted to hit us, they would have already. We make pretty easy targets, if you think about it."

Like a goat taking a slow walk they made their way up the trail. Turning a corner, they came up on a semi flat area. A number of mud huts sprung into view. A well sat in the middle of the trail two hundred yards away. They slowly pulled up and a host of children came out of nowhere to greet them.

"Alright boys, here's how this will work. A couple of the guys will watch the Hummers and set up a loose perimeter as we make first contact here with the locals. You just stick close to me and I'll try to keep the kids off you as we make our way."

They dismounted from the Hummers and made their way into the sea of children that gathered around them. Tim waved them off with his hand and Craig and Conner followed suit. They made their way further in to the square and a man came out to meet them. Tim prompted the translator and he initiated a conversation.

"He says he speaks for the village," the translator relayed.

"Tell him we need to speak to the village elder. The one who makes decisions for the village. Speaks for it." Tim motioned him with his hand.

"He says he is the one you are looking for."

Tim looked at him again. "Unless this village was wiped out under the Taliban, there has to be someone older that represents this village. He has to be somebody's kid or cousin or something."

The interpreter spoke with the man claiming to represent the village and the man turned and walked away.

"He said he will go get the elder," the translator told them.

They stood taking in the scene around them. Mud hut buildings lined each side of the road and animals walked about freely. The self-proclaimed leader of the village emerged shortly from a house with an elderly man that walked gingerly toward the group. He spoke to the translator who passed along his words. They stood and talked with the elder who invited them into his home where he offered them tea.

"We would like to give you some gifts and find out what your village might need," The translator relayed. A conversation about the village started. Tim explained some options the Army could employ to help the village if they were interested. The elder thanked him, but informed them they did not need anything. Craig looked around at the barren room that held nothing but a few meager furnishings on the dirt floor. This was a respectable man from the village and this was all he had. Craig could see how Tim would like helping these people. They were so poor they didn't know any better, but they were far from helpless. He could see it in the stern eyes of the elder. His weathered skin showed that he led a tough life and did not need the Americans to survive. Tim talked the elder into letting them hand out blankets to the villagers. They gave the blankets out and were repeatedly greeted with smiles from the villagers. They welcomed the Americans and thanked them with an innocent curiosity. They told the elder they would see what they could do about getting some medical help as well, since he gave little indication of what they might be in need of. The drive down was considerably faster.

"Well, what do you guys think?"

"I could see how you would like this. It'd be cool to be a part of building this place and getting people on their feet," Steele admitted.

"It just confirms what I've been saying. You guys are crazy. I'll take the city over some small village and goats in the mountains any day."

"That's good to hear. We'll be headed into the city tomorrow."

"Not quite what I had in mind." Conner frowned and shook his head.

"This city has some pretty cool stuff. There's a mosque that was built on the tomb of Mohammed's cousin. It's made from dark blue tiles. It's a pretty amazing sight."

"When it looks like Time Square, I'll be impressed."

"He's a hard case, isn't he?" Craig smirked and shook his head.

"Mark my words, tomorrow will be exciting. It's always something different when we go into the city."

17
INTO THE CITY

"Today, the mission is to go into the city and visit a school we're helping to rebuild. We'll meet with some town officials, discuss the progress we've made so far and find out what else we can do to help. I think you'll find it interesting, if you want to come."

"Count me in. I enjoy meeting the locals and learning about their culture. How 'bout it Conner?"

"Sure, I'll come along. Nothing to do here, anyway."

"Great, let's grab a bite to eat and head out. We'll hook up with an SF team and a translator then head to town in five vehicles."

There was a short briefing with all the players after breakfast. They performed a last equipment check and they loaded up for the short drive to the city. The Afghans eyed them as they passed. Craig was surprised by the intense glares they received from the locals as they drove deeper into the city. Since they were so far up North he expected a warmer welcome.

A couple of fifty caliber machine guns always set a good tone at least.

"Off to the right, you'll see that blue mosque I was telling you about. It's a big landmark in the area." Tim motioned with his head as they roared down the street.

"I think I saw that as we were flying in," Craig remembered.

"There is a lot of blue in the area, but that thing is hard to miss."

"I feel like I'm in the twilight zone with you guys. No way you guys have ever been to Times Square or seen New York at night. If you had you'd know this place is a dump."

"Keep talking, Conner, we all know that nothing compares to New York, but really what do you know? You never had been anywhere but New York before you joined the Army."

"Shows what you know, Craig. If you're in New York, you don't need to go anywhere else. Everything's already in New York."

"Alright you two, we're coming up on the school, so let's get dialed in."

They turned onto the street then slowed down as they drove. The street had the same weary, worn look with its mud buildings and empty stares. One building had a few more children outside playing than usual. Nothing else set it apart from the other buildings on the street. The group pulled up in front of the nondescript building and parked. A few vehicles were already there with some Afghan soldiers mulling around the area.

"We'll get out with the translator. Some of the guys will keep an eye on the Hummers while we're inside. The others will set up some security on the rear of the building," Tim reminded them as they dismounted from the vehicles and made their way to the building.

A young man met them at the door and informed them that the school official and city representative were inside the building. He led them inside to a small room. The smell of tea filled the air as they walked in. The young man left them with the officials who greeted them. The team sat down while Craig and Conner lingered in the hall. Two SF soldiers made their way through the hallway to the backdoor to recon the area.

"Peace be upon you," Tim greeted the official as the translator began his work. The men shook hands and introductions were made. The SF team leader and Tim offered the officials gifts as a thanks for hosting them. The official performed his role as host and showered compliments on his guests and offered them tea. The team picked up where the official left off and the dance began. They showered praises, recognizing the courage the officials had shown and hard work the city had done to expand educational opportunities for its people.

The conversation became businesslike and didn't interest Conner. He looked around, made eye contact with Craig then motioned Craig to the back. Craig nodded and they made their way out the back door. A few feet from the door stood a waist high wall with columns. A gate opened into a large courtyard where leftover snow still sat on the surrounding walls. Children kicked a ball and chased each other around the courtyard on the hard winter ground. Another waist-high wall enclosed the back of the courtyard where two Afghan soldiers stood watch by the gate.

Craig went to his left and leaned against the wall. He kicked up a leg up for support. He nodded at the two SF soldiers at opposite corners behind the waist high wall. Near the edge of the courtyard two more Afghan soldiers kept watch.

Craig heard some commotion inside the building and looked into the hallway to check it out. He saw the civil affairs team bringing in boxes of supplies from the hummers. *More icing on the cake for the locals.*

He smiled and propped himself back up on the wall. Conner walked into the yard. The kids stopped and looked at him as he walked up. He put his head through his weapon's sling and shifted his weapon to his back.

"Can I play?" he asked holding out his hands. The boy with the ball looked at the others for help. They looked hopeful and motioned to him to pass the ball. With a questioning glance the boy shrugged and kicked the ball over to him. Conner caught the ball with his foot and kicked it in the air, popping it off his knee. He hit it with his head back to the boy. The boy looked at his friends with big eyes and smiled at them. They laughed and smiled, then tried their hardest to copy his tricks.

"I keep telling you this is real football. I told you I was a stud in high school," Conner yelled over his shoulder.

"I know. You're real good about telling me how great you are at everything."

"Hear that kids?" Conner looked at the children gathered around smiling at him. "That's the sound of a jealous man."

Without any apparent understanding they joined him in laughter.

"Watch out Conner, looks like you're having fun."

He waved his hand and smiled back at the kids as they talked to him in broken English.

An argument erupted near the edge of the courtyard. The Afghan guards stopped a man who started to enter. Conner looked up and back at Craig. Craig stood on both feet and glanced at the SF soldiers. They had already taken casual positions of cover at the edges of the wall where it shot up in columns.

Conner looked at the children and back toward the gate, his eyes narrowed. He motioned the children away from the commotion. They obliged with little concern while one grabbed the soccer ball.

Conner walked up to see what the issue was. He pulled his weapon around settling back into his role as a soldier. Getting closer, he cradled his weapon naturally. His hand slid to the hand grip and he began to swing his weapon up slowly as he neared the gate. He made eye contact with the man arguing with the guards.

When the man noticed Conner, his eyes grew whiter. He shouted at the Afghan guards, pointing at Conner. His eyes narrowed and his brow dropped in anger as he raised his hands. One guard turned to run as the other tried to grab the man who pushed him aside.

"Allahu akbar," the man said softly at first. Then he let out a yell at the top of his lungs raising his eyes and hands toward the sky. "ALLAHU AKBAR!"

Conner instinctively let a round off at the man. The round hit him in the stomach and he began to double over in slow motion, still trying to look up.

Craig's eyes widened as he half fell behind the wall for cover. "Conner!" He yelled as he fell forward.

The peace was shattered as the explosion ripped through everything in its way. It felt like all creation screamed in the courtyard. Steel balls ripped through the air, shredding everything in their path.

The air was sucked out of Craig's open mouth. Everything seemed to run from the destruction. Adrenaline and fear spiked through everyone.

The men in the building rushed to the hall to see what happened. With weapons raised, they poured out the back and took positions on each side of the small wall. Some locals in the distance that weren't injured in the blast started to run away.

Craig's ears rang as a mist of debris fell over the courtyard. He rolled over on the ground and tried to get his bearings. Slightly dazed by the concussion of the blast and the shock of what happened, he sat up with his mouth still open.

The area erupted in chaos. Machine gun fire filled the air as the dust clouds billowed across the neighborhood. Small arms fire came from beyond the courtyard and dirt kicked up everywhere from the scattered shots.

"Sounds like two, maybe three out there," Tim yelled to Craig as he joined him behind the mud brick wall.

The Special Forces soldiers unleashed an arsenal on the attackers. M-203 rounds exploded in the distance. M4 and M-16 rounds zinged around as Craig watched in a daze.

"Where are they?" Tim yelled looking around.

"Can't really tell yet. I saw a flash off by the building to the right. Sounds like a couple out there," a Special Forces soldier yelled back. Tim looked over the wall and let out a couple of rounds in the general vicinity of the gunfire.

"Shit, this is some shit," was all he kept saying. He stopped and looked at Craig "You okay, man?" Craig nodded awkwardly. "Where's Conner?"

Craig shook his head no. "What?" Tim fired another burst over the wall and looked for muzzle flashes in the distance. The SF team had slowed their rate of fire as the haze settled. They were only taking intermittent fire now.

Craig got himself up on a knee and yelled angrily, "he's gone."

He popped his head over the wall and looked for a sign of Conner. There was too much carnage to make anything out.

"What?" Tim looked around and his face sagged.

"He was by the bomber," Craig yelled over the noise and let another burst out. Tears rolled down his dirty face.

The SF soldiers began to take control of the situation with unyielding fire on the incoming shooters.

The firing from afar ceased and an uneasy quiet settled over the street.

"Let's pick up and move out," the team leader yelled. They swept the area with precision, fanned out and set up a perimeter defense for their exit.

Craig felt sick to his stomach as the adrenaline pumped through his veins and turned his body chemistry upside down. He stood up to go find what he could of Conner.

"You don't want to see that." Tim grabbed his shoulder and tried to hold him back.

"You can't stop me," Craig brushed him off and stumbled over to find Conner's remains.

A gleam caught his eye. Among the debris and chaos, he walked to the object. He brushed the dirt away and picked up the gold chain that belonged to Conner. The cross dangled from the end of the chain and Craig's shoulders sagged. He looked around the scene and his face went pale. He turned away and was violently sick. Involuntary tears ran down his cheeks as he gazed at what was left of Conner and the others nearby.

"They were only children," he said to nobody in particular.

"Come over here." Tim ushered Craig away. Craig numbly followed like a drunk man leaving a bar. His head was spinning and the world closed around him. His ears were still ringing from all the noise, in spite of the relative quiet. Goats bayed in the distance while women and children cried as they absorbed the shock of the attack.

"Call this in and let's get these boys outta here. Grab what's left of that soldier and put him in the back and load up. We're getting the fuck out of dodge," the SF team leader ordered.

Covering all areas with weapons raised, they loaded into the vehicles. They barreled down the road leaving a plume of dust. Craig bounced in the seat, still dazed by the action. He stared off in the distance as his mind raced. It felt like the bombing didn't happen to him. Yet, it was the most intense experience he had ever had.

"I've never been in something like that."

"Yeah." It was all Craig could get out.

"I don't even know what we do about this," Tim stated vacantly.

They rode the rest of the way back to the compound in silence. The SF guys helped with Conner's remains before heading back to their area. Craig stepped out of the humvee and looked around still dazed. He looked around the camp searching for nothing in particular. His face reflected his feeling of emptiness. Tim thanked the SF soldiers for the escort back as Craig went back to the tent.

"I got in touch with Bagram. They'll have a plane here in the morning to take you back to Uzbekistan with Conner's remains."

Craig nodded.

They said something about an operation going on out West so the resources were a little thin. I don't know what they'll do when you get to Uzbekistan but I think they'll stick you on the next flight to Bagram."

"That's fine," was all he could muster.

"You want something to eat?" Tim offered hopefully.

"Nah, don't think I can eat anything."

"Yeah, not sure I can either."

That night was the longest of Craig's life. He couldn't sleep. As soon as he shut his eyes, all he could see was the aftermath and hear the screams. He stared in the darkness drifting in and out of sleep till the dawn broke over the mountain.

"Want some coffee?" Tim crawled off his cot and reached for the pot.

"Sure."

"You able to sleep at all last night?"

"Not really, you?"

"Nah, couldn't hardly shut my eyes." He pulled some coffee out of a can and filled the filter up. He turned the coffee machine on and the fresh brew filled the tent.

"The flight is supposed to be here around sixteen hundred hours. I'm making a bite to eat if you want something."

"Can't say I do."

"Yeah."

The day was long. Craig found himself sitting around replaying the events without meaning to. As he looked around outside he'd notice a smell, see a shadow, or hear a Hummer and it would set off a sequence in his mind. He'd awaken out of his daze in a sweat looking around, afraid and angry as he faced the event once again. He was mad that he couldn't seem to put it out of his mind. Even for a few minutes.

They were early to meet the flight since they knew the pilots didn't want to sit around for long. Not like they had anything better to do. Word spread about the mission going south and no one was excited about this flight. The C-130 was a dot in the distance as they watched it approach. Everything seemed significant as Craig stared in the sky. Such a small thing in the expanse of the sky filled him with wonder. He couldn't help but think how lucky he was to be sitting there. His heart sank with the thought of Conner not there to hop another ride somewhere fun. His throat was tight as he choked a little on the emotion of the past twelve hours. The plane taxied toward them and the noise became deafening. The gate lowered and a detail brought a casket out and met them at the Hummer. The soldiers lifted the body bag and set it in the casket. The special detail walked it back up to the plane.

"Take care, Craig."

"You too, Tim. Thanks." They shook hands awkwardly then Craig turned to get on board.

The blast of the engines pressed his uniform against him as he walked to the tailgate carrying his bag and Conner's. It was awkward to carry it all and it felt that way, too. Craig didn't look back as the gate shut. The engines rev'ed up for take-off and the plane shuddered as the pilot held the brake waiting to release the power. A couple of soldiers on board waited for the plane to continue its flight and stared uncomfortably at the new cargo.

The bird climbed steeply, escaping the ground, and banked hard to turn north heading back to Uzbekistan. The force of gravity pulled against them as they turned. Craig stared out the window at the landscape dotted with brown and white with the splash of blue in the center. The brown swallowed everything eventually, and gave way to the clouds.

Emotion surged within Craig as the pressure squeezed his chest. Thankful for the noise of the plane he gasped at the powerful feelings rising up. He choked on his emotions as the plane shuddered, lifting its weight above the clouds. Craig watched as the ripples of mountain waved in the wind as they flew overhead. Everything was so small. Even snow covered mountains looked like a child's toys. The C-130 rumbled on as he turned his eyes back upon the coffin. It was hard to keep his mind off of it.

The flight stretched time. It seemed like only yesterday he had arrived with dreams of great achievements. Now the thoughts of such things were as small as the mountains below.

I told him we'd be alright. What about his little girl? Why didn't I see something like this coming?

Anger stirred up inside him. Anger at himself. Anger at the terrorists. Anger at the locals. He was beginning to hate them all.

18
HEALTH AND PROSPERITY

Craig was restless on the short flight to Uzbekistan. The stress and lack of sleep had taken its toll. He tried to stay awake so he wouldn't have to relive it all. He found himself giving in and nodding off.

His right leg slipped out in front of him startling him back awake. Eyes wide and reaching for his weapon, he caught himself as he brought his head up.

He looked around and noticed everyone else was nodding off too. He wiped his forehead, clearing some of the sweat away. The plane was cool but he found himself sweating again and his heart racing. He shook his head and leaned back. A mass of clouds slowly passed underneath as they began their descent. He was relieved the flight would be over soon. He felt claustrophobic all of a sudden and wanted some space. He stretched his neck to let in more air. The pull of gravity squeezed him as the plane banked toward the landing strip. He sat up straighter to get even more air. The stress was oppressive as the plane leveled to land. The landing was smooth but the expected jolt made Craig gasp just the same.

"Specialist Steele." Sergeant Taylor greeted him at the tarmac. "There aren't any planes out of here today, but tomorrow morning at 1000 hours we'll have you on your way to Bagram. We'll take care of Conner 'till we get you back on the plane tomorrow. He will begin his trip to the states when they are through with him in Bagram. You'll be in your usual accommodations. We have a chaplain, if you need to speak with him."

"No thanks, Sergeant. I think I'll just head to the tent and get some rest."

"Understood. You just let us know if you need anything."

"Roger that."

He dropped off his weapon, ammo, and computer at the signal unit armory and headed to the visitor tent. He dropped his bags and lay down on the bunk. He laid there for a while in the empty tent.

He could catch his breath again. He breathed deeply and started to relax. He stared at the fabric and listened to the noise outside. He started to doze off in the relative calm. He awoke abruptly with a jump. *Dreaming again.*

He decided it would be better to have some company. He stopped by the morale tent and found it empty as usual. It wasn't even five so the day shift wasn't finished and the night shift was going to eat dinner. He remembered the little shop outside the tarmac and headed to see if they were still open.

"Hello, Craig," Svetlana greeted him.

"Hey there. I wasn't sure if you'd remember me."

"Of course I remember the chess king!" She smiled and giggled.

"Is Alex coming by today?"

"He will since I'm going to call him to tell him you are here."

"Oh no, that isn't necessary."

"But of course it is. He will want to see you. I think he wants a rematch." She dialed her cell phone and smiled at him.

"Alex! Guess who is here in the shop." She nodded. "Yes, it's him. He came by and asked for you. I think he is looking for a chess game." She covered the phone with her hand. "He wants to know if you can wait twenty minutes for him." He shrugged his shoulders and nodded. "Yes, he says he will wait. Ok."

"You have any more of that vodka lying around?"

"Of course, would you would like a drink?" She pulled out a tall, clear bottle of vodka from underneath the counter.

"As a matter of fact I would."

She pulled out two teacups. "The store will be closed soon anyway." She filled both and gave him one. She started to place the bottle back under the counter and he waved her off and patted the counter. She sat the bottle back down.

"To health and prosperity," he offered downing it with one gulp.

Her eyebrows rose as he finished the entire cup. She filled his cup again.

"I think you may not beat Alex this time if you drink so much."

"Maybe not, but I think it'll be okay." He exhaled deeply. The stress washed away with each swallow. His shoulders started to relax as he stood there drinking.

"You look like you needed a drink."

"More than ever."

She flipped the sign to "closed" and filled his cup again. "Perhaps you should have one more drink then go back to your tent."

"Nah, I'll be ok. Really, I just needed to get a little warm. So, you like this job?"

"Yes, why not? I need work. This one pays good money."

"Yeah, but is it what you want to do?"

"What do you mean what I want to do?" A look of concentration spread across her face as she tried to grasp the meaning.

"Is this what you want to do every day for work?"

"There is no other work around here as good as this." She turned and raised her arms as she looked around the store. "What am I going to do?" Work in a bakery or a factory? No, I will work here. Smile at you American men. Make you happy and make more money than I would at all those other places."

"That's a good game plan. You've got your act together."

"Yes, that is my plan. Work the easiest job and make the most money!"

"You sure you're not an American?"

Life didn't seem so bad now. He was laughing again. His mind was preoccupied. He was relaxing for a moment and it felt good. His body was beginning to feel at ease. The vodka was taking affect and the stress faded away.

The door opened. "Hello, Craig!"

"Alex! Dmitry! Good to see you."

Alex and Craig embraced, patting each other on the back. Alex gave him a customary kiss on each cheek. He finished the greeting with a slap on the back. Dmitry shook his hand vigorously.

"Ah, I see Svetlana has been taking care of you. Maybe I should let you stay here longer and I will tell everyone that you were lucky the first time."

"Let's go play, Alex."

"Very well, Svetlana. Close up and come join us."

"Sure, Alex."

"Now this time we will see if you are lucky or good."

"I'm both Alex. I'm definitely both." A flash of sadness crossed his face.

Alex smiled as they walked from the shop across the yard into the Uzbek military building.

"Sergei!"

"Alex! Ah, the American. I will get the game and the vodka."

"I will go first since you won last time," Alex told him.

They settled into a competitive silence. The clear bottle of vodka without a label sat next to the board. The war on the board was going well for Alex. A third of Craig's pieces were captured before he knew it. He stared hard, trying to concentrate but the vodka had flanked him and the game had become hazy. He knew he was in trouble as he stared at the board. He tried to focus, but it was too much work and grabbed his cup instead. Sipping the vodka now, he eased back in his chair.

"Alex. I have to say you've got me this time."

"This game is not looking good for you. Unless you are better than I can imagine."

"It's not over, but the rest is just the setup." Craig resigned himself to the defeat.

The bottle was half empty. Sergei had settled in to watch the match next to Dmitry and Svetlana. They passed the bottle from the store around and drank as they watched.

"Check!" Alex claimed victory with a big smile.

"That was a good match."

"I think you had too much vodka. You do not handle the vodka very well, yet but we will train you."

"What? Maybe, maybe not. It was fun though." He raised a toast.

"Yes, but now you must come with me to town and meet my friends. They will want to meet the American who beat me. Even if it was just one time." A proud smile spread across his face.

"Maybe after a couple more drinks." Craig finished his cup and set it down and stared back at Alex.

"Deal."

"Ha! You hear that Svetlana? You will have a great time. I will introduce you to my family. We will get one of Svetlana's friends for you." He motioned to her and she smiled.

"Looks like we're in for a big night, then."

"Yes, we will have a large night. We'll drink one more, then go."

"Wait. How do I get off base? I can't leave in my uniform."

"We have some clothes you can wear. You will be able to leave with us."

"If you say so."

"I am a businessman, Craig. I can get many things done."

"What do you do anyway?"

"I do many things. There are many ways to make money. That's not important now. Tonight we go on the town and I show you a great time! Come let's go. Sergei, go get Craig some clothes he can wear into town."

Sergei disappeared into the back and returned with a bundle then motioned Craig to the bathroom to change.

"How do I look?" He modeled the new outfit of tight jeans and a western shirt.

"That's better. Now you look like a Russian." Svetlana encouraged him with a thumbs up.

They crammed into the Tico passenger car that Alex drove. Sergei came along making them squeeze in three across the back seat. They placed Craig in the back on the passenger side so the guard wouldn't have a clear view. Craig could feel his heart pounding even through the fog of the alcohol. He became concerned as they approached the gate.

"You sure this is such a good idea, Alex?" He wondered if he had gone too far already.

"Oh yes, I'm telling you, I have many friends."

"Hey, Alex. Headed home for the night?" The American guard leaned over to chat with Alex.

"Yes, we are going to have a big party. You should come."

"I can't come tonight. Hey Dmitry." He waved inside. "You have to tell me sooner so I can arrange to get off work."

Craig rolled his eyes, surprised it might be so easy.

"Okay, next time maybe."

"Sure." The soldier casually looked in the vehicle.

"Enjoy that vodka tonight my friend."

"That I will. Have a good night." He patted the roof and waved them through.

"You too. See you in the morning."

Driving off the base they came to an intersection and turned right. They sped down the highway to the city lights in the distance.

"See, Craig, my friend. I can do many things. Now we are off to our party."

"I guess I have a lot to learn on this trip. So, where are we going anyway?"

"We are going to my house."

"But what's the name of the city?"

"It's Karshi, don't you know where you are?"

"I do. We just call it K2. Since two cities around here start with K. It's easier."

"I also have a lot to learn about you Americans, it sounds like." Alex shook his head.

Alex put in a Russian music cassette as they raced down the highway. The entire car sang along. Sergei produced the bottle of vodka and they drank from it as Alex drove. Craig tried to join in the songs and they laughed as he stumbled through the words. They pulled up to a little neighborhood apartment building where small balconies adorned the antique-looking structure. A lone satellite dish hung next to one of the balconies.

"Is that your place, Alex?" Craig pointed at the dish.

"See, I told you. Craig is a smart soldier. Yes, it is my place."

The stairwell was dark and smelled of urine as they made their way up the stairs. After the third flight, they stood outside a large metal door. Alex produced a key and let everyone in.

Just inside the entry was a small carpet. Alex took his shoes off and placed them on the rack next to the door. Everyone followed suit. Craig worked his boots off his feet and sat them next to the rack.

"Come Craig, let's get some food and some glasses for the vodka. Mama, Mama, this is the American I told you about."

A short plump woman with a headscarf greeted him in Russian, smiling and pushing back a few hairs that escaped the arrangement.

"Come, Craig. Mama already has food on the table." He led him to the table. Craig could identify some food but he had no idea about the rest.

"Mama has made you some of the best Uzbek food, but first we'll have chai and bread."

"Wow, this looks great."

"You haven't even seen the meal yet. This is just the start. Mama! Where is the vodka?"

His mother produced a bottle of ice-cold vodka. They filled glasses as everyone sat down around the table.

"To health and prosperity," Alex offered as they downed the first glass. He motioned to Craig.

"To new friends and old."

They roared and accepted the toast and began passing around the chai and bread.

"This is some good bread how do you call this in Uzbek?"

"In Uzbek we call this non. We like to drink chai with it, but also vodka."

"Mama, let's eat. I am hungry and we have to go dancing still." Alex called to his mother after half an hour of eating and toasting everything under of the sun. She brought out a platter of rice and lamb called osh palov and its fragrance filled the room. Salad, as they called it, of potatoes and cucumbers joined the main dish to top off the feast. Craig couldn't believe his eyes. He'd been eating and drinking for an hour already and it looked like he was in for a longer night than he expected. They ate and drank as the night wore on.

Two and a half hours later, after dessert, Alex announced they had to hurry because they had to pick up Svetlana's friend to go dancing. His mother complained that they were leaving so early, but he promised Craig would be back some other time and they would give him a proper welcome.

Craig said good-bye and thanked Alex's mother. She patted him on the cheeks and smiled big then rested her hands on her belly. She stood in the doorway and watched them disappear into the stairwell below.

Craig could see his breath in the glow of the streetlights as they piled in the car. He grabbed the bottle of vodka and took a drink to warm himself. The Russian music blared once again and they drove a few blocks to pick up Svetlana's friend. Svetlana darted off into the building while they waited in the car.

"Craig. Masha is a good girl. I think you will like her. She is a good dancer and looks good too, right Sergei?"

Sergei nodded with a smile and took another drink from his bottle of vodka. Svetlana reappeared with her friend. Masha was wearing a simple dress. Her black hair was down past her shoulders and the sweet smell of her hair greeted them as she got in the backseat with Sergei and Craig. Alex continued with the introductions.

"Masha, this is Craig, a friend of mine."
She smiled and batted her green eyes at him.
"*Min ya zavoot* Craig." He watched her eyes light up and smiled back.

19
PICKLE JUICE

The neon Russian sign stood out in the Uzbek skyline as they drove up. Craig could hear the bass pulsing outside as they parked the car.

"Alex, come in. Come in." The doorman half bowed to him submissively.

"Mitya this is the American I told you about," he announced as he showed off Craig.

"Ah, the chess king." The large man shook Craig's hand with a vise grip.

"Yes, this is him. Tonight we show him how the Russians in Uzbekistan live," he boasted.

They entered the dark club and smoke hung low from the ceiling. The music pulsed a techno beat. Masha grabbed his hand and pulled him to the dance floor. They pressed their way into the mass of bodies moving to the music. She looked him in the eyes and danced beautifully as he moved slowly watching her in a trance. Alex smiled as he danced next to them. He motioned him on as Craig swayed with Masha.

They all danced until they were soaked from the effort. They made their way off the floor to a table reserved for them near the front. More vodka was delivered and they toasted to the evening's success. They laughed about the dancing and toasted to it as well.

"Girls, go to the bathroom or dance or something," Alex ordered. The girls obliged and disappeared into the club. Alex then turned to Craig.

"So what do you think, my friend?"

"I think Uzbekistan is great! I'll have to come back sometime."

Alex smiled, pleased with Craig's assessment.

"You and I could do business, Craig."

"Oh yeah?" He strained to hear over the music. "What kind?"

"You could help me to get things that I can't find here."

"What type of things did you have in mind?"

"That would depend on you. You work in communications. Can you get me information on the transportation of certain items?"

"Transportation? No, I don't have access to that type of communication."

"What do you have access to, Craig? Anything that might be useful to me?" Alex waited.

"Not really. I tell you what, though. I will do some checking and let you know what I can help with."

"Ah, I knew you would understand my business. Some people don't, but they miss a wonderful life, don't they?" He noted pleased with the progress. They sat and watched the dance floor and the bodies moving with the rhythm.

"So what do you think of Masha?"

"She's beautiful," Craig admitted watching her dance on the floor. Her long brunette hair waved back and forth as she closed her eyes and raised her arms to the music.

"She is. We have many beautiful things here. She could be yours if you want. Every time you come to town."

Craig was uncomfortable. "What do you mean mine?"

"I just mean she can be available for you when you come."

"You mean like a hooker?"

"A hooker?" Alex repeated confused.

"Yeah, like a prostitute?"

"Masha?" His eyes grew large then he let out a roar of a laugh and patted him on the arm. "No, no, don't be so dramatic, Craig. No, she doesn't have a man. I can make sure she doesn't get one while you are gone either." He smiled and chuckled again.

"Hmm. That's not a bad idea. I mean she does look good." He watched her walk up.

"You've been sitting long enough." She pulled him out of his seat back to the floor.

"Alex likes you." Her slavic accent tickled his ear.

"Why do you say that?"

"He's been telling everyone about you. He was impressed that you were able to defeat him in chess. No one around here is able to beat him."

"Oh really? That's good to hear. I must be better than I thought."

"You must be a good general."

"General? I'm not even an officer."

"Chess is the game of commanders. If you can beat a commander, you must be one too."

"Is Alex a commander?"

"Yes he is."

"I guess I'm in good company then."

"You could be." She spun around and looked back with a smile.

"Definitely."

They made their way back to the table and toasted a few more rounds on the house. It was two thirty in the morning when they left.

"Are you having a good time, Craig?"

"You kidding me, Alex?"

"Good. We'll pick you up at six to take you back."

"Six?"

They pulled up to Masha's place and she got out of the car.

"Yes, you will stay with Masha until then. Before you go, you must have the last drink." Sergei gave him the bottle of vodka they used in the car as they made their way from place to place. Craig took a swig.

"Okay, now can we head to your place?"

"I can't take you home to my house, my mother would not be happy. I will see you in a couple of hours."

"Okay, see you later." He stood for a moment confused by the turn of events.

Masha grabbed his hand once again and led him through the dark entrance up the stairs to a fifth floor apartment. Opening the steel door into darkness she slipped off her shoes and helped him do the same. They made their way to her bedroom with the lights off. She smiled at him and began to take his borrowed clothes off.

"Wait. Do you have a boyfriend?"

"No, why?"

"I'm confused about you, Alex and Svetlana. I'm just trying to figure out what your motivation is? How do you fit in with them?" he stated, slurring the words.

"My motivation?" She threw her head back and laughed. "You Americans are so self-conscious. I am happy to be with you. What more do you want?"

"Well, if you put it that way."

He began to take his shirt off and she assisted. He sat down on the bed and she watched him patiently. He lay back and the room began to spin. He sat up, trying to regain control of himself.

"Is there something wrong?"

"I'm not feeling too well."

"You must not be used to so much drinking."

"That may be it. I just feel like the room is spinning. It's been a while since I drank so much."

"Come, I will fix you." She showed him to the kitchen and gave him a glass of clear liquid. He took a full drink, and his eyes opened wide.

He coughed. "What is this?"

"It is pickle vinegar. It will help. I will start some coffee too. You will feel better."

"I think I'm okay after the vinegar. You have any mint?"

She threw her head back and laughed. "You sure you are better now? I don't want to have to clean up a mess."

"That stuff was a wakeup call. I think I'm good now." He waved her off because he didn't want to endure another drink from the glass even though his head was still spinning.

"I tell you what. Make the coffee and we'll hang out while we wait till I get my bearings."

"Get your bearings?" She repeated and her brow wrinkled as she tried to understand.

"It's a saying." He laughed lightly. "Basically it means let me sit here 'till I feel better."

"Okay, I'll make the coffee."

"So you live here by yourself?"

"Yes."

"I thought that people didn't live by themselves over here very much."

"I didn't always. My mother died three years ago and my brother died before that," she stated matter- of-fact.

"I'm sorry to hear that. You've had a rough time."

"It is just life."

"Maybe. I don't know anyone who has lost all their family."

"Well, you Americans have an easy life. We have lived through communism and now are enduring privatization." She teased to lighten his mood.

"So what kind of work do you do?"

"I work in a department store."

"So how do you know Svetlana and Alex?"

"I was in school with Svetlana. Alex and my brother were friends."

"So, you and Svetlana hang out a lot?"

"Yes, we do things together all the time."

"Like go to the clubs?"

"We go there for Alex. He has business there."

"What kind of business does he do?"

"He takes care of a lot of people here. He sells a lot of things and helps keep order in the city."

"Really? People do seem to know him, I guess."

"Yes, ah our coffee is ready." She filled up two cups of coffee and grabbed some treats to go along with them.

"So, what do you think of our city?"

"I haven't seen very much, but I have enjoyed it so far."

"I see why Alex likes you."

"Oh yeah and why's that?"

"You are honest but smart."

"I'm not sure about all that, but thanks."

"It is true. So are you feeling better now?"

"The room has stopped spinning."

"You will not drink so much next time."

"Maybe."

"So Alex told me you are from Texas. Do they drink much vodka in Texas?"

"I don't. I drink more beer than anything. I drink the hard stuff a little, but not much."

"That's right. We don't drink so much beer like you Americans."

"So does Alex have a lot of American friends?"

"Some."

"Does he bring them all to town?"

"He takes some to the club."

"So is this some kind of routine thing you guys do?"

"Thing we do?"

"Yeah, he makes friends. You help entertain?"

"Oh no. You do not understand Alex. He doesn't take businessmen to his home. He took you home because he liked you. He asked me to come because he thought you were a good soldier. The type of man I should be around."

"He looks out for you?"

"Yes, he has taken my brother's place."

"He sounds like an interesting guy."

"Yes, he is."

"I feel better. How about we get some rest?"

"That sounds great. I'm tired."

She turned out the kitchen light and they made their way to the bedroom. The air in the room was cool as they crawled into bed. She laid her head on his chest and looked up at him. His eyes were closed. She smiled and closed hers too.

20
NEXT PLACE OF DUTY

Craig bolted up and reached for his weapon but only found air. The pounding on the door matched the one in his head as he looked around.

"Masha! Craig!" He could hear Alex through the door.

Craig was still a little disoriented from the night of hard drinking. Masha jumped off the bed to answer the door. He stared at her tall slender figure wrapped in her pale blue dress. Her tan skin was easy to see in the bright light. She looked back at him and smiled on her way to the door.

He shook his head and put his feet on the floor. His head was pounding and he was slightly dizzy, but he felt alright otherwise.

"Good morning, Craig!" Alex bellowed, with Svetlana in tow as he met him in the hall.

"Are you ready to go back to base?"

"I guess so, what time is it?"

"I let you sleep in. It's six thirty. We have to go now. My guard will be off duty soon and you have a plane to catch."

"You coming with us?" Craig looked at Masha.

"Yes." She beamed with a smile and grabbed her coat. She took his arm as they went down the stairs.

Sergei drove this time and Alex sat in the passenger seat. Craig, Masha, and Svetlana sat in the back. Sitting close to each other they talked while the car raced back to the base.

Craig was hung over but his head was starting to clear up. He wasn't angry now, just dazed from the booze. The thought he snuck off base in his drunken stupor was sinking in as he listened to Alex and Sergei talk in Russian. Butterflies sprang up as they approached the gate. The vodka made the decision seem trivial but now the decision felt very serious as they pulled up to the gate. An Uzbek guard accompanied by an Air Force security guard approached the vehicle. Craig squeezed Masha's hand tighter. The guards leaned over to speak with them as they came to a stop.

"Morning Sergei, Alex."

"Morning. It was a great night. Next time you must come with me. You will have a great time."

"I'll have to do that," the soldier agreed. He peered into the window and tried to see in the back. Alex moved his head toward the soldier as Masha leaned over to kiss Craig. The soldier smiled.

"Alright, Alex. You guys have a good day." He slapped the roof of the car and motioned them on.

Masha leaned back as they cleared the checkpoint and smiled sheepishly at him.

"You don't have to stop now," he teased and leaned toward her as she brushed him away and blushed. They pulled into the courtyard next to the Uzbek military building. They all went in and Craig changed back into his uniform.

"You look nice in any uniform," Masha flirted.

"You had a good time, Craig?" Alex prodded.

"I had a great time, Alex. I will see you next time." They embraced and slapped each other on the back.

"Craig, before you go. A toast."

Craig laughed. "Fine."

"To friends that are gone. To new friends that have come and the adventures ahead of us." Craig toasted as soberly as he could.

Alex smiled and looked around proudly as they toasted. Masha looked at Craig intently. The glasses rattled as they raced to put them down on the table.

They walked to the store and Svetlana opened it for business. Craig stood there for a moment then announced. "Next time Alex, we play before I start drinking!"

Alex laughed as Craig made his way to the door with Masha.

"It was my pleasure," Craig stumbled though in Russian.

"Mine too."

They embraced for a moment then he looked up at Alex who beamed like a proud father. Craig walked out into the morning light. He squinted and looked back over his shoulder then smiled at her. She stood in the doorway smiling back and watched him as he walked away.

He made his way to the tent and shook his head as he wondered how close he'd come to getting some real UCMJ. He shook his head in disbelief. A part of him was scared but the other part said screw it. The war had become real to him and things weren't so clear cut anymore. He wasn't sure about anything, but did know that friends were important no matter where they came from. He made his way to his tent and grabbed his gear. He barely made it to the flight line in time to sit and wait for the flight. He sat in the plywood constructed room to wait for his call to his flight. He drifted in and out of sleep until he finally heard his flight called.

He was numb from the whirlwind of events. The landing wasn't so rough this time around. Everything seemed less important now. The landing was low to the ground as usual but it didn't faze him this time. He sat back in his seat as they taxied down to the runway. He stayed still as the others started to gather their gear. The gate opened to the world outside and he stared at the rays of light breaking into the bay.

The plane was met by a host of soldiers on the tarmac. The pilots shut the engines down.

The detail draped the coffin with a flag as everyone in the cargo bay stopped to watch. Craig and the other soldiers stood still as the crew escorted the coffin down the ramp. They followed the detail and coffin at a distance looking uneasy, not knowing what to do. A couple of MPs and mortuary affairs soldiers met the coffin. They exchanged salutes with the plane detail then took charge of the casket. The soldiers on the ramp stared at the scene before them. Not really knowing what to do they stood watching, waiting to see what was next.

Craig recognized the officer in charge of the headquarters element, Colonel Allen, accompanied by SSG Hallis. Then he noticed the Colonel was standing next to the commanding general, Lieutenant General Cook.

"Welcome back, Son." The lieutenant general smiled sincerely and extended his hand to Craig.

"Thank you, Sir." He shook his hand then smartly saluted. The general returned the salute, and then Colonel Allen extended his hand.

"Glad you made it back, Son."

"Thank you, Sir." Craig started to grow uncomfortable with the formality.

SSG Hallis stepped forward to intercede on his behalf. "Let me get Conner's stuff." he offered. "Glad you're back, Craig," SSG Hallis added slapping him on the shoulder and steering him away from the flight line.

"Thanks, Sergeant."

"Don't you worry about anything. They'll pass Conner along to mortuary affairs so they can do their identification and paperwork, then he'll be on his way back home." Hallis continued. "Craig you take it easy the rest of the day."

"Okay, SGT Hallis."

"I want you to get yourself together over the next couple of days and we'll have you back to normal in no time. Just take it easy for now, okay?"

"Sure."

"Great, let's drop your computer off and you can head back to the tent for the day. We'll see how you are in a day or two and we'll put you on some light duty to get you back in the swing of things."

"Roger that," Craig mustered without any enthusiasm.

Craig sat in his tent and listened to the noise of the base. People walked by laughing and talking. Craig felt like he was in a dream, watching everything from a distance. The guys came in and out of the tent during the day.

"Hey, Craig. You alright dude?"

"Man, heard that was crazy."

"Craig, what was it like?"

The questions were innocent and sincere but it wasn't anything he wanted to chat about. He let out a quick "yeah" or "yep it was crazy" without leaving any room to carry the conversation further. The next day was much of the same then SSG Hallis told him there would be a ceremony for Conner in the afternoon. Craig reluctantly made his way to the flight line.

"We come together today to remember the sacrifice of SPC James Conner. He came here from...."

The words faded in Craig's ears. The scene seemed a bit out of place. He was surprised by the event and felt awkward standing near the officers with his NCO. A flurry of emotion swept through him as the chaplain began saying words about the next place of duty for Conner. He spoke of his sacrifice and how he displayed the ultimate devotion to one's country and fellow man. The chaplain kept it brief. Somewhere from behind, taps began to play and Craig's legs trembled with the emotion of the song. It was over quickly. The casket was loaded onto a plane crisply then the gate closed as the engines fired up. The plane taxied down the runway and lifted into the sky in a slow, determined climb. The crowd lingered for a moment then started to disperse with each left to his own thoughts.

Craig half stumbled back to his tent and lay down to catch his breath. He felt like he was suffocating. Minutes passed before he started to feel better.

"Sorry about Conner."

"Heard you have Haji duty tomorrow."

"SSG Hallis said I have some sort of duty. Guess, that's it."

"Well, nothing happening on duty except babysitting a bunch of Haj-is."

"Sure, nothing but a bunch of Hajis. That's all that was in Mazar-i-Sharif." Craig snapped with more bite than he expected.

"Sorry dude, I didn't mean anything."

"Forget it." He turned over on his bunk and tried to think of something.

21
AN INVESTIGATION

The next morning Hallis called him to the circus tent.

"You've got Haji duty, Craig," Hallis told him from across the table in the commo shop.

"C'mon Sergeant, I don't want to baby-sit a bunch of Afghans hammering nails all day long."

"Like I said, when you got back. I think you could use some low key duty 'til you get your feet back under you."

"Sergeant, look. We're not really doing anything here anyway. There's a war going on outside this wire and we're just sitting around."

"My point exactly. You just got back in from the Wild West. You need a little time to relax."

"I am relaxed, Sergeant."

"Great, you'll enjoy the duty even more then." Hallis leaned forward. "It's for your own good, Craig."

"Roger that, Sergeant," Craig snapped with an angry look.

"Move out Craig, you've got some baby-sitting to do." Hallis dismissed him, frustrated with his attitude.

Craig executed an about face and headed out for duty without another word.

Sunlight sprinkled over the valley as Craig walked down the dusty road. Soldiers from various units walked to duty spread out along the road headed toward the front gate. The morning seemed calm as Craig looked around at the orange sky and white clouds stretching across the skyline.

"Head to the gate and get a crew for the day," he was told after he reported for duty and signed in.

Like any good system, the contractor was the middleman making the real money in the whole setup. The contractors grouped the workers with the right skill sets outside the gate before they were lined up for inspection.

The front gate, where the workers came in, resembled a cattle shoot. MP's would let them in and the locals had to navigate the long stretches of steel fence. They turned again and again until they reached the gate. An MP met them and ushered them in a couple at a time to be searched. Two MP's in body armor and kevlar waited for them in the pen.

"Raise your arms, please," the MP said to the first local as he held up his arms to demonstrate. The Afghan complied and let the MP sweep his body with a metal detector like he was going to school in south Chicago. The first MP passed him along to the next MP who patted the local down thoroughly. The local looked entirely placid through the process, which made Craig distrust him. Craig would be ticked off if he had to go through such treatment to get somewhere. He wondered how the Afghan could look so content. The Afghans passed inspection and were led through a gate to a holding pen. When a group of ten assembled, they were assigned to a guard with a local Afghan contractor. Craig was assigned a contractor whose group was headed to lay the foundation for a building.

"Do you know where we are going?"

"Oh yes, we started working this site this week. We have already framed everything and just need to pour the concrete," the contractor informed him.

"Great, you know these guys?" Craig motioned toward the crew walking in front of them.

"Yes." He smiled. "I have worked with most of them before. They all know how to do the work."

"Great, I don't want to be bothered today, so handle the crew and we'll get along fine."

"Sounds good, boss."

"Yeah." Craig's eyes narrowed as he surveyed the group. They were shabby with ragged pants or traditional Afghan clothing. Their skin was leathery from years of working outside. The old men were slow moving and had empty looks as they walked to the job. The younger men looked intent and their eyes darted back and forth as they absorbed the layout and landscape of the base.

The contractor set everyone up doing different jobs. Some workers went about making concrete and pouring it into the molds already setup, while others began settling and smoothing it out. A couple of hours passed when a van pulled up and the contractor greeted it. He walked around to the back of the truck and pulled out a large metal looking vase. A couple of workers broke away from the work crew and filled it with water and built a fire. They dropped something in the pot to cook as Craig looked on. The men were an unusual assortment for a labor crew. Some men were clearly in their fifties or older mixed with younger guys in their twenties but they performed the manual labor side by side.

They talked amongst themselves as they worked. Once in a while they looked up at Craig smiled and laughed. He became more suspicious the longer he watched them.

An older man that oversaw some of the crew walked over to Craig. "Hello."

"Hi," Craig replied without interest.

"I have been to America." He squatted next to Craig and gathered his loose garment into his lap. The rest watched on curiously.

"Oh yeah?" Craig stared at the old man slightly amused.

"New York. I was there twenty years ago."

"It's changed a lot since you've been there," Craig stated flatly.

"Yes, I would think so." The old man paused and stared back at Craig.

The younger men eased up to hear the conversation.

A young man from the group squatted next to them. "I've been to America too."

"What were you doing there?"

"I was an exchange student," the young man boasted and looked back at his younger friends.

"That's great, did you enjoy it?"

"I was amazed at how lazy and spoiled you Americans are."

"Really? That's an interesting take." Craig turned to the old man. "So what did you do in America?"

"I studied there as well, but returned when my country was invaded."

"Did you fight the Russians?"

"Yes, I fought the Russians." He stroked his beard thoughtfully.

"I am Craig."

"My name is Abdul-Raheem." The old man proudly smiled and bowed his head.

Craig nodded in return.

"Your people are a great help here, but not always."

"I can believe that. Nothing ever goes as smoothly as we would like."

"Time is with us. You will come then go, but we will remain. It is the way of Allah."

"I hope we go too, but I hope we leave you people better off than you were."

The group broke for lunch and sat around talking and looking at Craig again while he continued his conversation with Abdul-Raheem.

"The Russians came one day and we did not know what they wanted. They kept coming and destroyed everything in their way like a fire. We had to fight to get rid of them. They made life hard, but Allah was merciful and we drove them out. Then the Taliban came and we fought them. Then Allah brought you and you helped us drive them out. There is no more fighting for now. So now I can come here, work and make money for my family."

"I hope you get very rich, old man. With all the fighting you have done, you deserve it."

The group returned to work as Craig watched them. The sun began to fade and the contractor rounded up the men and tools. They started the long walk back to the front gate as dusk began to settle. The men joked with each other and laughed. The exchange student made his way back to Craig.

"You like the Army?"

"Of course, why wouldn't I?"

"Maybe because you Americans have no business in the places you go and no one wants you there."

"Maybe you should get back with your friends." Craig shifted his weapon and felt his hands start to sweat. He brushed one down his pant leg.

The young man went on ignoring the suggestion. "You like your weapon?"

"Like I said, I think you need to get back with your friends." Craig's eyes narrowed as his voice rose. His breath was becoming shorter and his chest tightened. The others nearby glanced at each other and whispered among themselves. Craig moved his head from left to right taking in the scene.

"I like your weapon. Can I see it?" The young man didn't wait for an answer and reached for Craig's weapon.

Craig pulled back and shifted the weapon in his hands grasping the back of the shoulder stock with one hand and the hand guards with the other. One fluid movement and there was a crack as the butt-stroke from Craig's rifle hit its target. The young man crumpled to the street.

Craig's heart was pounding. Conner's face and the courtyard explosion flashed through Craig's mind. Craig began to kick the man on the ground. "What the hell's the matter with you?" He yelled as he kicked him. "You stupid bastard!"

The group of workers stopped and started toward him.

"That's far enough. Don't even think about it," he yelled as he raised his weapon and took aim at the group.

His eyes were wide and his face was flush. Tears of rage rolled down his cheeks. They stopped where they were. They stared at each other then stepped back.

The young man on the ground moaned and writhed in pain. The workers talked with each other and a few became visibly angry. "Move again and it'll be the last one you make," Craig spit the words out.

He slid his finger to the trigger as the group started to move. This made them pause again. Another work group walked up and Craig quickly found himself surrounded. He began to turn back and forth aiming his weapon at the crowd gathering on all sides. The soldier escorting the new group made his way to Craig and raised his hands. "Whoa, what the hell's going on here?"

"That guy grabbed my rifle, so I laid him out," Craig rasped. His throat was tight and his heart was pounding.

"Ok, take it easy." He looked around to assess the situation. "I tell you what. Why don't I take a look at him to calm the crowd down and you lower your weapon a little so everyone can relax."

Craig looked at the soldier. "Okay." His eyes relaxed and he lowered his rifle slightly. The soldier took a look at the moaning man.

"Looks like you got him pretty good. He'll live. I'm going to help him up and give him to his friends. You stay here."

The soldier helped the groggy man to his feet and shuffled him to his friends. Two put his arms on their shoulders to support him as his head hung to the side and he moaned.

A vehicle passing by stopped and someone jumped out. It was a Lieutenant. He started to jog making his way over from the Hummer.

"Damn." The other soldier noticed the officer rushing to the scene.

"At ease, soldier. Just what's going on here?" The LT yelled, running up with his weapon drawn.

The injured young man moaned louder. Blood trickled down his face.

"That local tried to take my weapon, Sir."

"So you tried to kill him for it?" The Lieutenant threw one hand up exasperated.

"If I wanted to kill him he'd be dead," Craig snapped.

"Over there by the Hummer soldier, and put that weapon down," the Lieutenant ordered.

"You got it LT." Craig lowered his weapon completely, looked back at the crowd then walked toward the Hummer.

Two MP Hummers arrived as the LT took charge.

"You need some help, Sir?" an MP offered.

"I need you to take this injured man to the doctor. I need someone to get that soldier's weapon and take him back to his command and inform them of this situation. I want an investigation into this incident."

"Roger that, Sir. Will do."

The Lieutenant made his way back to his Hummer.

"There will be an investigation into this, Soldier. You can't walk around trying to kill the Afghan population."

"Let's have that weapon, Specialist," the MP ordered.

"You can have it." Craig thrust the weapon at him and scowled at the Lieutenant.

The MPs whipped their Hummer around and took Craig back to the big circus tent. SGT Ensly was on duty and greeted them.

"What do we have here?"

"This soldier beat the hell out of a local while on guard duty, Sergeant. Looks like he was kicking the guy when a Lieutenant pulled up and got involved. I need to give you his weapon and let you know the Lieutenant is demanding an investigation into it, so you may hear some more about it."

"Alright, Sergeant. I'll take it from here," Ensly replied as he took the weapon.

"Well hero, looks like this just isn't your week, huh? Take a seat. You can hang out here 'til Hallis gets back from chow and see what he wants to do. If it was me, I'd send you back to the states because you're running around here acting like this war is about you or something."

Craig felt his temperature rise and he stared Ensly down.

22
R&R

"What's going on, Craig?" Hallis walked him out of the compound to get some air.

"Nothing, Sergeant. The guy tried grabbing my weapon and I reacted."

"Craig, you were kicking him when the Lieutenant showed up. Sounds like there's a little more to it than that."

"It was the heat of the moment. It was no big deal. The guy shouldn't have tried to grab my weapon."

"You might have carried it too far, Craig. This Lieutenant is some hard charger with some connections at that so, it's serious now."

"Ok, so what are you trying to say?"

"Hopefully, one of those guys you were walking with saw him reach for the weapon and we can get this cleared up. The way things are done these days it's guilty till proven innocent and you might get some UCMJ."

"What? You've got to be kidding me. I know I went off a little, but c'mon the guy went for my weapon! I had no idea what that guy was going to do if he grabbed it. There's no way anyone would have done anything different. What was I supposed to do, let him have it?"

"I know, Craig, I know. It would've been better if you had hit a soldier almost. Things with these Afghans can get real sticky, especially since you weren't outside the wire. The rules are a little different out there."

"So what now, Sergeant?"

"I think it will probably all blow over, especially since no one was there. It'll be his word against yours. It just sounds bad, especially from that Lieutenant's point of view. But he jumped the gun before getting the facts, so it's made this whole thing a little messy. We'll just have to ride this out."

"Okay."

Hallis stared at the night sky. "Hey, you've been here five months right?"

"Yeah."

"Ok, I'm going to talk with the Colonel and see if we can get you out of here for a while. You're due some rest and relaxation anyway. We'll probably need a statement from you but I bet we can send you home anyway. Sound good to you?"

"Sure, I guess."

"Well, don't get too excited. I'm trying to help you out here, kid."

"I know, Sergeant. I'm just ticked. Some jerk does something stupid and I get the shaft. I don't know. I guess I could use a break to get my head clear."

"Looks like you're off duty, so go hit the gym and relieve some of this stress, then head to the tent. I'll let you know when I find out something."

Craig took Sergeant Hallis's recommendation and headed to the gym. He was an hour into his workout doing some biceps and chest, going from dumbbells to the bench press, when a soldier approached him.

"Where's your weapon soldier?" the man in a PT uniform demanded.

"My NCO has it. Turns out I'm a loose cannon. Why? Is there a problem?" He barked as he sat up.

"Never mind, soldier." The man turned and walked away.

Craig shook his head and slapped the bench with his hand. He lay back and started another set of reps on the bench when SSG Hallis appeared to spot him.

"I talked to the Colonel. He says it's a good idea to get you some rest and he'll sign the orders. You'll be out of here in the next week or so. He thinks you're a good soldier. You should be thankful and take this time to get your head straight. C'mon two more," Hallis said with his fingers on the bar as he helped Craig up with the weight.

"I'll do my best, Sergeant." Craig breathed out with the last rep.

"You do that, Craig. You do that. Besides I'm sure there's some girl back home that will be thrilled to see you. That should be worth something." He smiled and walked away.

Craig thought about everyone back home. It would be good to see them. It had been a long time. He hadn't talked with anyone for a month, before the ambush. Craig made his way to the morale tent. A soldier at the front desk was the only person there. He wondered how someone got that job and made his way to the phones.

"Hey, Melissa, it's me Craig."

"Craig! Is that you? Oh my goodness!

"Yeah, I..."

"I can't believe it's you! Why haven't you called? I was worried, but Pete said he hadn't heard from you either so you must have been busy. Everything okay?"

"Yeah, I'm fine. I just wanted to..."

"I haven't heard from you since you left. What have you been doing out there?"

"I've been busy on missions."

"It doesn't matter, really. I'm just so glad to hear from you. How are you?"

"Me? I'm fine. Looks like I'll be heading home for some R&R soon."

"Really! When? I can't wait to see you!"

"I don't know, but I don't think it will be long. I'm due for my two weeks. My NCO said it looks like I'll be getting it here a week or so."

"Your NC' who?"

"The guy in charge."

"I can't wait! Call me as soon as you find out."

"Yeah, I'll do that. I just wanted to let you know I was coming. What have you been up to?"

"I'm great. I went to the mall yesterday and you wouldn't believe the dress I got. I was with Amy she got a great dress too. We had the best time. When you get home, I can..."

"That sounds great. Look, I've got to call my parents quick before they leave for the day. I'll call you when I find out more, okay?"

"Sure, I can't wait to see you. Call me when you can."

"Ok, I'll call you later, bye."

"Bye, Craig."

He hung up the phone and his heart was pounding. He stroked his chin and thought for a moment, then dialed his parents. The phone rang twice.

"Hello."

"Hey, Mom, it's Craig." His shoulders dropped as he relaxed.

"Craig! It's so good to hear your voice. I've been worried sick about you. We haven't heard from you since you got there it seems like."

"I know. I've been busy with missions."

"It's okay. We like to hear from you a little though."

"Yeah, I know. I'll work on that."

"You sound funny. Are you okay, Craig?"

"Me? I'm fine. Look, I'm calling because I'm coming home in a week or two and wanted to let you know."

"You're done?"

"No, Mom," Craig chuckled. "I've got some R&R coming, so I'll be heading home for a couple of weeks."

"Oh Craig, that's great to hear. It'll be great to see you."

"It'll be good to see you too."

"Craig, I know you and your dad have your differences, but he'll be thrilled to see you."

"You sure about that? Dad hasn't been happy with me since I decided to join the Army."

"He's just worried about you. We all are."

"Ok, Mom, if you say so. I'll give you some more details when I find out something."

"You take care of yourself, Craig."

"I'll talk with you later, Mom."

"I love you, Craig."

"I love you too, Mom."

Craig was on a plane to Germany within ten days. The flight back was long, but uneventful. The flight, to the states, was a civilian airliner straight to Dallas. He changed planes in Dallas to a puddle jumper headed to Lubbock. He didn't have much of an expectation as he walked down the ramp, then he saw them. His mom, dad, Melissa, along with a handful of other family members. They were all there to greet him. A sign above them read, "Welcome Home Craig".

His eyes rose in surprise. A smile spread across his face. His step was lighter as he neared the group. It was exhilarating to see so many people there to meet him.

"Yea!" A cheer erupted as they saw him. He wrapped his arms around Melissa and gave her a kiss. He lifted his head to see his mom and reached out to give her a hug. His dad grabbed him and gave him a big bear hug.

"It's good to see you, Son"

"It's good to see you, too." Craig's emotions overwhelmed him as he choked back some tears. He wasn't expecting the reception, but was grateful just the same. He dropped his bag and made his way around hugging aunts, uncles, cousins and friends.

"Let's go home, Craig." His mom grabbed him by the arm after he made the rounds. "We've got a full menu at home and everyone is coming over."

The mass of people kept Craig busy as he talked with them and told them how grateful he was to see them. He kept the talk about the deployment vanilla as they asked him questions. He was tired but his mom kicked the crowd out by six. His mom and dad left him and Melissa alone in the living room after the last person left.

"Wow!" Melissa sat on the couch and smiled at him.

"Yeah." Craig let out a sigh.

"That was some day, huh?"

"Sure was. I wasn't expecting anything like that. It was like Christmas morning or something."

"I'm glad, though. You deserve it." She snuggled up to him on the couch.

Craig's brow furrowed and his body shifted. "I don't deserve anything."

"I'm sorry, Craig. What's wrong?" She sat up confused.

"Nothing, I just don't want charity. I don't deserve anything."

"I didn't mean anything like that. I just meant everyone should be here to see you."

"I'm not special, I just made it home."

"Craig, what's wrong?"

"Nothing. I'm tired from the trip, I guess."

"Are you sure? You don't seem like yourself."

"I'm fine I just need to get some sleep." He looked around. "I tell you what, why don't you come by tomorrow after I get some rest and we'll hang out. I'll feel better."

"Ok." Melissa stood up from the couch with a puzzled look on her face.

"You want me to call tomorrow before I come by?" She slung her purse over her shoulder and turned her head back as she reached the door.

"Sure, that's fine. I'll see you tomorrow," Craig agreed, distracted as he followed her to the door.

She turned to face him and put her hands on his face and stared into his eyes. "Call me if you need me, Babe."

"I will." He kissed her and watched her walk to her car. She pulled her keys out of her purse then waved one time as she pulled back out of the driveway. He watched her pull away, half wanting to stop her and half hoping she'd hurry up. He was restless. A knot was in his stomach. It had been there for a while now and he wasn't sure what to do about it.

"Hey Craig, I was headed to the kitchen to grab a Shiner, want one?" his dad offered.

"Yeah, that'd hit the spot."

"Does Melissa need something?" He looked past Craig to the living room.

"Oh, no. She went home," he replied awkwardly.

"Really?" He thought for a moment. "Yeah, it can take some time to get used to everyone again when you've been gone."

"I guess so."

"You've got the thousand yard stare, Craig."

"Huh? Come again?"

"That's what we'd say about guys that have been out in the bush. It takes its toll. All the stress, fear, and exhaustion wears a man down."

"Oh, yeah. I guess I'm pretty tired."

"It leaves you with a hollow look. You recover in time, but when your mind goes back there that look creeps back sometimes."

"Flopping schedules every month and other things now and then can take their toll, I guess," Craig offered with little interest in the subject.

His dad took the hint and made his way to the kitchen talking over his shoulder. "They can. You have to make sure they don't get to you, though. It'll cloud your mind and you'll make mistakes. Out there, they can be deadly."

"I'll keep that in mind. It's good to talk with you again. I thought you were probably still mad at me about joining."

"I still think you shouldn't have joined." His dad handed him the beer. "You should have at least gone in as an officer if you were going to do it. But no, I'm not angry with you anymore. I just couldn't see any sense in you doing that. You should've listened to me."

"Yeah, maybe I should've done some things differently."

"It wasn't fun in my day. You had to go and didn't get a choice."

"It's not like that anymore, Dad. Times have changed."

"Maybe, but guys are still dying just the same."

Craig took a swig of his beer. "Yeah. Think I'll try to get some sleep."

"Alright, night Craig."

"Night, Dad." Craig grabbed another beer and headed to his room.

The phone rang two times. His mom answered.

"Should I go get Craig? It's one of his friends from high school." He heard his mom ask from down the hall.

"No, he said he's going to get some sleep. He can catch up with them tomorrow."

Craig sat staring out of the window. He sipped his beer as he wondered how long it would be before he could sleep through the night again.

23
SHORT ON TIME

The alcohol and the sheer exhaustion lulled Craig to sleep for a handful of hours. He woke up while it was still dark outside. He was still in his uniform and decided to take his boots off. Still wide awake, he headed to the fridge to get another beer in hopes of sleeping the rest of the night.

His father was sitting at the kitchen table, staring out of the back door. He surprised Craig.

"Hey, Craig. Did you get some sleep?"

"Yeah, I got a few hours." Craig placed his empty bottle on the counter top. He opened the fridge for another Shiner black, sparking the cap he looked at his dad.

"Me too. You know, you coming home from a combat zone stirred up a lot of memories. Made it hard for me to sleep."

"It gets easier with time, right?"

"It does. Sometimes it's harder than others. That's why I didn't want you doing this, Son. I didn't want you to have these sleepless nights." His dad swore and went to the fridge to grab another beer for himself.

"I'll be okay, Dad."

"I know, but some day you'll understand. You'll have kids and you won't want them to have to go through the things you have."

"It's like you think I've done something wrong. I didn't do anything wrong." His voice rose as his defenses went up.

"Okay, Son. It's nothing to get upset about." His dad raised his hands to calm Craig down.

"There's plenty to be upset about, Dad. Regardless of what you think about the Army, you should respect my choice."

"I do, Son. It's just that, I've been there and didn't want you to go through it."

"It's too late for that. I already have." Craig took his beer and headed back to his room. He sat in bed flipping the channels for a while. He noticed it was 4:00 am and he wasn't getting sleepy. He changed his clothes and decided to go for a drive. He went to the kitchen and grabbed a six pack of Shiner along with the keys to his mom's car. He didn't know where he was going, but he felt better just stepping off the porch.

He decided to drive out to the lake like he did back in high school. He hung out there with his friends, but sometimes would go by himself to think about things. The drive always gave him some time for his mind to wander. He thought about how he wanted to go to Europe someday and visit every country. It seemed so exotic. His buddies were all for it as long as there were sexy women speaking foreign languages.

Travel didn't quite have the same zing now like it did before. He pulled up to some grass near the water and hopped on the hood of his mom's Chevy Cavalier. He laughed at himself as he sat there. The Army wasn't working out quite like he planned. He hadn't seen France and hadn't planned on being in a bunch of dirt holes halfway around the world either.

Things were different before 9/11 when he joined. Back then there were sales pitches of college funds and world travel. It seemed like a great combination. He could do the things he always wanted, be a soldier, travel and get paid on top of it. Now it was duty, stars and stripes. He didn't have any regrets, but the world was very different now.

The heat of the sun on his face woke him from his sleep. A couple of empty beer bottles were on the hood next to him and the sun blinded him as he opened his eyes. He ducked, covering his eyes and looked around. It was 8:30 in the morning. He felt better after getting a few hours of sleep. Feeling energized, he headed home to get some breakfast.

"Hi Craig, I thought you were in bed." His mom greeted him as he walked in the house.

He threw the keys on the table. "I went for a little drive."

"Are you hungry? I could fix you something."

"Sure, that'd be great. Dad head to work already?

"Yes, he went in early so he could get home quicker."

"Alright, I think I'll hit the shower."

"Ok, it'll be ready when you get out."

The house smelled great. The aroma of fried eggs, apple wood smoked bacon and freshly brewed coffee filled the air. Craig's stomach agreed that it was time to eat.

"Did you have a good time with Melissa yesterday?" His mom smiled from across the table hoping for some detail.

"It was good to see her."

"Yes, she's a nice girl. Are you going to spend some time with her to-day?"

"She's supposed to come by."

"Great, if you want you can ask her over to dinner tonight and you two could go out after. That reminds me, Pete called last night, but you were already in bed. I'm sure you'll want to catch up with him too."

"I need to call him up. That could be some fun."

"You should. You should have some fun while you're home. We were thinking about taking you skiing this weekend if you wanted. We could go to Taos or Ruidoso. You could ask Melissa if she wants to come too."

"Ok, we'll see. I haven't skied in a while. You wouldn't believe all the mountains I've seen with snow, but I haven't been able to ski a single one. You might just have an idea there. That could be fun."

"Great, I'll let your dad know. I'm going to the store to get some ribs, corn and potatoes. Do you need anything?" She grabbed the keys as she got up from the table.

"Nothing I can think of."

The phone rang and Craig answered.

"Craig, it's me, Melissa."

"Hey, Melissa." He waved to his mom. She beamed and headed out of the front door.

"My classes will be over at eleven o'clock. You want to get some lunch? I was thinking we could go to Picantes."

"Oh, that sounds good. I'm in. Swing by when class is over and pick me up, I'll be here."

The wind had picked up by the time Melissa showed up and a brown haze filled the sky. The air was filled with dust as they drove down thirty-Fourth Street to Picantes. Craig could see the green sign and red topped building in the distance. They pulled up to the asphalt parking lot marked with little holes and loose rock showing its disrepair. It once stood as an empty tribute to a fast food failure but the building had been converted into a Tex-Mex heaven and the result was delicious.

The smell of peppers and fajita meat cooking escaped as they opened the door. The walls were decorated with sombreros and dried chilies. They took a seat in a booth and were greeted shortly by a petite Hispanic girl. She delivered chips and salsa and took their drink orders.

"If there is anything I miss about Lubbock, it's this place."

"I know what you mean. When I get back from Dallas it's one of the first things I want to have when I get back to school."

"It's the best I've found so far."

The waitress returned with their tea and took their orders.

"I'll have beef enchiladas with tomatillo sauce."

"And I'll have the combo fajitas." Craig handed her the menus.

"So, what's the food like over there?"

"Not the worst I'm sure, but the salad gave me food poisoning once. Guess I should have realized the dark green slimy parts weren't normal."

"Yuck, that sounds awful. Food poisoning in a place like that. What about those box lunches they give out?"

"Box lunches?" He looked confused. "Oh, you mean the MREs." He chuckled.

"That's right, I couldn't remember the name."

"It doesn't take long to get tired of those. They're pretty bad. You have to keep lots of water in your body when you eat those. Over there it's so damn hot, it's about impossible to stay hydrated. It makes for a bad combination. I did get some great food in Uzbekistan once though."

"Uzbekistan! You got to go there?"

"It was just a few weeks ago. We had a mission and I got to hang out with some locals. It was pretty fun."

"Wow, I'm not sure I could find it on a map. What did you do?"

"Nothing really. Did a little work then went shopping at a store just outside the gate. The girl running it had some friends show up for lunch. They do the craziest stuff sometimes. They just closed the shop for lunch. Anyway her friends and I got along so well they asked me to eat lunch with them. We drank vodka, played chess and just hung out."

"That's so like you Craig. You can fit in anywhere."

"I don't know about that but we had a lot of fun. There was this one time we were in Kyrgyzstan. They gave us these coupons for beer. We started drinking before the sun went down and by the time the lights came on we were singing George Strait Songs out loud. These Air Force guys didn't think too much of our singing and came over to tell us about it when..."

The crackle of the sizzling fajitas interrupted them as a smoking cast iron skillet full of chicken, beef, peppers and onions was placed in front of him. Melissa's enchiladas looked good too and he thought for a moment he might have to order more.

"You haven't seemed very happy since you've been back."

His mouth was full and it gave him a moment to think before speaking. "I've just got a lot on my mind."

"Anything you want to talk about?"

"Not really." He paused for a moment. He knew he had to give her something, so he continued. "Well there is one thing. I don't feel like I'm really doing anything over there."

"What do you mean you're not doing anything? You're over there doing your job. It's more than a lot of people." She defended him.

"I'm doing my job. I guess I just don't think my job is that important. I only took the job I have because my parents didn't want me to get shot at. There's a war going on and I just play with computers for the most part." His volume grew louder as he spoke and the anger began to surface. "Fly here and there, but that's about it." He waved his hand in disgust.

"But, that's important. There are lots of guys that can't do your job," she argued back.

"A trained monkey can do my job," he snapped.

She looked at him sadly, and then looked away.

"I was just trying to say I am proud of what you are doing."

They ate in silence for a little while.

"I'm sorry. It's my fault. I'm just wound up. I'm trying to relax. Really I am." His face softened as she looked at him. "Besides, you didn't want me to join either."

"That's right, but it doesn't mean I don't think what you're doing is important."

Craig knew she meant well but realized they weren't getting anywhere fast. He decided to let it go. He finished his fajitas and remembered his mom's idea of the ski trip.

"My parents were talking about going skiing Friday, want to come?" He redirected the conversation skillfully.

"That sounds great! I'll skip my classes so we can go early."

"I'll let them know."

Her smile broadened and he felt better. He was having a hard time balancing his frustration and emotions against everyone's excitement. They were so elated to see him and he didn't want to disappoint them.

"I could use a drink," he stated with a sigh.

"It's a little early for that isn't it?"

"I'll be headed back soon so I'm on a little short on time these days."

"You sure you're ok?"

He looked away. "I'll let you know."

24
A SUPPORT GROUP

The roads were winding as they climbed the mountains at a snail's pace. The trees were so thick he could only see the mountaintops once in a while. A heavy snow was falling making the drive treacherous and slow.

Craig stared out the window in anticipation. "This is going to make some great powder."

"I don't think I've been skiing since that ski trip that I chaperoned you on in junior high school," his dad reflected.

"I'm glad we decided to do this. I think we're going to have a great time." His mom looked around at everyone excited.

"There's some diamonds out here with our name on them, Dad."

Melissa cringed at the mention of skiing diamonds. "Diamonds? I think your mom and I will slow ride some greens and sit in the lodge drinking some hot chocolate while you boys attack the mountains."

"I've been itching to ski. I kept seeing all these tall mountains over there covered with snow, but I just couldn't get near them."

They checked into the lodge and settled in. After dinner they sat out on the porch sipping hot chocolates and whiskeys. Steam rose from the outdoor heaters that burned the falling snow. The conversations lulled as the drinks were finished. The day's drive had taken its toll. Yawns and goodnights were exchanged as the snow kept falling. They made their way to their rooms in the disappearing light to sleep off the long drive.

The first runs of the day started at nine o'clock on the mountain. The chairlift rattled and swayed as it took them up the mountain. Craig reached into his puffy winter coat and pulled out a silver flask. He took a long drink and the vodka warmed him.

"Ah." He leaned back.

"You've been drinking a lot since you've been home. Don't you think you need a break?" Melissa advised him.

"Want a drink?" He smiled. "I'll have a nice break when I go back."

"You didn't call me Thursday night. Just because you are out with friends doesn't mean you don't need to call me. That's the second time this week."

"We were just out having fun."

"What? I'm not fun? I guess I don't get what they do for you that I don't."

"Well, for one thing they don't gripe about me drinking or not calling. I guess what they do is just be my friend."

"I don't know what you call them, but I think you've got some problems and you're going to get yourself in trouble if you don't watch out."

"I can handle myself."

The lift reached the second stop and they jumped off. His parents were right behind them.

"Well ladies, looks like this is where we go our separate ways." His dad tried to lighten the mood as Melissa shot Craig an angry look.

"Yep, see you guys at the bottom," Craig added as he shoved off with his ski poles to warm up on a blue run.

"Looks like you guys didn't have a good ride up the mountain," his dad called to him as he caught up to Craig.

"She doesn't like me drinking and not checking in."

"You have been drinking a lot since you got back. She might have a point. You could slow down a bit."

"That's a conversation for another day," Craig countered as he looked down the steep slope and leaned into it. Going over the edge onto the trail his blood surged through his body. The cold against his face bit more and more the faster he went. The sting faded as his mind became more focused on the trail ahead. The trees became a blur as he flew past them. His legs burned with fire as he turned back and forth racing his dad down the mountain. His heart was pounding when he reached the bottom.

"Whooo!" He let out a roar.

"That was a heck of a ride, huh Son?"

"I'd say it was. We have to do it again."

"Let's go."

The lift swung underneath and they jumped on as it started the climb back up the mountain. The wind swirled the snow into puffs that curled up and blew across the slopes, frosting them on the way. Craig reached into his jacket again to warm up.

"So, let's talk about this drinking, Son. What's the deal?"

"What? It's just a little drink to keep me warm."

"Don't be coy, Son. You've been drinking like I breathe air since you've been back. You need to get it off your chest."

"Get what off my chest?" Craig took a swig and looked away at the trees.

"Ok Craig, you're the one who has to deal with it. I just want to help."

"Everyone wants to help. So they keep saying."

They sat in silence. They watched the snow and listened to the lift creak as it swayed in the wind.

"Did you have to deal with anything when you got back?"

"Yes, I did. I can't say it was all roses and sunshine either. But then again I didn't have anyone like you do."

"Oh, like parents who were proud of you and what you were doing?" Craig responded with sarcasm.

"You got me there. Maybe I haven't done the best job with you joining and all, but I'm here for you if you need me."

"Thanks for the support, Dad. Glad to know you're on board now. Don't you think it could be a little too late?"

"I didn't have any support when I came home, Son. I had to deal with it my own way. It wasn't the best, but it was all I had."

"Didn't Grandad help you out?"

"Granddad couldn't help me; he never recovered from his time in the Pacific Islands. I don't know what's happened with you over there, but he saw things that he couldn't talk about. There's a lot of evil in the world and he saw a lot of it firsthand."

"Sounds like we have something in common." Craig's eyes narrowed and he reached into his pocket for another drink.

"You could if you aren't careful. He became more angry and bitter as time went on. He didn't know how to find his way out of it. Your uncle and mother helped me a lot but it took time. There's not a fix. It's really just a process of figuring it out."

"Yeah, I'm working on that. If everyone would just give me the space to do it."

"I hope so. If you don't you can drown in it. I knew guys that came back and got lost, did dumb things, or just drowned in all the confusion and pain. Seen too many funerals of guys like that. I don't want to see you end up like that. I was headed down that road once, too."

"Alright then." His voice rose and a hand went up in exasperation. "You dealt with it your way so let me deal with it my way."

"You're being hard-headed, Son. Look, just don't screw your life up in the meantime. I'm offering to help you. I didn't get that option. This drinking is becoming a problem. It's not hard to miss."

"This drinking is not a problem, Dad. To some people it's a six pack to me it's a support group, either way we get what we need."

"Cute Son, real cute."

They jumped off the lift and headed toward a diamond run.

"I tell you what, Dad. To get you off my back." Craig stood up straight. "I'll tell you what's on my mind if you can beat me down this hill. You can't tell Mom, though. You in?"

"I'll go along with that. No matter what?"

"No matter what." Craig's eyes beamed confidence.

"You ready?" His dad extended his hand to shake on it.

"Bring it, old man." Craig shook his hand. His dad smiled back. Without a word he popped the latch on Craig's right ski and pushed him over.

"Hey, you can't..." Craig grabbed his ski and fumbled to put it on.

"See you at the bottom, kid." His dad went over the edge and down the slope. Craig scrambled up but it was too late. His dad was a quarter of the way down before he even got his ski back on.

"Ready to go again?" His dad smiled as Craig skied up.

"I guess we should have defined some rules."

They got on the lift for another run and Craig pulled the flask out of his jacket.

"Give me a swig of that, will you?" His dad took a big drink and handed it back to Craig. "That hits the spot. I was getting cold."

"After two runs, you should be plenty warm by now."

"Well, spill it already and quit trying to dodge the subject."

Craig looked at the skiers below as they made their way down. "What kind of action did you see when you were in Vietnam, Dad?"

"Action?" There was a long pause as the lift swayed back and forth.

"It was pretty crazy. There were no safe places. The front lines were everywhere. The North Vietnamese would hit us no matter where we were. You never knew where it was coming from. It could be pretty scary sometimes. Since we didn't put a boot down on every inch of soil like we used to, it made things a little hairy sometimes."

They rode in silence for a few moments until his dad continued. "You've had that look lately, Craig."

"What look?"

"That thousand yard stare."

"That again?" Craig shifted uncomfortably.

"I had it too. It'll pass, but you have to give it some time. You need to get some good sleep and talk about whatever is bothering you. If you don't, it can eat you alive. You're already headed down that road. I drank a lot when I got home too. I wasted a lot of time trying to drown it all out. Thing is, no matter how much you drink, it's still there when you get done. You can save yourself a bunch of trouble if you'll just let it out."

"I keep hearing that."

"Well, maybe you should listen."

"Alright, Dad." He paused and stroked his chin. He took a deep breath and blurted it out. "You ever get anyone killed?" Craig's stare extended into the snow.

"I hoped it hadn't come to that. I didn't know it was that bad where you were."

"It wasn't. We went somewhere else and it hit the fan."

"I had some friends that got killed. Some died in some of those mortar attacks from nowhere. It'd drive us crazy. We never knew when they would hit, then it would happen and you'd look up and a couple of your friends would be dead. There were lots of sleepless nights between the shelling and the nightmares. It's been a long time, so it doesn't ride my mind now like it did back then. It still does sometimes." He looked off into the trees.

"It hasn't been very long for me. I can't even sleep through the night."

"It'll get better. I just can't tell you how long it will be before it does."

"But I got a guy killed, Dad." His gaze drifted into the white emptiness.

"What happened?"

"We missed a plane and got stuck in Mazar-i-Sharif. While we were there, we hooked up with a civil affairs unit. They do goodwill projects with the locals. The whole hearts and minds angle. I talked our civil affairs contact into letting us go on some missions with them. I thought it would be fun. It was, but on the second mission we went out on we got ambushed. It was a simple mission, but some Al-Queda guys had a different idea. I was with Conner, he was a buddy of mine. We were at this school and he walked over to check out some commotion when a suicide bomber tried to get into the area. The bomber just walked up and blew himself up. Connor didn't have a chance." His mind drifted as the last words trailed out. The sound of the snow falling mixed with the rattle of the lift.

"I can't even imagine. Sorry to hear that." They looked at the trees topped with snow and the skiers trickle down the mountain like snow.

"You didn't kill him though. They did." The chair creaked under the motion.

"Maybe, I don't know. It doesn't make me feel much better, though. I talked him into going on the mission. He really didn't want to go. He didn't like that kind of stuff. He had a little girl." He wiped a tear off his cheek. "Tell you what, Dad. I'm trying to figure this all out, but in the meantime why don't you just let me get through it like you did. Your own way."

They jumped off for another run at the diamond. The tall mountain was steep. Even with the clouds the snow was bright. They breathed in the cold air and watched the skiers below dance their way down to the bottom. It eased some of the stress to see such a beautiful sight.

"Sure, Son, you make your way. Just be careful."

"I always am."

His dad smiled. "You have been. So don't go blow it now."

25
THE ANSWERS

"That was a good trip, wasn't it?" Melissa watched him kick some leaves on the sidewalk.

"It was great. Way too short, though." He breathed deeply. The contrast of the snow-filled mountains and the sixty-three degree West Texas winter day brought a smile to his face.

"It was good to see you having some fun. You haven't seemed like you have had much fun since you've been back."

"It's not that. It's just that it's taking a little time to unwind."

"Have you unwound enough to talk to me?"

"Maybe, what do you want to talk about?"

"What are you going to do, Craig?"

"About what?"

"About life. About us."

"What are you talking about?" He stopped and stared at her.

"Well, since you've been back you've been spending more time with your friends drinking than you're spending with me. I just want to know what your plans are." She stopped walking and stared intently at him.

"We just got back from a ski trip together. What more do you want? I don't have any plans. I'm not sure what you want from me here." He pieced the words together haphazardly.

"I want you. You haven't been here this whole time."

"What do you want? Huh?" His voice grew louder.

"It's this attitude. You're angry. You're drinking all the time. What's going on?"

"I'm sorry for bringing some stress into your perfect little college world. There happens to be a war going on and I happen to be part of it. I'm sorry if it's a little inconvenient to deal with."

"All this anger scares me, but I can handle it if you'll just let me know what's going on."

"This anger scares you?" He grew incredulous. "This is nothing. Maybe you should go back to college."

Tears began to roll down her cheeks. "I don't want to Craig, but you aren't giving me much of a choice. You don't want me to be a part of your life right now. I get it. I could wait if you would just let me in, let me know something. Anything. You aren't letting me in on any of it. I'm confused." Her voice grew softer.

He looked away. His stomach turned and wrenched. "I don't know what to tell you. You know I enjoy being with you."

"No, I don't know that. How can I?"

"We have fun together."

"That's not enough and you know it. You have to give me more. Your friends are getting more of you than I am and I won't settle for that."

"Look, I'm not looking to get married or anything."

"I'm not either, but I expect more than this."

He shook his head. "I don't know what to tell you, then. We can hang out and have fun but I don't know when things will be different."

"I don't need it to be different; I just need to be part of your life."

"I can't figure it out for myself, much less make you part of it." He threw up his hands and shook his head in disgust.

"You stopped calling me." Her voice grew louder as she detailed her frustration with him. "You're only home for two weeks and you're hardly spending time with me. If it wasn't for your parents, I wouldn't have seen you at all this week. All these things add up. You can't expect me to think we are fine when you aren't even making an effort."

"Ok, so you want an answer of some sort." He shot back. "How about this, I don't know what's going on and if you can't wait long enough for me to get my head straight, then maybe this isn't what either one of us needs."

"I could wait if you would tell me what was going on in your head. Just give me an idea of what is in store. I'm not going to wait around for you to get your mind right if you don't want me to be a part of it. If you don't want me to be a part of the hard times, we won't get very far anyway."

"So, I guess, that's it then."

"I guess so." She turned to walk back to her car parked in front of the house.

"Melissa. I just don't..."

"Don't worry about it, Craig. You don't really want me anyway." She yelled over her shoulder and ran to her car.

"It's just that I don't have the answers you're looking for." He yelled at her and started to walk toward her car. She didn't stop. She kept going until she reached the car and got in.

His stomach turned as he watched her. His lower lip trembled and his eyes watered as he watched her shut the car door and drive off. He clinched his fist in defense, confused by the emotions swirling through him. His instinct was to run after her, but he braced himself and resisted the urge. He stood there dumbstruck wondering what just happened. His head was light at first then pounded from the fallout of the conversation.

I'll call her later. She'll calm down.

The cool breeze soothed his headache as he walked back to the house. Birds talked to each other in the trees lining the street. He headed straight to the fridge, grabbed a beer and went out on the back porch to think.

His mom called to him through the kitchen window. "Everything alright, Craig?"

"Yeah, why?"

"It didn't look like Melissa was too happy when she left."

"She'll be fine."

"I hope so. Are you okay?"

"What is with everyone?" He stood up from the porch. "Can't I just hang out and enjoy my time while I'm home without everyone wanting answers about something?"

"We hate to see you miserable."

"Even if I am, I'll get through it at some point. Sorry this isn't a happy, fun vacation for everybody."

"Oh Craig, you know we just want what's best for you. You'll be going back soon and we just want to help. So does Melissa."

"Melissa and I are going to take a break for a while. It's probably for the best anyway. I need some time to clear my head and can't do it with her badgering me with questions and demanding answers all the time."

"That's fine, Craig. You do what you want to. You always do."

He smiled. "I guess you're right about that." She came out to the porch and gave him a hug.

"We just want what's best for you. Don't forget that."

26
FLAG WAVING

"Hey Pete, what's up?" He answered the phone half asleep.

"Craig! Dude you have to come hang out. I'll come by and pick you up if I have to."

"When can you swing by and pick me up then?"

"I'll ditch my classes and swing by in a few minutes."

"Okay, later." Craig rolled over and looked at the clock and it was almost noon. He went to the kitchen for some lunch when he smelled a turkey sandwich cooking in the cast iron skillet.

"Morning, sleepyhead."

"Morning, Mom."

"You have any plans today?"

"Pete's going to swing by and pick me up and we're going to hang out."

"Oh, that's nice. I like him. He's a nice boy."

"Yeah, that smells good. How much longer before it's ready?"

"You can have this one now, if you want."

"What are you boys going to go do?"

"I don't know; hit the strip and a club maybe."

"Melissa going with you?"

"C'mon Mom, I told you we're taking a break. It's a guy's night."

"Thought you'd have had plenty of those by now." She smirked and sat down with him at the table.

"They haven't all been fun. This will be just plain fun."

"Can't you have fun with Melissa?"

"Mom, can you stop pushing me to hang out with her?"

"She's good for you, Craig. I just want a good girl for you."

"I'm going without her tonight. I don't want her around right now anyway."

"I thought you liked her."

"I do. Look, I'm not getting married anytime soon, so no sense in pushing it."

"I know. I'm not trying to get you married. I just want some stability in your life. She's a good influence on you."

"I have lots of good influences in my life, Mom." A knock at the door interrupted the discussion. "Speaking of influences."

"What's up Pete?" Craig grabbed his hand and gave him a half hug and slap on the back.

"We need to go out and have some fun tonight. Celebrate that you are home."

"Twist my arm. Mom, looks like I'll see you later."

"Ok, you boys stay out of trouble."

"We will," they said in unison as they walked out of the door and got in Pete's truck.

"What do you have in mind, amigo?" Pete backed the truck out of the drive way and stopped the truck.

"You have any liquor at your place?"

"Sure a little whiskey and some beer."

"Let's hit the strip then. I don't want to run out."

"Easy enough." Pete took his foot off the brake and started to drive. "So how do you like the Army so far?"

"It's pretty good. Can't complain."

"You were all gung-ho when you left here. So what's it like over in the desert?"

"Yeah, I guess I was. Things are different now. It's good to be home, though."

"I thought you'd be so tired of all that Army stuff. Thought maybe you'd seen the light and be ready to get back in school now."

"Nah, I don't think I'll be heading to school anytime soon."

"Probably not as many good looking women out there in the desert though, I bet."

"That's true, but you'd be surprised. There are some real gems every once in a while."

"Works for me. You keep every once in a while and I'll take every time I turn around."

"Talk it up, college boy."

The city was dry so to get alcohol it took a brief fifteen minute drive out of town to the Strip. It was a West Texas Vegas looking stretch of liquor stores. Neon signs and brake taillights would fill the horizon every Friday and Saturday night with lines of the faithful. It was early in the day still when they drove up, but there was already a steady stream of traffic headed to and from the stores.

"What did you have in mind anyway, hero?"

"You can drop the hero bit. Got an NCO that calls me that and I don't really like him. Drink wise, I could go for some vodka. Grab a couple of bottles and I'll pay for it."

"Vodka? No way man. I'll pay for all of it. But vodka? You feeling alright? I figured you'd want a case or two of Shiner?"

"I drank a bit of vodka over there. Guess I kinda got used to it."

"Drinking over there? I thought that they didn't do that stuff in the Army anymore."

"You wouldn't believe it if I told you."

"So you mean I'm hanging out with my friends telling them about how hard core you are and the tough life you have but you're telling me it's like a big frat party over there?"

"Nah, it's nothing like that. But there are some times when you get to mix with the locals. They drink like fish over there and their habits rub off on you. That's all."

"So when you were drinking were there any chicks around?"

"Yeah, there were some females."

"Females, man all this military language is weird. It makes you seem older or something."

"I guess I've picked up some odd habits."

"Some more than others. So, were there some hot chicks over there or what?"

"There were some here and there."

"You get any mileage with any?"

"No, but I did meet this one beautiful Uzbek girl that made me think. I was just beginning to scratch the surface, but I didn't get very far."

"Yea?" Pete smiled. "What happened?"

"It's kinda funny. I was hitting it off with this one female that I met, but drank too much and got a little sideways."

"Nothing happened? You're off in a war and you get a chance with some hot thing and you get sick? Man, you need help!"

"Told you it was kinda funny."

"Funny? Dude, that's just sad. A perfectly nice woman and you can't hold your liquor."

"You have no idea. Those people drink like we breathe air. We drank vodka for eight hours or something."

"I don't know, man. You go off join the Army, can't hold your liquor, can't deliver when the women are around. You've picked up some bad habits."

"Tell you what. You go join the Army and spend some time deployed and let's see what habits you pick up."

"Listen, joining was your first mistake. I thought you would have figured that out by now. Not enough hot women in the Army to get me to join."

"You're a real patriot, Pete."

"Patriot? Nope, I'll leave all that flag waving to you. I'll enjoy the freedom. You go earn it. Speaking of earning it, this is on me. What are we getting?"

"I just need a couple of things. A couple of these." He grabbed two bottles of vodka and a twelve of Shiner black.

"That's all we're getting?"

"That's what I'm drinking, what do you want?"

"You trying to build up that tolerance before you get back over there? I guess grab me a bottle of that Rain vodka too and a case of the Shiner Black."

They checked out and took the loop back across town to Pete's apartment. Just west of the loop on 19th street they pulled into an apartment complex.

"Did you move, Pete?"

"Yeah, got a roommate. We split the rent here. You remember crazy Steve? He was the safety in high school, took Mark's place."

"Oh yeah, I remember him. He was a pretty tough dude."

"Yeah, that's him. He's a good guy. A good roommate. He's got a girl but there's not any drama, so it works real well."

"Looks like a nice little area."

"Mostly college students out here, so it's a pretty fun place"

The walked up the stairs to apartment one hundred twelve. Pete fumbled with his keys until he found the right one and let them in. The room was bare except for the necessities. A table stood behind the bar with a couple of chairs around it. A creme colored fabric couch was in front of the entertainment center with a large TV sitting on top. A red chair sat alongside the wall. The sparse room was topped off by a keg in the corner.

"You been partying much?"

"Not a lot."

"You just keep that keg around for emergencies?"

"That and special occasions." Pete loaded the beer into the fridge. "So what will it be Nintendo 64 or Playstation2?"

"What? How did you get a PlayStation?"

"I heard those were hard to come by."

"My uncle was in Japan and picked it up for me for Christmas."

"PlayStation it is then. What games do you have?"

"Metal Gear Solid 2 and Gran Turismo 3"

"Gran Turismo? Let's do that."

"Gran Turismo it is, then."

"So whatcha going to drive?"

"Think I'll take a Viper, you?"

"I'll take it easy on you and drive a Porsche. Just give me a track with some scenery. Ah, wait. Let's pour some drinks first."

"I got it, whatcha need?"

"Give me some vodka on the rocks."

"Starting out hard?"

"Only way to go, you?"

"I'll grab a Shiner, but one on the rocks coming up."

They raced through California and Europe. They were making their way through the turns and twists of Italy when the doorbell rang.

"You expecting someone?"

"Yeah, I told a couple of people you were coming over, so they wanted to stop by."

27
HARD TIMES

Craig sat back on the couch and let out a sigh. Pete went to the door and greeted the new arrivals.

"Hey Craig, Betty's here with a couple of friends."

Craig got up off the couch and met her in the hall.

"Hey Betty, good to see you."

"You look great, Craig. Glad you came home for a while."

"You still hanging with this guy?" Craig motioned toward Pete.

"All the good ones are running off trying to kill Bin Laden," she teased. "I want you to meet some of my friends, this is Tanya."

"Hello." He shook her hand.

"Hey."

He watched the bleach blonde walk past him in tight, form-fitting jeans. She carried two four packs of wine coolers and sat them on the bar.

"This is my friend, Allison."

"Hey there, Allison."

"Nice to meet you, I've heard a lot about you." She walked in with two more packs of wine coolers to join Tanya.

Betty leaned over, "Are you still dating that girl, Melissa?" she half whispered.

"Not anymore." He felt better about it already.

"Well, this can be a real fun coming home party." She went to the kitchen and winked at her friends. They giggled and looked back as they put the wine coolers away.

He looked at Pete and rolled his eyes.

"I know. You're the lucky hero tonight." He smacked Craig's shoulder on his way to the stereo to set the mood.

"No hero, but you sure are making it hard to just sit back and relax."

"This is the way to relax. This will be worth it anyway."

Kenny Chesney sang about where he came from, setting the mood as the group got comfortable.

"Can I get you ladies a drink while these wine coolers chill?" Pete offered over the music headed to the refrigerator.

"What do you have in mind?" Tanya looked with interest.

"Craig, what do you suggest?"

"Cape cods all the way around"

Pete looked at the girls and laughed. "Okay, so what's that anyway?"

"Vodka with cranberry juice. Here, let me help." Craig stepped up to the bar. He pulled the cranberry juice out of the refrigerator and put ice in three glasses. He added some vodka and topped it off with cranberry juice.

"Got any lime?"

"Don't carry lime here."

"Here you go ladies." Craig handed the strong drinks to the girls who looked at each other and sipped gingerly.

"You make a strong drink these days," Betty noted.

"Hard times call for hard drinks."

"It's not bad here is it?" Allison flicked her hair and smiled.

"Maybe not for you." He finished off his vodka and poured another.

The girls looked at each other. Tanya had a twinkle in her eye and looked at Betty. Betty shrugged and Tanya finished off her drink.

"Pour me another, soldier boy."

"Alright then, Tanya. Now that's what I'm talking about. A woman who's not afraid to step out and take the drink by the glass."

Encouraged by Tanya, he poured her another drink and made himself another.

"Some other people are going to show up, but are you ladies up for a little game while we wait?" Pete waved them over to the small table behind the couch.

"You trying to get me drunk?" Betty asked playfully.

"Of course, to the table ladies!"

They settled in around the small table between the bar and the couch. Tanya sat between Craig and Allison as Pete pulled a folding chair from his desk and joined the group at the table.

"Did they make you hard core, Craig?" Betty looked at her friends with a smile.

"Yeah, something like that." With a serious look he rolled and sunk the first quarter into the glass.

"First rule. No one can say drink or any other form of the word." He downed his shot glass of vodka and threw a shrewd grin at everyone. Betty looked at Pete as Craig got up to get the bottle of vodka to refill his glass. Pete shrugged, smiled, and waved her off with his hand.

"Let me help." Tanya got up from the table and grabbed the cranberry juice from the bar.

The quarter made the rounds and it was hit and miss. The rules increased and the vodka flowed.

"You sure are drinking a lot more these days, Craig." Betty sized him up.

He stared at her. "You're right, consume your beverage." He smiled.

She laughed, "I was being serious."

"I am too."

She shook her head, laughed, and downed her drink as she shot Pete a glance. Pete was saved by a knock at the door.

"Hey, Corey! Who else did you bring?"

The group came in as Corey introduced them.

"This is Monica and her friend, Lisa, and my buddy, Nathan."

"C'mon in guys, we're playing quarters. Let's move the game to the coffee table so we can all fit." Pete finished introducing everybody as they moved the game. They gathered around the couch pulling the chairs in front of the TV.

"Okay, new game. Hard core Craig here has been running the game and it's time to turn the tables. We could use some help."

The new game started and the rules became more creative. The demand for drinks to be consumed kept a steady pace. The group got louder as the game wore on.

"Anyone that's in the Army has to drink when someone makes a shot!"

"You can't make that rule, Nathan," Pete objected.

"Yeah, you can't make a rule that makes someone drink every time," Betty joined.

"That's not fair." Allison whined.

"You have to consume, Betty!" Craig laughed. "I can take it if you join me smart guy," Craig challenged.

"Deal, hero."

Craig's eyes narrowed. "I've had enough of the hero stuff."

"What? I heard you were single handily winning the war over there," Nathan answered as he blew the warning off.

"What do you say we take this party to the next level," Pete interrupted. "Let's hit the rodeo,"

"Alright!" Betty jumped out of her chair and clapped her hands. She grabbed Allison next to her. "C'mon, time to go dancin'!"

They piled into Pete's truck and Corey's SUV and headed across town to the club.

Trucks filled the parking lot. Cowboy hats were everywhere. Men and women were decked out in boots and jeans, from real cowboys in pressed western shirts to the college boys in their button downs. The strong aroma of Coors Light and Polo cologne filled the air. The music was so loud they had to yell to hear each other. Their excitement built even more as they gathered around a table.

"C'mon!" Betty grabbed Pete and took him out on the floor.

Nathan and Lisa followed them. George Strait was playing and they two-stepped out onto the floor.

"I'm going to get a drink. You want anything?" Craig looked at Tanya and Allison.

"Sure, I'll take a blue Hawaiian"

"Make that two," Allison chimed.

He headed to the bar. Most everyone had a Coors or Miller Light.

"I'll take vodka on the rocks and two blue Hawaiians"

The cowboy on the stool next to him looked over and nodded. He nodded back aware that he didn't really feel like being out in a crowd. He was glad to be home but wasn't really in the party mood.

"Why didn't you return my call?"

His head sank.

"Melissa? Hey, what are you doing here?" He lifted his voice with each word in an attempt to play it off.

She glared at him. "I could ask the same. What are you doing here?"

28
THE PROBLEM SOLVER

Garth Brook's song serenaded couples on the dance floor. Craig looked at them two-stepping slowly to the ballad. He knew this wasn't going to be good.

"Well? This is how it is?" She demanded.

He turned his head and looked at her. "Pete wanted to celebrate me coming home. I thought we were just going to hang at his place."

"You look it." She looked down at his pull over and tennis shoes.

"You got that right." He looked around. "So, who are you here with?"

"Jennifer. She thought we should go have some fun since you didn't call me back and it looks like we're done for a while."

"Sorry, I just haven't been up for doing much."

"Could've surprised me."

"I wasn't planning on going out. I mean look at me."

"Whatever, I don't know what's going on with you, but I hope you figure things out."

"I just need some time. I've got a lot on my mind"

"So, are you here with one of those girls I saw you with?"

"What? No, those are Betty's friends. She just brought them along."

"Oh, and I guess they aren't going to want to dance."

"What? I don't know. I'm just here because Pete asked me to come along. I'm just planning on drinking."

"That's about all you want to do these days."

His heart was beating faster and the club seemed silent as the tension built between them. He noticed her eyes moisten and felt bad even though he didn't want to.

"I've got to go." She turned and walked toward the door. Jennifer was nearby and shot Craig a nasty look as she escorted her out. He wanted to chase her, but sat there frozen. Feeling guilty, angry, and confused he couldn't move.

"Romeo! That'll be twelve dollars," the bartender barked.

"Huh?" He replied shaken out of his daze he turned back to the bar.

"That'll be twelve dollars."

"Oh yeah." He picked up the vodka and slammed it back. "Another vodka." He put a twenty on the bar. "Keep the change."

He made his way back to the table with the drinks as he tried to figure out what just happened. He knew deep down it was already in motion. He just had to go through the pain and discomfort of it first.

"About time!" Nathan declared.

"Here you go, ladies." He looked at Tanya.

"You want to dance?"

"Thought you wouldn't ask."

They made their way to the dance floor and joined in the mass of bodies swaying in rhythm to Garth Brooks. He could see Tanya enjoying herself and he was even more frustrated at the way things were going. She was pretty. Her beautiful hair gleamed in the club lights. Her lean body pressed against his as they moved back and forth. His blood pumped faster as the thought of getting past the niceties. He knew she would be willing. He twirled her around as the song ended and they made their way back to the table.

"Looks like you guys are having fun," Betty said with a twinkle.

"I'll be right back." Allison got up to get another drink from the bar. "Wait for me," Tanya called as she went to join her.

"Was that Melissa I saw earlier?"

"Yeah, not sure what to do about her."

"Don't sweat it," Pete advised.

"It will work itself out, but be sweet to her Craig, she's a nice girl," Betty cautioned.

"I'm trying. It's just she wants too much. I need someone who can take a break."

"Well, Tanya won't crowd you, man. She could help you figure it out." Pete smiled then took a swig of his beer.

Betty shot him a harsh look. "What do you know? She's a nice girl, too. You be careful not to hurt either one, okay?" Betty demanded.

"I'm not planning on it. I'm just trying to figure things out."

"Enough of all this talk let's get a pitcher or something. Hey, where's Nathan?"

They looked around and couldn't see him anywhere. Tanya and Allison made their way back giggling. "Here you go." Tanya handed Craig another vodka and then sat beside him. *The night might not be a waste after all.* They drank a pitcher while Craig opted for more vodka. The club started to close so they decided to make their way to the cars. They ran into Nathan outside the club with a girl he'd met.

"You coming with us or what?" Pete asked.

"I think I'll get a ride with Crystal and we'll meet you there." Nathan flashed a big smile, pleased with himself.

"Okay, we'll see you there." Pete waved as he walked Betty to the truck.

"Hey, Crystal, who's this?" A tall cowboy demanded as he walked up.

"Oh no," she gasped.

"Hey man, I was just..."

"No one's talking to you." The cowboy interrupted without even looking at Nathan.

"Is there a problem here?" Craig jumped in.

"Who are you?" The cowboy was thrown off guard.

"I'm the problem solver. You have one?"

The cowboy laughed, "I don't think you know what you're getting yourself into partner." He looked behind him at three other cowboys that looked on with interest.

"Hey, I got this," Nathan insisted.

"Yeah." Craig shrugged then turned to the cowboy, "Oh yeah, I'm not your partner."

He cold-cocked the cowboy with one shot full of pent up anger. Two of the cowboys, watching, rushed him. The third grabbed something from the truck bed he was leaning against.

Craig avoided the first one with a side step and a push. He gave the second an uppercut as he ran into him. They both rolled onto the pavement. Craig jumped up quickly and smiled. He felt like he was in his element.

He started to look for the third one when he felt something slam against the left side of his head. He tried to see what hit him as he fell, but was blinded by the warm liquid running down his face. He knew he should do something, but couldn't quite remember what it was as he crumpled to the pavement.

Pete reached the guy as he pulled the heavy chain back one more time for another hit at Craig. Pete grabbed the chain, pulled the cowboy toward him and hit him at the same time. The cowboy fell backward onto the pavement like a tree.

Craig rose to a knee and shook his head. He knew he needed to get up so he started to stand. The cowboy he gave an uppercut was on his feet about to lay into Craig when Nathan kicked him in the lower back. The cowboy grabbed his back as he fell to the ground.

"Damn, Craig," Pete cursed and pulled him to his feet. He half dragged him toward the truck. He threw his keys to Betty who had a frightened look on her face. Tanya and Allison were mirror images as they stood with shocked looks at the sudden violent exchange that had played out.

"Where's your car?" Nathan grabbed Crystal.

The guys on the pavement struggled to recover. They made it to their feet but they were through and headed for their trucks. Club security was trying to get through the crowd that had gathered to watch the fight.

"You made it home, but you may not make it back to the Army if you keep this up." Pete scowled as they piled in the back row of the quad cab.

"Here put this on his head." Tanya gave Pete a rag she found in the floor.

"What the hell hit me?"

"Some guy decided to take a tow chain to you. I think you got the hook."

"Feels like someone's poured hot oil on my head."

"That'd be the blood I'm trying to keep from messing up my truck."

"Sorry man, is it bad?"

"I think we'll have to get you to the hospital"

"Hospital? Nah, I'm fine."

"You may be, but that cut on your head isn't. Want me to take you home first?"

"Might as well get me to the hospital then."

It took twelve stitches to get his head back together. They headed back to the apartment and the girls said goodbye and left. The drama of the night had exhausted them all. Craig sat on the couch touching his head without thinking.

"Ow. Yeah, I think this is going to leave a mark."

"Don't think I've seen you drink that much before, Craig. You sure you're doing alright?" Pete sat in the chair across from him.

"I get better as the night goes on."

"Keep going like that and your liver's going to look like a raisin."

"If I live that long."

"What?"

"Nothing, so when did you become such a lightweight drinker?"

"I'm not a lightweight. I'm just not in the sumo class. You sure you're alright? You seem different."

"Yeah? You're different too. Didn't know you became such a woman while I was gone."

"See, that's what I'm talking about. Aside from the heavy drinking, you seem pissed off about everything. Like you're about to boil over. Kinda looked like those cowboys were just the lucky jerks to get it. They deserved it, but you were going to lay into Nathan earlier if we didn't go to the club. Tonight it looked like you were looking to get into a fight no matter who it was."

"Yeah, I've got a little steam to blow off. It's been a long month. I think I just needed to get some air. But coming home has been good. I'm just trying to sort some stuff out."

"All these women got your mind messed up?"

"What?"

"Women over there, the one here. Looks like they've got you all wound up."

"I've got to figure that out too."

"That chick you fell asleep on?"

"I didn't fall asleep on her."

"Sounds like you've got some interesting things to figure out alright."

"Life has just gotten real complicated in general."

"You know I'm no teetotaler, but at the rate you're drinking you're going to make things worse if you keep this up."

"Well this vodka won't solve it but sure will help move the night along. That's kind of the point now anyway. I figure I'll work out the details later."

"Think I'm about done for the night. You want to crash here on the couch?"

"How about dropping me off at my house. I don't want to miss a night of sleeping in a bed while I'm home if I can help it."

Pete dropped him off at home where he let himself in. His parents left the hall light on so he could find his way to his room. He made it to his room and stripped off his bloodied shirt. Sitting on his bed he touched his head and winced. *Making some real progress here at home.* He smiled and lay down. He was asleep before he knew it.

He woke up late the next afternoon. His body ached from the fight and the stitches were sore.

He could smell dinner cooking in the kitchen. He got a quick shower to clean up and went to the kitchen to see what smelled so good.

"Oh my goodness! Craig! What happened to your head?" His mother gasped. One hand went to her mouth as she tried to suppress her shock.

Craig winced. He expected her to be upset, but it still wasn't fun. He could see the concern on her face and tried to reassure her.

"It's nothing really. You should see the other guy." He laughed trying to gloss over the moment.

"Craig, what happened to you? Stop making jokes I'm serious," she demanded as tears welled up in her eyes and made their way down her cheeks. "What's happening to you Craig?"

"It's nothing, Mom." He waved her off. "We were at the Rodeo and some guys started a fight in the parking lot. No one got in any trouble."

"I wish you wouldn't go out there. It's nothing but trouble. You're making me scared. You don't seem like yourself anymore. "

"I know. I'm fine though. I'll be gone in a couple of days anyway. So don't worry about it. So what smells so good?" He tried to change the subject.

"While you were sleeping off your wild night I've had a brisket in the oven. I have some potato salad, coleslaw and baked beans to go with it if you're planning on being around," she snipped.

"Sounds great. Yeah, I'm kinda tired. I think I'll hang around here tonight if you don't mind." He smiled.

She smiled back and he hugged her. "Of course I don't mind."

They ate dinner and sat in the living room. The light from the TV flickered on the wall and Craig stared without any interest. There were a host of emotions and questions eating at him. He wasn't sure what they all were but he could feel the turmoil inside. He knew the ambush was part of it, but there was something more and he couldn't put his finger on it.

It didn't make much sense to him, but he was ready to get back. The stress of the questions that came with the quiet was harder to deal with than the possibilities that came with being deployed. Each one threatened to unleash a torrent of emotions that he was trying to sort through.

He wasn't sure how to handle them and was afraid of where they might lead.

He was afraid. Not of dying or getting shot at. He was just afraid of the unknown. The uncharted waters of extreme emotions he had never known before. That was part of it. Then there were the questions rolling around in his head and feelings he couldn't put his finger on. His beer was empty before long so he headed to the kitchen. He decided to kick it up a notch and get a little quicker buzz and opened the liquor cabinet.

He pulled out the vodka and grabbed some cranberry juice from the refrigerator. He poured himself a strong drink and headed out to the back porch. The sun was setting. The wide West Texas sky began to explode with color. A bright orange began the show, then the colors mixed and blues and purples began to shade the clouds. A pink ribbon at the bottom of the clouds unraveled slowly as he gazed at the sky. Music from the neighbor across the alley filled the air. Kenney Chesney kicked off a serenade taking the sun down as Craig sat trying to decide what the problem was. The splashes of colors were overcome by the dark purple then darkness consumed them all. Craig sat looking at the stars and wondered if he was making the right choices.

Overcome by the weight of the past few weeks his shoulders sank. His lip quivered as he worked hard to keep the emotions at bay. He wiped a couple of tears from his face and pushed his hand down his pant leg.

"Mind if I join you?" His dad came through the backdoor with a glass in his hand.

"Sure. As long as you're not planning to interrogate me."

"Your mom already warned me. I just thought I'd join you for a drink. I saw you had the vodka out. "What did you make? The cape cod?"

"For the most part, no lime."

"Why don't you come over here and I'll start a fire to take the evening chill off. I'm getting too old to be sitting on the porch steps. I need something soft and cozy."

"My butt was getting numb anyway," Craig acceded.

His dad sat his drink down on the end table. Between the porch and chairs was an outdoor fireplace. He threw some logs on and started a fire.

"That's more like it." His dad stared with satisfaction as the flames grew taller.

The flames leapt up from the fireplace reaching into the night air. Huddled around the glow for the warmth it offered, they sat in silence and enjoyed the fire.

"I think I'm not happy with the job I'm doing," Craig confessed finally breaking the silence.

"What, you don't like flying all over that godforsaken piece of earth?"

"Actually, that's the fun part. I think I want to get out of this support role and into the combat. I guess after seeing some of what's going on, I want a bigger piece of the action."

"That's not quite the response I was expecting. What do you mean by a bigger piece of the action? Infantry or maybe that civil affairs group?"

"I don't know. Those missions with that civil affairs team were interesting. They mix with the locals and work with the SF a lot."

"Never really heard of them before you told me. Sounds like it would be interesting."

"It was. Part of me wants to punch back at the bad guys though. I was thinking infantry might be fun for a while. Especially with all the action going on these days."

"The guys I knew in Vietnam didn't think it was that much fun."

"I know, Dad. There was a whole lot of drama about that war we don't have, though. We're out hunting a bunch of guys who attacked us. A bunch of murderers and their bosses. Your war had a bunch of political drama."

"There's always political drama, Son, but I know what you mean. So, it's either help'em or kill'em, huh?"

Craig laughed. "Something like that."

"Well, you could get killed walking across the street anywhere, so you might as well be doing what you want and have a good time with it. But you can't do either one today, can you?"

"No."

"Then don't sweat it too much. The Army won't move too fast for you, anyway. It's hard to get that big machine to move fast when you want something done. There's nothing to get bent out of shape about while you're here. I think you've got some time to think this all through. You've got enough stress without creating some for yourself."

"Good point. I guess I can put it on the back burner for a while."

"You'll have a better time if you do. Just let things flow a little bit."

"I was before everything hit the fan. I don't know, I guess I just got caught up a little with all that's happened. It was like I need to make some changes, and quick. I might not have that much time you know?"

"You only have the time that God gives you, Son. No more, no less. Try to remember that and you'll find it's all a lot easier."

"God? C'mon Dad." He waved him off with his hand. "Conner believed in that stuff and it didn't do him much good."

"I'm sure it didn't hurt either. Doesn't matter Craig. Put whatever name you want on it. Call it fate if you want. If it's a bullet in Afghanistan or a car wreck in Texas, if it's your time, it's your time."

"I guess." Craig took a long drink.

"Speaking of time, you've only got a couple of days before you go back. You get enough fun to last you 'til you get home?"

"Think I'm ready to get back. I've had all the time off I can stand. None of this seems that important right now. There's a lot going on over there."

"I know what you mean, but it's going to happen whether you're there or not."

"I know. I just don't want to miss out on anything. Besides, you know how it is. You don't want to leave your team when they're still in the middle of it."

29

GI JOE

It was already dark when he stepped off the plane in Bagram. He walked down the tarmac with his ruck sack on his shoulder carrying his civilian clothes. The valley was deep into winter and snow lined the runway. The smell of the dirt, the diesel fumes and odd smell of Afghanistan were familiar now. In some strange way it felt good to be back. The heaters rumbled in the night as he entered the tent and unpacked in the dark. The flight had been long and he was ready to get some sleep.

Craig was up with the sun and made his way to the circus tent to check in. Hallis leaned back in his chair and gave Craig a long look. "Looks like the trip did you some good."

"Yeah, I think it did."

"What happened to your head?"

"Oh, this. It's a souvenir I got while I was home." Craig rubbed the fresh scar that was still healing with a smile.

"Nothing that involved the police, I hope?"

"No, Sergeant, just some fun with some cowboys."

"We're not going to have anything like that happen here are we?"

"Think I'm done with all that excitement for a little while. I've had enough to last me for a while."

"Good to hear. Since you're not on the shift rotation right now I'm sending you down to Kandahar. It's that time of the month so you might as well jump right in."

"Roger that, Sergeant."

"I already had Parker check on the flights and you guys will be out of here late this afternoon. You can get the computers ready in the meantime."

"Will do, Sergeant."

They flew into Kandahar just before dusk. The flight was smooth until a goat herder somewhere decided to take a pop or two at them as they began their descent. The pilot began counter measures. The plane slammed from the left, then to the right, throwing everyone around in the back. The quick drop to the airstrip felt like the Superman at Six Flags. The bottom dropped out, then they slammed down to the tarmac. The rumble of the engines and the vibrating shudder was a rude wakeup call as they pulled to a stop.

"Another day in paradise," Parker announced and stood up.

"We haven't gotten to paradise yet. If you think this is paradise, you have no imagination."

"It's all in what you make of it, Craig. There are women everywhere. If there's a woman around, it can be paradise."

"Maybe, it can depend on the woman."

"That sounds like a personal problem, Craig. If you can't find paradise with a woman, you might need some help. They can all take you there."

"Did I miss the drinks on that flight? I mean, you must've been drinking. Some women aren't worth the time of day. Much less a taste of paradise."

"Seriously, Craig. It doesn't matter what the woman is like. Hot, cold, wild or shy they all can take you right to paradise if you know what you're doing."

"From what I remember about paradise it, has nothing to do with women."

"Well, that might depend on your religion, but that's not the point. If you don't know that, then you're not paying attention or you just don't know what you're doing." The banter carried them from the tarmac to the road. Laughing at each other, they continued to spar until they reached the SF compound. "Where are we, Craig?"

"The SF compound."

"We stay with the SF down here?"

"Yeah, they have the best of everything down here."

"You sound like their salesman or something."

"That'd be an easy job. These guys live like kings."

"No kidding?"

"You'll see."

The compound was dark and Jesse wasn't in his office, so Craig led Parker to the guest tents where they unpacked and put in for the night. The morning brought the lure of the freshly cooked breakfast so they headed to get some eggs and bacon. They spotted Jesse at a table eating with some soldiers. He nodded at them as they fell in line to get some breakfast.

"Good to see you, Craig. You boys come by the office when you're done."

They nodded and Craig cleaned his plate like he was back in basic.

"C'mon Parker, finish up."

"What's the hurry? We don't have that much to do down here do we?"

"More than you know, just hurry up."

Parker shook his head and stuffed his face a little quicker since Craig was hounding him.

"Good morning, Jesse." Craig greeted Jesse who was pounding away on his laptop.

"Hey fellas, how goes it?"

"Pretty good. This is Parker." Craig motioned to his left.

"You boys here to visit the local units again?"

"Roger that. We'd like to go on a mission with you guys while we're here, if you can arrange it." Parker looked at him wide eyed for a moment.

"A mission? I don't know if I can arrange that in a day. How long are you guys here?"

"A couple of days."

"Ok, I'll see what I can do. Eddy will be glad to hear it. He thought you might find the Special Forces a little better than the average guy. He can spot guys that have what it takes a mile away."

"Glad to hear it. Nothing average about any of this so far. We'll head out and get our work done ASAP just in case you can swing something for us."

"Alright, I'll see what I can do."

"Wait, you want to do what?" Parker's pitch rose with each word as they left his office. "No offense but haven't you already had enough excitement outside the wire?"

"No way, man. I want to see how the pros work. Aren't you curious? It'll be like watching cops, except you're doing it with them."

"You're not talking me into going out with the SF."

"Nothing will happen. Besides, these guys can handle it."

"That's all you bro. I'm not interested. If I wanted to do that stuff I'd have joined the infantry or something. Does Hallis know about this?"

"He will when we get back, I'll tell him later."

"Wait." Parker raised his hand and stopped Craig. "So what's my silence worth?"

"I tell you what. You let me go on this mission without letting the word get out and we'll head anywhere you want to go within reason."

"How are you going to pull that off? We'll have to head back to Bagram."

"We can get our work done today get a mission in tomorrow and head out the next day. Then we can go somewhere for a day or two and head back. Once we got our crypto delivered we can go anywhere as long as we're back within six or seven days."

"Ok, I'm game, but it's your butt on the line if anything goes wrong. Wait, you mean you're willing to risk getting in serious trouble to go running around the hills with the SF when we could go to Turkey or somewhere? Instead of hanging out with hot Air Force chicks you want to run around with a bunch of bearded hillbillies? What's wrong with you?"

"Nothing. I just want to see what it's like."

"Alright. You go play GI Joe for one mission. ONE mission. Without me. Then we go visit some hot women."

"Deal. That's all I want."

Craig woke up early the second day hoping for some good news.

"Any word from the captain?"

"Yeah, he said you guys can tag along on a mission tomorrow. He doesn't have any details, but knew you would understand."

"Sweet I'll be ready. My compadre doesn't want to come, so he'll just stay here and probably go look for some women."

"A man's gotta have his priorities. I can respect that. Eddy said you guys might need to head over to the weapon shop and pick up something a little less bulky. Something that might not get you killed in case anything happens. I can take you when you're ready."

Jesse took him by the weapons room and picked up an M4 and four empty magazines.

"I think this will do. Let's put some rounds in these mags and get you out to the range this morning so you can get used to it. Give that M-16 to SSG McCoy. When you get back from the mission you can swap it back out." Craig obliged willingly and loaded the mags with the rounds McCoy gave him.

"This is nothing like my unit. I had to sign for rounds when I got them. Much less, this many and a weapon too."

"The rounds are already signed for before we ever get them. We don't have time to be filling out paperwork about rounds and having to account for them in the field. It'd be like we were in the Army or something." He laughed. "Alright, we're off. Let's go see how you like this weapon."

Jesse grabbed a Hummer and they drove out to the makeshift gun range.

"I think you'll like this weapon. It has a smooth trigger motion. The lighter weight makes it a lot of fun to shoot. This weapon is very versatile compared to that dinosaur you haul around. There are a lot of options for the weapon too between laser sights, grenade launcher, the forward grips and such. We won't get into all of that, but you'll have plenty of fun with this. The other stuff is something to look forward to. The barrel on this weapon is about six inches shorter than your M-16 and almost two pounds lighter. You can fire whenever you're ready."

Craig looked around. It was just him and Jesse. He put in some ear plugs and gave Jesse a thumbs up. He walked up, loaded a magazine and chambered a round. He selected single shot and put a couple down range. He began to get the feel of it and flipped it over to semi-auto, then finally stepped it up to full auto and emptied the magazine. He lowered the weapon and looked over his shoulder with a big grin. "That's what I'm talking about."

"Smooth huh? This has to be one of my favorite weapons. Not as powerful as some weapons but it's a lot of fun. It has the same round as the M-16, but don't worry though, it'll kill most people you run into anyway. Especially when you know how to place it."

"Can I unload a couple of mags?"

"Go for it. You have three more. I keep telling you, this isn't the Army."

"I'm starting to get it now." He took the time to zero the weapon with the second magazine. He confirmed his zero with the third magazine. Finally he kicked off the last mag on auto holding the forward grip and unloaded it. "Whooowhooo!"

"I know you think this is a big deal, but this is what we do all the time," Jesse chuckled. "Once you go SF you'll never want to leave. Most of the time the only way guys leave is because they get hurt, killed, or have to retire. It's just too much fun to get out. There's nothing in the civilian world that can touch this. Let's go get some chow. All this work has made me hungry. "

Back in Jesse's office they sat down and heated up some Ramen for lunch. Jesse put in the movie, "The Godfather", to watch while they ate.

"You guys get settled with a weapon already?" The captain poked his head in the door.

"We traded out that dinosaur of his for an M4. He should be good to go. He'll need to swing by and get some more rounds, but that's it."

"Smells good in here. If it wasn't for Ramen, I couldn't make it through college. I don't think I'd make it through this deployment without it either."

"Beats MREs," Craig agreed.

"Eat up then, Craig, we'll be moving out in an hour. I'll give you the details when you're done. So swing by my office."

Craig sat up. "An hour?"

"Yeah, we got a little cleanup job to go do and I thought you'd like to go along. You can still come tomorrow if you want."

"I told Parker I was only going on one mission. We have a deal. After the mission we're headed somewhere he can find some Air Force women before we go back to Bagram. This will give us the time to get a flight somewhere good."

"Sounds like a plan. See you at the office in a few."

"Roger that, Sir."

The weapons sergeant loaded Craig up with more rounds and two grenades for good measure. Craig's pulse quickened as he attached the grenades to his load bearing vest. He was headed out into the wild and was armed for a real fight for the first time. The prospect thrilled him.

The captain's office was a multi-use area. The executive officer shared the space as well as a team sergeant. The captain's desk had a few books, laptop, and assorted papers. Lying between the books and the laptop was an area map mostly closed as it curled up at the ends.

"Craig, come on over." Eddy waved him over as another soldier walked away. "Ok, you're role on this mission is to shadow me. Don't do anything unless I do it. This is just a local issue but sometimes when our allies are intimidated or want to hassle some of their competitors they ask us to do some work for them. Our higher ups somewhere get a little mileage from these things. They like to remind the locals they're on the right side when we flex some muscle. So this is our turn to get out and flex. So you see this road headed out of town?" Eddy pointed to a line on the map leading south out of Kandahar. We're going to head out this road about an hour and find the guys causing trouble and have a chat with them."

The team sergeant stopped by the door. "Eddy, we're ready."

"We can finish in the Hummer."

"Yes, Sir."

He entered the yard and saw five Hummers lined up. Ten men with beards growing at different stages dressed in their eclectic gear waited for the order to ride.

"Craig, I'd like you to meet Rick. He's the team leader we'll be tagging along with."

"Hello Craig, what's your day job?"

"Commo, crypto courier."

"Seen any action out here?"

"A little."

"Alright. If this deal goes south, you just do what we tell you. You'll need to pitch in if things get hairy. Understood?"

"Roger that."

Rick turned to the group and said with the wave of his hand, "Mount up."

30
DAYLIGHT AMBUSH

"There's an entrepreneurial group that decided they wanted to start collecting toll money from people on a road a few miles out of town. Like I said, the locals didn't want to get involved with it for whatever reason, so we've been tapped to go clear the roadblock," Eddy informed him loudly over the rushing wind.

"So, what's the plan?"

"We thought we'd just go up and chat with them and see what happens," Eddy told him with a straight face.

"Really?"

He nodded.

"I thought there'd be something a little more strategic."

"This isn't rocket science. We'll pull up in a basic defensive formation and take proper measures but these guys are just local crooks. These guys aren't para-military or anything. They're just out to make a buck. That's the downside of these favors we get called in on. Not as much planning as we like but generally there's nothing to them. This shouldn't be too complicated. You never know of course, if someone gets trigger happy the whole thing could end up sideways. That always complicates things, but hopefully these guys aren't too dedicated to this new job and they come along peacefully."

They headed south out of Kandahar. Racing down the highway, they passed relics of wars gone by. Burned out tanks and pieces of Soviet hardware stood out among the flat land. They hardly took notice of the village Mandi Sar as they passed it. It wasn't quite, "The ride of the

Valkyries" from Apocalypse Now, but he felt like he was flying just the same.

"They're supposed to be between here and the mountains along this stretch of road," Eddy explained as he dragged his finger along the road on the map. "A predator in the area confirmed their location just the other side of this hill." He jammed his finger at a point in between narrow curved lines on the map. "It should be about twenty more minutes from here. No sign of any additional people in the area, so it doesn't look like they have any backup if things get hot."

Craig nodded as the wind rushed through the windows. The anticipation had Craig keyed up when they left. Halfway there the initial adrenaline shot started to fade. It was silent in the cab except for the continuing rush of air blasting through the window. Although they drove eighty miles an hour, time seemed to slow as he felt the wind on his face. He looked to his left at the SF soldier next to him in all his combat gear and felt a sense of awe. He looked at the front of the cab at the sergeant driving the Hummer and could hardly believe he was there.

It was like a dream. Finally on a mission with the SF. The Hummer started up an incline and the vehicles slowed to forty miles an hour. The predator confirmed their approach. They were easing up on two trucks about a mile away. The terrain made a saddle on the other side of the hill. The low spot in the middle was a good place to catch unsuspecting travelers off guard. It was too late to do anything once the prey reached the low spot because they were committed.

One Hummer pulled over near the top of the hill and a sniper team took a position where they could watch the exchange. Another Hummer with a mounted fifty caliber machine gun pulled over to the side just over the crest where they could assist if needed. The rest of the group came over the hill at a manageable speed. They saw two vehicles on their right on the opposite incline as they went down into the dip. The bandits would have the high ground, giving them the chance to dictate an engagement if things went haywire from the start.

"Let's see what these boys want." Eddy loaded a round in his nine millimeter and holstered it as they pulled off the road. Two Hummers pulled up at an angle blocking the two bandit vehicles while pinning them in if things turned bad. Another Hummer took the center position with the fifty cal machine gunner resting on his weapon. The bandits seemed confused by the soldiers' appearance. They looked around nervously at each other. Their leader calmed them by walking out in front of the vehicles to greet the soldiers. Reassured, they lifted their weapons a little higher. Eddy sat for a moment assessing the situation.

"Craig, hand me that big bag of M&Ms. Grab one for yourself and come on."

Craig handed Eddy a bag of plain M&Ms and took the other as they exited the vehicle. Eddy opened the package dumped some in his hand a popped them in his mouth. "Follow my lead, Craig." He walked forward without looking back.

"Hello." Eddy greeted the bandit leader in the man's native tongue. The man's face couldn't hide his surprise at the greeting.

"We're on a sight-seeing trip," he added in English.

"What sights American soldiers with guns go to see out here?" the bandit offered in broken English.

"You would be surprised."

"I would, there is nothing out here."

"Have you ever had M&Ms?"

"No, what are these M&Ms?"

"Delightful little candy chocolates. Try some." Eddy extended the bag then ate some more to set the tone. The bandit extended his hand and took some. He held up a blue one and looked it over it carefully. He popped it into his mouth and his eyes softened as he chewed. His teeth were covered in chocolate when he smiled at Eddy who smiled back. The bandit popped the rest in his mouth then extended his hand a second time. Eddy obliged and refilled the hand.

Rick walked up and offered a Dr. Pepper and the man took it from him and his eyes opened wide as he swallowed. Eddy waved for the man behind the leader to come get some M&Ms too. The man stepped forward and shared in his leader's delight. He grew even more animated about the treasure he had discovered. He called to the others and waved for them to come over and Eddy and Craig were handing M&Ms to the crews of both bandit vehicles before they knew it. The leader grew comfortable and invited them to sit down to eat and drink with him. Two soldiers on the left flanked the vehicle slowly. They eased their way behind the group and before long Eddy had established a daylight ambush with M&Ms and Dr. Pepper.

"We'll be needing your weapons," Eddy informed the bandit leader after the mood was sufficiently relaxed. Surprised the bandit looked around and realized that all of his men had walked up and were eating and drinking. He barked at his men and slapped the one closest to him across his head. He surveyed the situation and saw that he had been out maneuvered. He resigned himself to his fate and told his men to hand over their weapons as they shared his surprise.

"Tag'em and bag'em boys," Eddy ordered as the bandits began to hold up their weapons without relinquishing their goodies. The team let them finish their treats then zip tied them and loaded them into the Hummers.

"Well, what do you think, Craig?" Eddy looked back at him with a satisfied look.

"Not quite what I expected, not sure I really know what to think after that."

"It's not always guns and grenades. You have to find creative solutions, so you don't lose people out here. Don't get me wrong we like the excitement too. Blowing things up is great but it's not any fun when people on your side start dying. Sometimes it can't be helped. But if it can, it's worth avoiding it."

"I would have never guessed that would be the tactic today. Not in a million years. I think I know even less about you guys now."

"I didn't think you'd have a good appreciation for it until you saw it firsthand. With small groups like these, different things like this can work fairly well."

"That's just the craziest thing I've ever seen."

"So you still thinking about getting out of the Army?"

"More than ever."

"You should be. You go take your vacation to find those Air Force babes and think it through."

The return trip was much of the same. Air blasted them as they drove along. They didn't stop anywhere and went straight to the detainment center to off load the bandits they captured. Eddy spoke with the detention center personnel while the team unloaded the bandits from the vehicles.

"What's going to happen to them?" Craig asked after Eddy climbed back in the Hummer.

"They'll probably be out in a day or two. They're not the bad guys we're after. They're just local hoods. We want the connected Al-Qaeda guys. Who knows, one of these guys might know someone though, you never know."

"So, that's it?"

"Pretty much. This was a good mission, since nobody had to fire any shots. Especially since these guys were local criminals. I'd hate to lose someone out here for basic police work. When bullets start flying, the bad guys aren't the only ones who die, you know?"

"I thought all you guys did was the hard core kill'em all stuff."

"Don't get me wrong, if a mission doesn't go right we'll come down hard. We'll unleash everything we have, so when the smoke clears the bad guys aren't the ones walking away. The standard operating procedure when we walk into engagements like this is to gain the tactical advantage then drop the hammer. It keeps things simple. If those guys got jumpy before we had them flanked, then at least we had an overlook with the sniper team and fifty on the hill and we had them cut off so it wouldn't have lasted long. I just used the same standard tactics, but with a little creative application."

"Parker's never going to believe this."

"Not everyone's cut out for this stuff. We're not looking for robots and guys that can only follow orders."

"What are you guys looking for then?"

"Take today for instance, we're looking for men with imagination and the ability to think on their feet. You can go a long way in Special Forces if you have those qualities. The rest goes without saying. Things like mental toughness and discipline. Discipline is probably the most important things. Most men can't endure the pain it takes to get here. If you decide to take a shot at it, I can get you a training slot. You'll have to dig deep to get through it. It'll be the hardest thing you've ever done, but it'll be worth it. Well, looks like this is our stop." They drove around to the rear of the building and combat parked the vehicles along the wall.

"Thanks for letting me tag along, Eddy."

"No problem. Always happy to shed some light in somebody's life. Let me know if you want to give it a shot. I'll get the ball rolling for you."

"Roger that."

Eddy walked into the building leaving Craig to think about all he had seen and heard. He could hardly contain his excitement about his new adventure. It beat anything he had experienced before.

"Parker, you missed it."

"Missed what?"

"I got to go on a mission today after all."

"Today? You better start packing then. We've got a plane to catch!"

"What, you kidding? I still have to turn this weapon back in."

"Well, you better get moving. We made a deal. One mission and we were headed out."

"Okay, okay. Don't you want to hear about the mission though?"

"Tell me all about it on the plane, man. Better yet, tell me when I have a female under each arm and it'll be even better. I'm packing right now and headed to the flight line to get us a ride."

"I'll join you within an hour or so. I'll have to go check with Jesse to make sure I get this weapon clean like they want."

"Alright, you know the drill. Don't be more than two hours or you might get us bumped."

"I'll do my best. You better stop wasting time, so I can get this weapon back."

"Fine, see you there."

Craig found Jesse back in the commo shop as usual.

"Jesse, you ever leave this place?"

"Me? Why would I want to? I've got cold drinks, food, phone and the internet. Air conditioning and a woman are the only things left that could make this any better. How was that mission?"

"It was great. Those guys are crazy."

"Tell me about it. What did they do this time?"

"They laid an ambush with M&Ms and Dr. Pepper in broad daylight. I wouldn't have believed it if I hadn't seen it with my own eyes."

"Standard operating procedure out here, man. They pull off some crazy stunts sometimes."

"Captured six guys without firing a shot."

"So, you gonna stick around for the other mission tomorrow?"

"I'd like to but Parker is holding to me to the one mission quota. He's already heading down to the flight line. That's why I came by. I need to clean this M4, pack and get to the flight line."

"Hand it to me." Jesse moved some papers off his desk and took the weapon. He quickly pulled the magazine out, cleared the weapon and began disassembling it.

"There you go, Craig." He gave a satisfied look at his work.

Craig cleaned it efficiently and reassembled it.

"Looks like you're on your way." Jesse gave an approving nod after he looked it over.

"Thanks for the help, Jesse. I had a great time."

"Anytime, Craig. Drop by next time you're in town and we'll see if we can get you on another one."

Craig went to the arms room to retrieve his M-16. He looked with longing at the M4 as the weapons sergeant cleared the weapon, eyed it, grabbed Craig's weapon and handed it back to him. The bulky M-16 felt awkward after handling the lighter M4. Craig sighed and headed to the flight line to find out where he was going to spend the next couple of days.

"Man, I was beginning to think you weren't going to show and we were going to miss this flight."

"I just had to take care of business. So where are we headed?"

"Germany, man. We're going where you can really do something."

"Germany? They don't have any flights from here going to Germany."

"I know that, I talked with Lisa about it." He motioned over his shoulder at a brunette Air Force clerk who made eye contact and smiled at them. "She told me what flights to take to get us there. She also told me about some friends to look up when we land. While you were hanging with the SF bro, I was on some missions of my own." He continued with a smile. "So, we head to Kuwait, and then hop on to Germany. Since we can get out tonight it will all work easy. Otherwise, we were headed to Kyrgyzstan. I heard there are some hot women on and off base over there."

"Alright, Germany it is. I just hope your fly girl gave good intel."

"She hooked us up. You can believe that. She called her friends there last night and told them we were probably coming. I just didn't know when."

A short layover in Kuwait for a handful of hours and they were on a C-5 to Germany before he knew it. Craig sat down expecting a sleepless flight, as usual. It felt like a commercial airliner. He half expected a stewardess to come by any minute with a cart full of snacks and drinks.

He sat in the still, red glow of the fuselage. His body was exhausted. The rush of excitement from the unexpected mission and the natural drain of travel finally overtook him. The gentleness and hum of the engines, as they soared through the night sky, rocked him to sleep.

"Sprecken zee doytch?" Parker awakened him with a smile. "Let's get this party started."

31
A STRONG MINDED MAN

"You know you're a real..."

"C'mon Craig, we have frauleins to blitzkrieg. We don't even need to get temporary quarters here, my girl, Lisa, took care of that. She told her friends about us and gave me their number. That's where we're gonna be staying."

"Okay, lead the way, Romeo."

They checked their weapons and commo equipment in and then found a phone. Parker flipped through a little book where he scrawled the names and numbers of all his women. He spoke for a moment then hung up.

"Alright, my man. They'll be here in about ten minutes." He rubbed his hands in expectation.

"I hope they look good, at least."

"You kidding me, bro? Did you see Lisa? Man, she showed me some pictures of her friends and they were fine! I guarantee you this will be more fun than that mission you went on."

"Bring it, Parker. Let's see what your girls have to offer. Sounds like I win either way."

Two women dressed in standard Air Force issue greeted them at the gate. A blonde named Ashley and a brunette named Jessica. Parker gave Craig a glance that said, "I told you so" and picked up his bag.

Ashley greeted them. "Lisa told us you were on leave from Afghanistan and needed a place to stay for a couple of days."

"That's right. You still have space for us?" Parker knew the answer but asked anyway.

"We have some room on the floor," Ashley taunted. "Good enough for us. We're hard core," Parker shot back. Jessica led them to her white 96' Ford Explorer and they loaded their bags and piled in.

"You boys hungry? We can stop so you can eat something."

"I could use a bite, how about you, Craig?"

"I'm in. They didn't serve us that in flight meal they used to."

It was mid-morning when they stopped at a pub near the base.

"What's good here?" Craig looked around the pub with curiosity.

"Besides the beer?" Jessica baited.

"What? Just because we're a couple of Army guys, all we do is drink beer and watch football?" Craig contended.

"Well, you'd be the first soldiers I've met that didn't," Ashley teased. "But the sausage and the brats are a safe bet pretty much anywhere in the country."

"Do they have hamburgers and French fries?" Parker looked concerned.

The girls giggled. "Not exactly, just ask for the Hamburg steak."

"I'll take a brat and some dark beer and keep'em coming," Craig ordered.

"I'll have a Hamburg steak and some beer, but make mine a blonde." Parker winked and smiled at Ashley. She giggled in return. The day was off to a great start.

The smell of perfume welcomed them as they entered the two bedroom apartment. The decor had a definite feminine touch. The sweet aroma from the candles and puffy throw pillows told them they had walked back into the world of females. The apartment was small but met basic needs with a kitchenette and living area that separated the two bedrooms. They dropped their bags by the couch as they walked in.

"Okay, we did talk with Lisa about this. You boys will have to fight over the couch, but we do have some blankets for the guy that gets the floor," Ashley told them after giving them the quick tour. "I hope you boys can get along while you're here or we'll have to separate you."

"Do what you have to, Ashley. Just be sure to play nice," Parker teased. The banter between Ashley and Parker continued and they ended up on the couch chatting. Jessica smiled at Craig and they laughed together at the pair off to a fast start.

"So, does your friend always drop cheesy lines?"

"It seems to work for him. Your friend is going along with it."

"She can get caught up sometimes. We'll have to keep an eye on those two."

"They could be in the other room before you know it. So how did you two end up here?"

"We both were looking to get off base. It was more an arrangement of necessity, but we have fun together. We're just not party girls so you know."

"Wait, what do you mean, you're not party girls? We're not going out?"

"I'll go dancing but I'm not big on the bar and club scene."

"I'm sure you say that to all the guys."

She slapped his shoulder for that remark and pretended to be offended.

"I'm just here because Parker worked out a deal with me. I'm not a big party animal anymore either."

"I'm sure you say that to all the girls," she mocked. "But you didn't look like a rookie at the pub with your John Wayne keep'em coming attitude."

"Got me there, but that's different."

"I hate to break this up, but we have to go to work. We're not on leave like you heroes." Jessica interrupted the conversation on the couch.

"She's right, we need to get out of here." Ashley hopped up from the couch and smiled at Parker.

"You make yourself at home. You can use our beds while we're not here. If you're good we'll try to get off work early," Jessica encouraged them as she opened the door.

"That's right, you boys relax and rest up. We have a busy night planned and you'll need your strength," Ashley flirted.

The door closed and the girls headed back to work. Craig clapped his hands together and looked at Parker. "I have to give you credit, Parker. You picked some winners, this time."

"I told you, man. Just think. If they looked that good in uniform, they're going to be smokin' hot tonight. Lisa showed me a couple of pictures in Kandahar, but I had no idea they'd look this good. This is going to be a great trip."

"Let's get some shut eye then, we might have a big night after all. I could use some more sleep. That flight wasn't nearly enough."

The early morning light was shut out of the apartment by the curtains the girls had put up. They each took a bed and slept soundly until the early afternoon. Craig flipped on the TV and Parker scoured the kitchen for something to eat.

"Man, I don't think these chicks know how to cook," Parker announced looking in the fridge.

"We're only here for two days. I think we'll be able to get by. Check the cabinets to see if they have any mac and cheese."

"Score!" Parker celebrated. "I found it. You get in here and fix it."

"What? Don't you know how to fix mac and cheese?"

"I don't cook, man. My mamma always told me to find a woman that knows how to cook. You know how to cook, don't you?"

"Cook? That isn't cooking. The directions are on the box, for crying out loud. If you can read, you can fix it yourself."

"C'mon, man. Help a brother out and just cook it. I don't know what I'm doing in here. I tell you what, you hook me up with some mac and cheese and I'll make sure that you get some time alone with Jessica tonight." A smile spread across his face and he raised his eyebrows.

"I tell you what. Just to get rid of you I'd make that deal. Jessica will be the icing on the cake."

"Some mighty fine icing at that. She does have some good features. With both of them looking so good it might be hard for me to pick. I might just have to take both and find you someone else."

"Yeah, right! I'm not sure about her. But she's definitely not your type. Besides I don't think she's much of a party chick."

"Way she looked, I could work with that. She's a woman, isn't she?"

"I'm going to make that mac and cheese just to shut you up."

They watched cartoons until the girls got home and changed to go out for the evening. They headed to a local pub that was popular with the Air Force personnel. It was dark inside. The smoke was thick and the evening rush was just getting started. Waitresses danced around the tables and patrons with mugs of beer and trays loaded with food. The sweet smell of beer hung under the smoke as they took seats at a corner booth.

"You boys should have come on the weekend. We would have had some time off," Ashley complained.

"Next time we get out this way, we'll keep that in mind." Parker scooted closer to her as he settled in.

"So, what do you guys do anyway? Lisa said she only sees you guys once in a while."

"We could tell you, but we'd have to shoot you," Parker teased. Craig shook his head.

"Seriously, what do you guys do?" Jessica prodded.

"We run crypto to a bunch of different places," Craig explained.

"Is that dangerous?"

"It can be," Parker interjected as he looked at Ashley and puffed his chest.

"It's not that serious, but anything can happen," Craig admitted sipping his beer. "So what's with you good-looking women all joining the Air Force."

"We're smarter I guess," Jessica answered. "Why did you guys go and join the Army?"

"The world needs heroes," Parker boasted.

"Okay, it's starting to get real thick in here. Be careful where you step, ladies." Craig looked at Parker and shook his head.

"You guys are cute. When you guys are ready, we'll hit the club. Right, Jessica?"

"I'll come tonight. I have to keep my eye on you." She looked at Craig. "These guys could be trouble."

Parker and Craig drank enough to feel like dancing and they were off to the club.

"You guys dance much?" Ashley yelled over the pulsing music as they were making their way to the floor.

"I've got moves that you've never seen," Parker bragged. "I'm pretty sure Craig does to." He laughed.

"C'mon Jessica, I don't bite." Craig took her hand and he led her out on the dance floor in spite of her surprised look.

Parker backed up the talk as he showed off his moves. Craig surprised them all with a few of his own while they laughed at some of the others.

"Parker, I think you joined the wrong branch. You're more Air Force material with all of your finesse," Ashley surmised as they left the club.

"He's definitely the finesse one!" Craig laughed.

"Don't worry Craig, you hit the nail on the head. You're Army all the way!" Jessica confirmed. They laughed as they jumped in the Explorer for the short drive back to the apartment.

"Why don't we go for a walk in the park? It's still early." Ashley grabbed Parker's hand as they got out of the car.

"That's a start." Parker shot her a sly smile.

"Sounds good," Jessica agreed. "Just remember we do have work tomorrow."

The night was cool with a slight breeze. They walked down the boulevard in the early evening light. The pairs fell into a natural separation as they enjoyed each other's company.

"So, what's with you Army guys always being so gung ho?" Jessica chided.

"The guys that talk the loudest usually aren't doing that much."

"Oh, that's how it is. He's the talker and you're the quiet man of action?"

"You could say that." He laughed. "Hey, where are they going?"

Parker and Ashley had stretched the distance between the pairs and taken a left off of the main path.

"They're taking the loop through the park. It's the prettier way around."

"It's a good night for a walk." He looked up at the stars beyond the streetlights. "Want to take the loop?"

"Sure, soldier, let's go."

The trail was well worn but even in the low light he could tell the grounds were taken care of.

"So, why did you join the Air Force?"

"I don't know. I just didn't know what I wanted to do when I got out of high school. I joined thinking I could figure it out as I went. How about you?"

"I went to college for a couple of years, but partied too much and my parents told me to go get a job, so I joined the Army."

"You didn't want to go get a normal job?"

"I always wanted to be in the Army. It's in my blood. One of those family traditions."

"Oh really? I guess I can understand that. My brother was in the Army. I joined the Air Force when he was getting out. So, do you like it?"

"I'm not sure. I like some things about it. Others, I don't."

"I think you get that with any job. It's the people that you work with that make it fun."

"Or can make it miserable. I like a lot of the guys I work with. My senior NCO is great. He's a real fair guy. Guys like that, I can work with. The others, I could do without. But you're probably right though, you get that with any job I guess. How long have you been in?"

"Three years. My time is up when I leave Germany."

"You going to re-up?

"I haven't decided. I like the Air Force. I get to do a lot of neat things and I can hop a flight anywhere. Some cool things like that make it hard to give it up. How long have you been in?"

"A year and half."

"You're just getting started then."

"Yeah, I joined, went to Basic and AIT then I got deployed before I even had time to figure out where everything was."

"Sounds a lot like my brother. He was infantry and after he joined he went to Macedonia right after training. He loved it."

"Why did he get out then?"

"He got married to a girl that didn't like him being gone all the time."

"That would do it."

"Here we are." Jessica motioned toward the building in front of them as they exited the park. They made their way to the apartment door.

Craig panned the street. "No sign of them. Shall we?"

"Wait, I'll knock before opening the door." She rolled her eyes and grinned.

"That might be a smart thing to do. I don't think we want any surprises." He chuckled.

There was no response to the knock. They entered the apartment and a light glowed under Ashley's door. They could hear voices muffled by softly playing music.

"Well looks they really hit it off. I don't want to break it up do you?" Jessica threw her keys on the bar.

"I'm not going in there." He raised his hands.

"Okay. Then it looks like you have the couch tonight."

"I don't bite," he teased.

"Maybe not. I like you, but you'll be gone in another day. I have more respect for myself than that."

"Wow, alright then, got any extra covers?"

"Sure do, and all the blankets you want."

The next morning the girls were gone before the guys woke up. Craig slept soundly on the couch.

"What?" He heard Parker exclaim. "What happened here?"

"Thanks for waking me up." Craig complained as he lay with his eyes shut.

"Sorry man, but you have some explaining to do."

"Why, what?" He rubbed his eyes and tried to adjust to the light. "What are you talking about?"

"I took care of my business. I got you guys alone and you ended up on the couch. I mean I can't do everything for you. Help a brother out." He hit Craig with a throw pillow.

"It's not like that. I told you, I don't think she's like that."

"Like what? What is she? Mother Theresa?"

"No, nothing like that. She's been around the military and she knows how these things go. She's just not into one-night stands."

"I'll have to talk with Ashley about this. Then again, maybe you should just work it a little more. I could tell she's into you."

"I'll be fine."

"I don't want to have to hold your hand, Craig. I mean, I thought you were a tough dude. I wouldn't have guessed this."

"Like I said, I'll be fine. She's just a strong-minded woman."

"Well, she needs a strong-minded man, then."

"That's what I was thinking."

32
A BUNCH OF ROCKS

The girls got off work early that day and they took a short trip to Homburg.

"So where are we going anyway?" Parker tried to get some details from Ashley.

"We thought you guys have been stuck in such ugly places, it was time to see something beautiful."

"You took care of that when we got here," Parker retorted.

"No, really. We thought you would like to see some beautiful places before you headed back to the desert." Ashley grabbed him by the arm.

"Alright, you win." Parker raised his hands in surrender. Ashley pushed him and he put his arms around her. Jessica turned her head from the rear view mirror and looked at Craig. His eyes met hers and she quickly looked back to the road. Parker and Ashley continued to tease and flirt with each other. The sunlight on the rolling hills made the grass glow with a green brilliance that seemed so far-off in his memory. Old buildings stood as monuments to mark the history that had passed through this place. Craig sat in silence, enjoying the view, caught in the dream-like panorama. He could hardly believe the sharp contrast of colors. Greens were bright and vivid next to the dark earth that lay beneath it. The gray stones gave way to brilliant blue sky dabbed with white clouds. "Here we are." Jessica pointed to the ruins of a castle as they pulled into a parking lot.

"You sure?" Parker looked around smartly.

"What, I don't see anything but a bunch of rocks."

"Be nice!" Ashley slapped his shoulder. "We thought you guys would enjoy this place. It's so beautiful. You just have to see the valley." She pulled him from the car holding his hand.

"And he's the one with finesse, huh?"

"Alright, soldier, you ready to storm the hill?" Jessica teased.

"Lead the way!"

They walked through the ruins of the old castle feeling small between the large stones and remnants of walls. They exited the ruins and stood where the valley opened before them. Wealthy barons and countesses of old commanded the heights of the entire valley from where they stood. The hills eased into the valley covered in lush grass. Cows fed in the distance and trees brushed the sides of the hills with thick dark greens and shadows of black.

Craig reached for Jessica's hand as they stood overlooking the valley. She pulled her hand away, then said sorry with her eyes and slowly slipped her hand back to his. He looked at her and just under her collar the light caught her necklace and the gleam made him move his head.

"What's wrong?" She looked down at herself.

"Nothing, the sun just caught your necklace." She moved up a little to get out of the light.

"Oh, my dad gave it to me. She pulled out the chain where a golden cross hung from the end.

The sight made his head light. His smile faded.

"Is there something wrong?" She looked at him concerned as she dropped the necklace back into her shirt.

"It's nothing, I had a friend that had a necklace like that." He recovered. "It looks better on you."

She squeezed his hand tightly without looking at him, then relaxed. He felt the pulse of her hand as they stood motionless.

Parker looked around briefly and blurted, "We going to stand here all night or are we going to hit the club?"

Jessica and Craig looked at each other and laughed. "You have some real talent."

"What? What are we going to do? Sit here and look at rocks all night?"

"C'mon you big lug." Ashley's eyes apologized to Jessica as she pulled him away.

"I guess he's right." Jessica took Craig's hand and followed them.

"I guess so. You guys have the rest of the evening planned or was it just the view?"

"The whole evening. This is the Air Force, remember? We don't just jump into something without looking first."

"Alright, sounds promising."

She giggled and walked away letting her fingers slip from his grasp as he followed her back down. "So we thought you boys would like a good meal. We heard the Air Force is much better at providing good food, so we thought we'd keep up the tradition." Ashley opened the trunk and pulled out a large basket and handed it to Parker. Parker and Craig glanced at each other. They realized they were in for something different. Jessica grabbed some blankets and handed them to Craig then she pulled a small case out and a bottle of champagne.

"Does the Air Force pay more too?" Parker looked around in disbelief.

"Well, there are some advantages to living in the area. Besides my family comes here every time they visit me. When we were living in Germany, we'd come by once a year. We got to know this place pretty well."

"This should be interesting." Craig held the blankets up to Parker and smiled.

A grassy spot near the overlook was the perfect spot. They laid the blankets down around a piece of stone which became their table for the evening. Jessica unpacked champagne flutes and put them on the table. Ashley pulled out some plates and filled them with Caesar salad, beer braised lamb and sauerkraut complemented by mashed potatoes. The meal was topped off by a slice of Black Forest Cake.

"That's the best meal I've ever had." Parker leaned back on an elbow and sipped his champagne.

"Wow! That's all I can say," Craig agreed.

"This was good, but really. You boys need to get out more," Ashley reprimanded.

"She's right. You boys need a little culture."

"Easy now. Just because we don't eat don't eat five-star meals doesn't mean we don't have some culture," Craig argued.

"Really? C'mon. We know you boys are just frothing at the mouth for some beer."

"That's quite the judgment there," Craig contended.

"Am I wrong?" She held her ground.

"Let's get out of here." He looked into her eyes.

"I second that." Parker started to pick up the dishes eagerly.

They left the castle as the sunset spread an orange glow through the valley. The clouds rewarded their descent with a beautiful display of colors ranging from white to pink. Ashley and Parker disappeared into her room when they returned to the apartment. Craig and Jessica sat on the couch since it was still early. Soft music escaped from underneath the door to Ashley's room. Jessica blushed and looked around uncomfortably. "Want to watch a movie or something?"

"I tell you what. Why don't we get out of here and walk back to that bar," he suggested.

She smiled as she brushed her hair back. "That sounds good. We could go through the park. I love that place." She grabbed her bag and shot a glance at Ashley's door. "Should we say something?"

"I don't think they'll come out tonight, so you don't need to worry."

They took the long way through the park on the path that wrapped in and out of the trees.

"Well, I have to say that I'm glad you came to Germany for a couple of days."

"Me too. I'm bummed we have to go back tomorrow. This has been a lot more fun that I was expecting."

"What were you expecting?"

"A lot of time at the club with loud music. Some loud, obnoxious, but good-looking girls. A lot of nonsense from Parker to top it off."

"Well soldier, do tell. What happened?"

"Well, this friend of Parker's set us up with some friends of hers and one was a knockout. She really surprised me, because she was so down to earth and witty. We really hit it off and I had to leave before I knew it."

"Revealing."

"And what about you? What were you expecting?"

"I was expecting to be bored to death with a couple of macho, he-man woman haters just looking for a fast time. I dreaded having to keep one off of me for a couple of days. I was surprised though, one had a brain and actually used it. I found him quite charming."

"Sounds like we're really starting to get somewhere. Now, do tell."

"Since I grew up I the military, I know how this goes. When I was dating in high school a lot of soldiers would talk with me for a little while, then they were gone and that was it. So I don't really expect anything different here."

"Wait, you're a military brat? You've been holding back!"

"Oh yeah, didn't I tell you my dad was in?"

"No, but don't throw us all in together. I'm not some guy who disappeared on you."

"You will, though. So the real question is when or will you ever call? Do you have a girlfriend back home and are just having some fun while you're away?" Jessica stopped and looked at him.

"Whoa," he let out and held his hands up. "Are we done with the light conversation now?"

"I just wonder. Parker probably has a couple. One or two everywhere he can get one. You seem a little different, but you might have one or two somewhere. You are a guy after all."

"I had a girl I was hanging out with a little but nothing too serious." He looked away and started to walk again.

"I don't want to pry." She followed him. "I like you so, I just don't want to get something started that we can't finish."

"It's okay. I got to go home on leave a little while back and I didn't really handle going home very well. She wanted more than I could give in two weeks, so we're not together anymore."

"If you're not around the military it can be hard to understand how to handle all the transition. My mom always gave my dad his distance when he came home. It's like he had to decompress or something. Like he had to relearn how to be around everybody when he came back from being around nothing but macho guys for months. Not to mention the times when it was really stressful. I learned a lot about deployments being around the Army growing up."

"And you still wanted to go into the military?"

"I grew up around the Army." She let out a light laugh. "My father was Airborne, so I saw a lot of the Air Force side and they always seemed to have it better."

"That could be true. I think the Army's catching up, though."

"I don't know about that, but things are looking up."

The bar's atmosphere was subdued when they arrived. A light crowd filled the assortment of tables with a few patrons at the bar.

"Wow. I guess I should expect deep questions like these from you, but I think I need a beer for this conversation." He waved to a barmaid who delivered a mug.

"What's the matter, too much to handle?"

"You probably have a point about the guys you've dated in the past. Maybe some fly by night romances. I can see that. Heck, that's Parker all over. But I'm not even looking for anybody right now. That's the kicker, because it looks like I found something I wasn't looking for."

"Oh? Just what were you looking for?"

"I was just here because that's what it took to get Parker to keep quiet about a mission I went on with a Special Forces group. But this has worked out better than I expected."

"You went on a mission with Special Forces? You guys work with them too?"

"No, but we drop crypto off to those guys. They're real cool. Always ready to help out. They've offered to let me go on missions and even get me a slot for the assessment before. They do some pretty wild stuff. You wouldn't believe the mission I went on if you heard about it on the news."

"Well, don't leave me hanging, what was the mission was like?"

Craig chuckled. "It was crazy. Some highway robbers setup an ambush in this dip between some good sized hills and had been stopping traffic and making them pay a toll. I was supposed to go on a mission the next day, but this one came up and I rolled out with them. We traveled out to the spot where the bad guys had setup. Typical Afghans, they had their AKs but they weren't very disciplined. The team offered these guys some M&Ms and some Dr. Pepper. When the bad guys were sucked in by the new food and drinks, the team surrounded them and disarmed them."

"You're right. That's pretty crazy, if I heard that on the news, I wouldn't believe it. Weren't you scared?"

"Scared? Of course, I was scared. I think everyone out here is running around scared at some point. We just push through the fear and do the job anyway, right?"

"I guess so. Sounds like a typical guy thing. I don't really have any stories about anything that involve weapons or bad guys, so I don't think I can really say. Why did you want to go out with the Special Forces on a mission?"

"It's a combination of things I guess. I grew up hearing about them, they were the studs in the movies. Then after I was deployed I started meeting them and they were the most relaxed people I had met in the Army. They were easy going and treated each other with respect, like grown men not trying to prove anything. They even call each other by their first name. On top of that, they do cool stuff and get the best of everything. They have the best food, the best weapons. I bet they get the best doctors, too. There just isn't much not to like about them."

"That does sound pretty exciting, but I bet they deploy all the time."

"Deploy? Since 9/11, I think we're all going to deploy no matter what group or unit we're with. At this rate, at least I would be enjoying myself eating good food and playing with cool toys along the way."

"So, are you going to become a full-fledged hero and join the Special Forces now?"

"I don't know. I've been thinking about it. They are impressive. It would be a good group to run around these war-torn countries with. Especially if I'm going to be doing it like I am now, anyway. I mean, if it hits the fan, I would rather be with the guys that know how to really drop the hammer."

"Have you thought about the infantry? My dad enjoyed the infantry."

"I had planned to move over to the infantry when this enlistment was up but I'm not sure. Those Special Forces guys see a lot more action."

"You really are thinking about it, aren't you?"

"I have been."

"Well then, what's holding you back?"

"I don't know. My parents weren't even glad I joined the Army. The reason I didn't go in the infantry to start with was to get them off my back about the whole thing. I don't think they would really like me doing something like that. That girl I had been dating wasn't too excited about it either."

"What did they have against Army?"

"Mom was just scared I'd get killed or something and my dad was in Vietnam, so he wasn't a fan of the idea either."

"Must have been hard to go against your parents."

"I was wasting their money in college, partying too much, anyway. They were tired of it, so I thought I might as well do something I really wanted to do. Too many war movies as a kid, I guess."

"A lot of people just don't understand."

"Exactly. A lot of people don't understand," he agreed emphatically. "Like having my dad and granddad's pictures hanging around with their uniforms on. It was all so cool looking."

"It gets in the blood at some point. You're probably an adrenaline junkie, too."

"Wow, you're pretty good. You going to read my palm next?"

"I can, but that will be extra." She laughed. He extended his palm and she took hold of it.

"This will be worth every dollar. You tell me what I'm going to do and I'll pay your tab."

"Alright, deal. Well, it looks like you have a way with the ladies, but you've hit a dry stretch. You have had some adventure and are headed toward more. Oh, wait, one more thing. Looks like there is a spark in your life that you should fan into a real flame."

"I don't know why we're hanging around here," Craig responded. "Looks like we have some fanning to do."

"How do you know it's me?" She teased.

"You're burning me up, so I'm pretty sure I've got that piece figured out." He paid the tab and they walked arm in arm down the sidewalk. A quick detour put them on the path for another long walk through park.

"How often do you guys get back to Germany?"

"Not much. Looks like I have a reason to make it a priority, though."

"Well, I'd like to see you again if you can work it in."

"I'll see what I can do. I will be back in a couple of months for sure when we head back to the states. We should be able to do something then, if not sooner."

"That would be great." She looked deeply into his eyes.

"Yes, it would." He leaned forward to kiss her and she met him and they embraced. After their lips touched and bodies pressed together, she pulled away quickly. She smiled, looked down and raised her hand with a finger extended.

"Alright, soldier boy. You know I'm enjoying you, but like I said before I'm not easy and I'm definitely not going to be a rebound girl."

"It's not like that." His eyes were sad as he looked at her.

She cupped his face. "You don't think that now and I wish it wasn't true. We still need to let that old flame die before we fan this new one."

"How do you know it's not dead already?"

"It may be, but these things usually take time to get over. I think it'd be better if we waited a little while. I'd like to have something more than a flyby with a guy like you."

"Well, I guess that's something." They started walking arm in arm again.

"It could be, if you play your cards right."

"Well, if I do go SF, I'll already be experienced in various methods of torture."

"That's right. Keep that attitude. I'm doing you a favor."

"Not yet, but we can work on that."

The good byes were quick since the girls had to get to work the next morning. Steele and Parker waited for their flight in relative silence, each mulling over their adventure. Once in a while Parker would look at Craig and snicker. "The couch. Man, I can sleep on the couch at home."

33
A DIVERSION

"Steele. You got mail." Parker threw the envelope and it twisted in the air and fell at the foot of Craig's bunk.

"I don't get mail. Wonder who that's from?"

"Got me. Don't care unless it's a package. That obviously isn't," Parker remarked and lay down on his bunk to flip through a magazine.

Craig sat up and grabbed the letter. He flipped it over and his heart skipped a beat when he read the return address: Evelyn Conner. His mind raced. He sat the letter next to him on the bunk then glanced at it again. It bulged at the bottom. His hands were trembling. He brushed a hand down his leg. He looked up at Parker who was absorbed in his magazine. He grabbed his weapon and slung it over his shoulder and stuffed the letter in his pocket.

"Letter any good?" Parker looked over the magazine as Steele was headed outside.

"Didn't read it. Be back in a while." Steele walked out into the early evening and breathed deeply. He couldn't imagine why Conner's mom would be writing him. It scared him. He didn't know what to think. He walked down the dirt road then made his way back to the morale tent. He wanted somewhere he could be by himself to read it and that was as good as it would get tonight. He walked into the tent and heard a movie playing. The volume was loud. A few people watched the movie with their backs to him. He made his way to the phones, took his weapon off and leaned it against the table. He looked back and no one was paying any attention to him so he sat down. He pulled the letter out of his pocket and laid it on the table. He stared at it. A minute passed as he wrestled with the idea of opening it or not. He knew he had to. He didn't want to. He thought about just doing it later but was curious. What was in it?

He opened it and pulled out the letter. A gold necklace with a cross fell out and dropped to the table. He half gasped and looked around. He thought someone was playing a trick on him, but knew no one was near him. He looked back down. His stomach turned then knotted up and he squeezed his teeth shut. He struggled for control of his breathing as he tried to reign in the emotion swelling up inside of him. He was caught off guard by the letter to begin with and now this. He left the necklace on the table and unfolded the letter.

Dear Craig,

You may not remember, but I met you at the Christmas party last year. Jimmy always enjoyed you. He told us a lot of stories about his cowboy friend from Texas.

It brings me peace to know he died for a good cause and even more that he was protecting children and his friend.

When they sent his stuff home we gave his necklace to his ex-wife to keep for our granddaughter so when she is old enough she can wear it. Family and friends are the only important things in life so we wanted her to have it to remember him by.

He told me how you always looked out for him and he could depend on you. He would tell all his buddies from the neighborhood how tough you were and you were going to be a combat soldier someday.

I don't know where you will end up, but I thank God for all you did for my boy while he was with you. I bought you this necklace to wear in his honor as you move on as a soldier looking out for other boys who need to be looked after sometimes.

Thank you for being a good friend to him,

Evelyn

Tears hit the bottom of the letter. The gold necklace was distorted through his teary eyes as he looked down. He wiped them away with his sleeve and sniffled as his nose ran. He picked up the necklace and it glistened in the light from the movie behind him. The cross spun on the chain and Craig noticed writing on the back. He stopped it. Down the back read John 15:13. He knew it was from the Bible, but had no idea what it meant. He looked around and saw a Bible called *The Message* on a book shelf and flipped through it to the verse.

"This is the very best way to love. Put your life on the line for your friends."

He sat back in his chair in shock. The knot in his stomach had let go and now he felt exhausted. He wiped away a tear that still escaped as he took in the letter and verse. He could breathe again. He looked around but all eyes were on the screen. He shoved the letter and necklace in his pocket and grabbed his weapon and headed back outside to get his mind clear. He walked down to the tarmac and watched the planes come in and head back out. He held the necklace in his hand and struggled with the thought of putting it on. In the pale moonlight, he decided the least he could do was honor Conner by wearing it and tucked it underneath his t-shirt.

"Morning, sleeping beauties." SGT Ensly strutted as he entered the tent. Steele didn't get much sleep and struggled to wake up. Ensly stood next to his bunk. "I have to send somebody to Kuwait to pick up some Top Secret crypto so I thought since they have Scud missiles firing off then we should send a hero to pick it up. You're the only one I could think of," Ensly snorted and spit tobacco juice at the foot of Craig's bunk. "You and Parker need to get your bags and head to the flight line. You'll be picking up a case and bringing it back. Think you can handle it, Hero?"

"Roger that, Sergeant."

"Sure you will." He turned and shot Parker a glance. "Get packing Parker, the hero needs a sidekick," Ensly ordered as he left the tent.

Steele glared at Ensly as he left. His glare faded and he smiled at Parker. "You ready to get out of here?"

"Best news I've had all day." Parker sat up and started to get dressed.

They caught a C-17 headed to Kuwait and napped along the way. Half an hour from Kuwait the load master came by.

"They're having some SCUD launches and aren't allowing us to land in Kuwait right now. We're going to head to Germany. You'll have to get another flight back."

Steele looked at Parker. "It's Friday. We might get a whole weekend."

A big grin spread across Parker's face and he put his hands behind his head. "I love the Air Force. I could get used to this."

34
A BACKBONE

"I'm so happy to see you!" Jessica exclaimed as she meet him at the terminal and gave him a big hug.

"Me too."

"How did you end up here again?"

Parker interrupted as he looked at Ashley. "That information is classified. A need to know basis only. I'm sure you understand."

They all laughed.

"Looks like you'll fit in with those special ops guys. Running special ops and living by your own rules already," Jessica observed. "We have a lot of catching up to do since you've been gone."

"Oh really? It hasn't been that long." Craig's eyes shot upward as he thought about it.

"You men don't know what relationships are all about. You have to keep in touch so we can keep things balanced. I'll teach you all about it someday, if you're ever around long enough."

"You don't say? I thought we were good since the last time we talked."

"That's my point. You guys don't have a clue how we women work, but lucky for you, you met a smart Air Force girl."

"I guess I'm lucky, then."

"You got that right!"

Parker looked at him with surprise.

"Wait a minute; is there more going on here than I know about?" Parker feigned shock.

"Don't worry about them." Ashley reprimanded. "You have plenty to worry about right here."

"Sounds good to me." Parker smiled and gave her a quick kiss.

"Let's get you boys home and fix some dinner." Jessica blushed as she looked at Craig.

"From our last visit, I thought you didn't even cook," Parker argued.

"Oh, we can cook. We just weren't going to waste much time and energy on you guys," Jessica informed him.

"That's a nice touch." Craig winced.

"For all I knew you were just a couple of soldiers passing through. We didn't know you'd amount to anything." Jessica shoved Craig in the ribs.

"Oh, now that I am back for a second time, I am worthy of your time in the kitchen?"

"Something like that. Keep it up, Cowboy, and I'll have you walking to the pub for dinner."

"Okay, okay," he conceded. "What are we having?"

"We thought you'd appreciate some homemade pizza and some beer." Ashley piped in.

"You know the way to a man's heart." Parker hugged her as they walked.

They picked up their bags and walked to the Explorer. Craig was excited to see her again. He didn't know what to expect, but things were off to a good start.

"Well, you get to cutting and I'll get to cooking." Jessica handed him the onions and grabbed the mushrooms to rinse them off.

"Oh, I thought you girls would be making it all." He looked at the onions laid out before him.

"Are you being serious?" She asked playfully. "My daddy always helped my mom in the kitchen."

"Ashley already made the crust, we just need to get the toppings cut and throw the pizza in." Jessica laid out the plan.

He grabbed the knife. "I'm willing to help; I just didn't realize you needed me to help."

"Okay, soldier." She stopped and put her hand on her hip. "Looks like you have even more to learn. I don't need you to make this or anything else for that matter. But I'd like you to help." She put her hand down and smiled at him. "It's more fun when you have someone to do something with. Don't you think?"

"Sure, I guess. I don't think my dad ever helped my mom cook much except when it came to the grill. She took care of those things."

"If that's what it takes just pretend we're grilling, because if we're not doing it together, then you might as well head out and pick up some Pizza Hut or something."

"Okay, okay. Are all you Air Force women so determined?"

"Of course. So get started over there," she teased with a smile.

He embraced his new mission with gusto and began cutting onions, mushrooms, and tomatoes thinly as was allowed by the knives they had on hand.

"Good job," Jessica admitted.

"What? You didn't think I knew how to cut vegetables or something?"

"Well you didn't exactly give me a lot of hope that you were all that domestic."

"I'm not domestic, but I can use a knife, if that means anything."

"It says something. Let's get this pizza in the oven."

"Thanks for the help, Parker." Craig shook his head at Parker on the couch drinking a beer with Ashley.

"There wasn't any room over there." Parker laughed.

Craig turned to Jessica. "So, what did you have in mind tonight?"

"Well, I thought after we made this stellar pizza, we could enjoy a glass of wine on the couch and maybe watch a movie. What do you think?"

"Some wine, then dinner and some beer to go with that. What, are you trying to get me drunk?"

"It would take a lot more than that, now wouldn't it, soldier?"

He opened the bottle of wine and poured both of them a glass. Ashley and Parker had already made their way to her room by the time Craig and Jessica made it to the couch.

"So, tell me all about this Special Forces training that you keep talking about."

"Well, first I would have to go to the assessment course. That will last three weeks. When I am selected to move on, I'll be headed to the qualification course. When I make it through the Q course I should make it through the whole process. I think so, anyway."

"Sounds like you're pretty confident."

"I am, this is what I wanted to do all along."

"So, how long is all this supposed to take?"

"How long? It will take depends on the training I get selected for. It could take six months to a year and a half. Plus there's language training and additional schools that go along with the unit assignment."

"Sounds like you know all about this Special Forces stuff."

"I ask a lot of questions every time I get a chance. They probably think I'm like a little kid asking so many questions."

"That's smart. You'll know what to expect at least."

"I don't know."

"Well, I hope you get a chance, for your sake."

"What's that supposed to mean?"

"I mean if you don't make it, I think you'll be miserable. Your face lights up every time you talk about joining Special Forces. I'd hate to see it if you didn't."

"I guess you're probably right about that. I get pretty excited about the whole idea."

"Of course you do. You boys like to run around and prove yourselves and blow things up."

"I'm not trying to prove anything."

"Sure you say that now. I guess we'll see someday."

"I don't know about that. I'm just being me and doing what I want to. So what are we going to do the next couple of days, cook and drink wine?" He changed the subject.

"Would that be so bad?"

"Guess I could think of worse things." He put his put his arm on the back of the couch. "You really are gun shy when it comes to relationships."

"I may be, but I'm pretty sure you're willing to help me overcome that problem."

"I'll drink to that!" He raised his glass and they toasted as they laughed.

The aroma of cooking cheese made its way to the couch. Subtle flavors of sweet tomato sauce and onion danced in behind. The smell was so thick in the room they could taste the pizza. They set the table while the pizza cooled.

Jessica knocked on Ashley's door to let them know the pizza was ready but no one came out.

She pulled a beer from the fridge and poured it into a gold rimmed German beer glass.

"You really do know the way to a man's heart."

"It doesn't take a GPS to figure that out." She handed him the glass and smiled.

"Maybe not, but I have to say you're off to a great start."

She cut the pizza and pulled a piece onto his plate as the browned cheese stretched then lazily joined the slice.

"This has to be the best pizza I've ever had."

"It tastes better when you help make it, huh?" She laughed.

"That too."

"I was thinking we could watch Casablanca and have some brownies and ice cream for dessert, if you are interested."

"You kiddin'? Twist my arm."

They settled onto the couch and got cozy as they watched the drama unfold. Craig's mind wandered a little as he drank his second beer. He was feeling good and enjoying the time with her. He felt comfortable and was surprised by her easy going nature. He was attracted to her physically at first, without question. Their time together was unfolding the layers of her personality and it was making it even sweeter.

She surprised him at every turn. He didn't expect her to challenge him in the kitchen like she did, but he didn't hold it against her. On the contrary he respected her more because she wasn't going to let him slide by and stood up for herself. He wasn't lazy about things like cooking, but he sure didn't think he should waste his time doing something someone else was willing to do. But she had spunk. She was the kind of woman he was interested in. One with a backbone. One with some fire. One that could bring something to the table.

She didn't bring a lot of demands to the relationship so far either. She wasn't demanding anything that he couldn't give. He was pleased with how things were going. He wouldn't mind getting her in bed, but she was different. He couldn't put his finger on it yet, but there was something about her. She had something that made him think it was worth the wait so far. *I've been through worse stuff. I can make it through this maze to win the prize. Who knows it might be tonight.*

He could smell her as she shifted next to him. His heart sped up a little as the fragrance teased his nose. The movie was fine, but he was having a hard time concentrating. All he could do was think about her as they sat there. He would make his way from her toes sticking up in the air on the coffee table down her legs to her waist. Over her shoulder her profile flickered in the light of the TV. The movie ended before he knew it and Bogart and the French captain walked down the runaway into the fog.

She turned her head and looked up at him. He smiled and leaned toward her. They enjoyed a long, slow kiss. His right hand made it to her waist. He began to move it and she backed away from him, interrupting the kiss. Her hands went up in front and she shook her head. Her eyes became tender and she looked down.

"I'm really enjoying you. I'd love for you to touch me, but we need to be real slow." She raised her head back up.

"What's up? You still waiting to see if I'm really done with Melissa?"

"Well, that's part of it."

The frustration was obvious as he asked, "Okay then, what else?"

"Lots of things. I'm not going to sleep with you just because you're a good-looking guy and I like you."

"I didn't think we'd sleep together tonight," he huffed, half trying to convince her.

"Look, maybe you need to know some more about me. I really like you. I enjoy hanging out with you." She paused.

"So, what's the problem?" he insisted.

"I don't want to go too far too fast."

"Too fast? I'm not sure we can go much slower."

"You don't understand."

"Okay if I don't understand, then tell me what I'm missing."

"I can't just have sex with you."

"Oh, why not? Something wrong with me?" His face flushed.

"No, it's not that. Look, I'm a follower of Jesus. I can't just jump into bed with a guy."

"Don't think I've ever heard that one before."

"It's not an excuse, it's just something you need to know."

"That's great and all, but what does that even matter?"

"It matters a lot. It means we won't be having sex until there's a ring on my finger for starters."

"What? No sex!" He exclaimed. She looked away. He could tell he hurt her somehow. They sat in silence for a moment as he digested the idea. He inhaled deeply and let it out.

"Okay, maybe I can deal with that, but what else?" his tone softened with each word.

"Well, what else do you want to know?"

"I don't know. Just how far into this Jesus stuff are you?"

"I'm all the way in."

"Wait a second here. You're drinking wine, you're going to the club with us and your roommate is no saint. So, what exactly are you getting at? You'll do anything except have sex with me?" He sat back further into the couch with a look of satisfaction having trapped her in her hypocrisy.

"I know, it can be confusing if you don't know what it means to be a follower of Jesus."

"Oh, I'm waiting." He took another drink of his beer. "Tell me all about it."

"I can drink and I can dance, but I do these kinds of things within limits. I don't go running around getting drunk and won't become a stripper, but those are the extremes. If you want a simple way to think of it, it's like this. If it's an extreme of any behavior for the most part, it's probably something I'm not going to do."

"Alright, so you can kiss and stuff too?"

"Yes, but even something like a kiss I am careful with. I'm not just running around kissing a bunch of guys."

"But why not? What's wrong with it? I'm not saying you have to go be a stripper, but what does it hurt to have sex?"

"Don't be so extreme."

"Extreme about sex? It's a great thing. You don't want to miss out on anything do you? That sounds extreme to me."

"No, I don't want to miss out on anything. But I want to wait 'til the right time to do them."

"I don't know about all this. You should have told me this before. It's like you've been leading me on or something," he accused.

"I'm sorry, Craig. Maybe you're right. This was all a favor to a friend at first, but then you turned out to be a great guy. You're not like Parker or guys like that. He wouldn't have wanted to be with me after I didn't have sex with him the first night. That's not the kind of guy I want. I'm not looking for a one-night stand."

"You've said that before. I'm not looking for a one-night stand, either. I want to have a relationship with you. It's just people usually have sex when they're together. It's not like I'm out there having sex with every girl I run into. I like you, too. That's why I wanted to spend time with you while I was here. You've given me a lot to think about, though."

"I'm sorry. I tried to talk to you sooner about it. We've just had so much fun, and I guess I was scared you wouldn't want to be with me anymore." She looked tenderly at him.

His heart melted as he looked at her. He never had a girl throw Jesus at him to keep from having sex with him before. He knew he liked her a lot and they had a great time whenever they talked or went out to do something.

"I just don't know what to think. I guess this would be a good time to call it a night. I'll have to think about all of this."

"Sure, I guess it's a lot." She stood up and grabbed her empty glass. "I understand."

He started moving the cushions around on the couch to make himself comfortable. She turned off the kitchen light and paused at the end of the couch.

"If you want to go back to the base tomorrow, I'll take you."

He looked at her and shook his head. "I don't know. Just give me a little time to think, okay?"

"Sure, good night, Craig." She left him alone in the dark and closed the door to her room.

35
RULES OF ENGAGEMENT

A restless night of tossing and turning on the couch ended when Jessica came out of her room dressed for a morning jog. Craig turned over to see her making her way to the door.

"Going somewhere?"

"Just a little jog. I'll be back in a while. Didn't mean to wake you." Her tone was firm and her words short.

He sat up on the couch and let out a sigh. "Why don't you give me a chance to change and I'll join you."

"If you want to, that's fine." She walked to the kitchen and poured some orange juice while she waited.

He changed and they made their way out of the apartment onto the street below in silence. The morning was cool and the air was damp. The clean air was a nice change. No dust kicked up by never-ending traffic going up and down a little strip of dirt. No JP8 jet fuel fumes to inhale. He could even make out a hint of perfume as he jogged alongside her. She took him down the street that led to the park. They headed onto one of the trails that weaved through the park. He was feeling uncomfortable like he did something wrong, but wasn't sure what it was. He just ran along for a while but felt like he was missing something not being able to talk to her.

"So, we going to talk a little or what?" he finally blurted out looking straight ahead.

"I wanted to give you time to think. You had a big night." She wiped the perspiration from her forehead and shot him a look.

"Look, you just caught me off guard. That's all. I mean things were going so well and then you just put the brakes on."

"I didn't want you to think something was going to happen that wasn't. I didn't plan to ruin your big night." A flash of anger crossed her face.

She increased her pace a little, and started to get a lead on him.

The weeks of travel and sitting around the tent eating food odd hours were starting to take effect. He was already feeling it a little. *I won't make selection if I can't keep up here!* He increased his pace to catch her.

"I didn't think the Air Force was very big on PT."

"What, you think you guys are the only ones that do anything?"

"Hey now. I've seen the Air Force doing PT and I've never seen them do anything this hard."

"You forget. My daddy was a soldier. He taught me how to run and like it." She grinned.

"It's good to see you smile again."

"It's good to see you sweating. You're in luck though, this is where we start walking back for the cool down." She slowed to a jog, then to a walk. They both worked to catch their breath as they walked down the street back to the apartment. The morning light finally made it over the hill and bathed the old homes and trees in golden rays.

"Sure is beautiful in the morning, isn't it?" he noticed out loud.

"It makes the run worth it every time."

"I have to admit you're a better runner than the females in my unit. They give you women a bad name."

"How's that?"

"Most of them can't even finish a simple jog, much less a good run."

"Maybe the Air Force is tougher than you thought."

"Don't push it. I'm just saying you're in good shape."

Back at the apartment there was still no sign of Ashley or Parker. Jessica and Craig took turns getting cleaned up and met in the living room.

"So what's it going to be soldier? You going to stick with the Jesus freak or you headed back to base?"

"Thanks for not putting me on the spot and everything."

"I just don't want to waste anyone's time here. If this isn't something you can handle, then we need to break it off."

"Can't handle? I'm not saying that. It's just that. Well. I mean, what does it mean for me that you're one of those church people."

"One of those church people, huh?"

"Now, I didn't mean it like that."

"No, it's okay. So, since I'm one of those church people what does that mean for you? That's what it all boils down to right?"

"I guess so."

"It just means we keep doing what we've been doing, but we don't do much more physically."

"Ok, so we hang out, but no sex? That's pretty much it?"

"I honestly didn't think you'd be so shocked by this. You were more like Parker than I suspected, I guess."

"Wait a second, now. I'm nothing like Parker."

"Well, you could have fooled me. As soon as sex was off the table you were stuck trying to figure out if you were interested in being with me or not. I'd say that's pretty close to Parker's take on things too."

"It wasn't that. I mean yeah, I was surprised about the no sex bomb and then you ambushed me with the whole church thing. I needed a little time to get my head straight. I mean that was a lot to dump on a guy."

"So how many church people do you know?"

"My parents go a couple of times a year. My aunt and uncle go too. My aunt is big on it, I guess."

"So all you see is that they go to church?"

"What are you getting at?"

"I mean isn't there more to it than they're just church people?"

"Sure, I guess."

"So, you really don't know what following Jesus is all about and you're ready to judge me and end a relationship just because you've got some preconceived idea of what it means?"

"I know what going to church is all about. I've been a couple of times. They sing some songs, some guy talks about how much everybody needs help and then asks for money."

"You're a bit sketchy on the details, Craig."

"Okay, fine. Let's get to the bottom of this. You tell me what this church stuff is all about then."

Jessica raised her hands and turned away. "You know, maybe we should just go get some breakfast. We're going at each other pretty good right now, we might need to cool off."

"That's a great idea. I'm starving. Let's go get something to eat. While we're there you can tell me all about it."

"You sure? I don't think you really want to know."

"I didn't before, but at this point I want to know what has you so fired up. At first you hacked me off, but now I guess I should hear you out at least."

"Don't do me any favors."

"Alright, let's just talk about it over breakfast, okay?"

They walked down the street a way to a little nook that served breakfast. The sausage and a pile of pancakes were delivered as they sipped their steaming black coffee.

"So, you going to hold me in suspense all morning or what?"

"I wanted to give you time to get settled."

"Settled as I'm going to get. What's this Jesus thing all about?" He stuffed his mouth full of pancake and looked her in the eyes.

"I had this friend, Amanda that I used to do everything with when we were in junior high school. We did the usual sleep overs and talked about boys all-night. We went out for the same sports. We were connected at the hip." She looked around the room slowly till her gaze fell back on Craig. "In tenth grade she went home from school with a friend of ours one day. Someone ran a stop sign as they went through an intersection.

She was in the backseat. She died in the intersection." She paused again. Her mind was lost in memories and seas of sorrow until he pulled her back out.

"I'm sorry about your friend. That just sucks."

"Thanks. That's pretty much how I saw it, too. It shook my world pretty hard. I couldn't get out of bed for a week after the funeral. I was so lost without her. We were best friends. My dad came home not long after we found out. He took some leave and let me just cry for days. I'd never had someone that I loved die like that. Just here one second and gone the next. A week later though, my dad told me it was time to get back to school. I could hardly stomach it, but I did it. They sent me to counseling and everything, but that just seemed to open a can of worms. I wanted to know why she died. What's the point of living, if the people that you love could just be gone in an instant? I was confused and angry. Some people, trying to be nice, told me it was God's will and that just made me even angrier. What kind of God would kill my best friend? What kind of God lets something like that happen anyway? I sure didn't understand and I didn't want anything to do with a God that was so heartless."

Craig had stopped eating. He was completely captured by her story. His own pain was brewing into a storm as her story unfolded. His unhealed heart ached with the words and the questions struck home like lightening.

"I kept my distance from those people. My aunt Linda and her husband John came to visit a couple of months after Amanda died. My aunt was one of those churchy people, as you would say. But she didn't tell me it was all God's plan or anything like that. I knew she wasn't cold like that. She told me how sorry she was and how awful she felt for me. One Sunday afternoon, after she and Johnny came back from church, we started talking and I told her what those people said about Amanda dying. She had the saddest look on her face and just said, 'I'm so sorry Jess, those people didn't know you and the pain you are going through. I'm sure they meant well, but sometimes people just don't know what to say. Instead of keeping their mouths shut like they should, they just say something anyway because they feel uncomfortable, too. I'm so sorry they hurt you while you were in so much pain.' She hugged me and I cried some more."

Jessica dabbed a tear that had formed and started its descent down her left cheek. Craig sat there motionless caught in his own torrents of emotions and waves of pain as they echoed the feelings she described.

"Then she told me that despite what I thought, God loved Amanda and he loved me too. I couldn't make sense of it, but I let her talk. It kind of stirred everything back up, but it felt good to talk with her about it. Not long after that another friend that we ran around with, Julie, and I became better friends. We started hanging out a lot. She went to a church youth group and I started to go with her. One day a guy talked about how he had started wondering what life was all about. He looked around and saw all that was wrong with life and all the pain in it and wondered the same things I was wondering. How could a God allow such things? He flipped it on me when he said why shouldn't God allow such things? He told us to think about ourselves and answer honestly. Were we really good people? He said to look at all the evil people are doing to themselves and others. Throughout history it was all the same. As much as we like to think we're good, we're only fooling ourselves. He told us how even one lie was enough to miss out on going to heaven because God is perfect. That didn't really matter because the list of things we did wrong was a lot longer than that. I couldn't argue with that, so I listened to what he had to say. He said the penalty for all of our wrongs was to die. To die forever. He told us that because of the wrongs we have done, we are separated from God and can't be with Him. But God wanted to be with us and sent Jesus to pay for all of our wrongs. Jesus lived the perfect life and he could cover all of our wrongs by dying in our place. That was hard to believe, but he went on. He finished by saying if we just accept Jesus as our leader in our lives and trusted his payment for all our wrongs that God would lead us through this life. He would change us into the people he intended us to be all along." She let out a deep sigh. "Now, this didn't answer all of my questions, but God just spoke to me sitting there. He said what do you have to lose? I didn't jump, but I had to admit it wasn't going to cost me anything to believe except my denial of His existence. I went home and thought about everything I'd heard. My aunt had given me a Bible a long time ago, so I opened it up to some of the places he talked about and I just couldn't deny it anymore. It was staring me in the face. This guy, Jesus, who I'd heard about a little here and there all my life was either crazy, a liar, or was who He claimed to be. I finally fell to my knees in my room with the Bible on the floor and said 'Jesus, I believe you are who you say you are, be my payment and lead me through this life."

"Just like that? I mean we went from God killing your friend to now you're on His side?"

"No! It took some time to work through the pain still, but the more I thought about it all the more it made sense."

"I mean you just let Amanda's death slide? Don't you think you're letting God off the hook?"

"No, it's not like that. I ..."

"Sounds like it to me. I mean some guy tells you you're not any good, laying a guilt trip on you about your life and next thing you're joining the club?"

"It wasn't exactly like that." Jessica shook her head.

"I thought you were smarter than that. To get duped by a guilt trip."

"It wasn't a guilt trip. It was true. Think about yourself. You know you're no saint. None of us are."

"I'm not a saint, but I'm not a bad guy either, I'm no Bin Laden."

"It doesn't take that extreme, and if you search yourself, you'll know what I'm saying is true."

"Wow, I thought last night was an eye-opener, but this blows that away. I'm trying to give you the benefit of the doubt and all, but this really is a lot."

"Why's it so hard to accept? Can't someone believe in God and be okay in your book?"

"I believe in a God and everything, but I'm not going to church and all that stuff and making some guy the leader of my life. That's my job."

"What are you so defensive about?" Jessica's eyes grew wide.

"Me? I'm not defensive, this just doesn't seem to add up. It's like you didn't even think this stuff through. It sounded like you were on the right track but then you just caved in."

"You sound like you're the one who's angry about something." Jessica sniped.

"I'm angry about plenty, but that's beside the point." Craig argued back.

"I think that just might be the point."

"I'm not going to talk about me. We're talking about your Jesus thing."

"Well, that's it. It made sense to me and I haven't regretted it."

"So, now life is just happy and easy?"

"Oh no, it's not even close to easy and happy. I still have problems. Life still throws me curves, but now I know that whatever happens I'll never get lost again like I did when Amanda died. I still don't have a lot of answers, but I know who does."

"Well, that's great, I'm glad you got religion."

"I stopped denying my creator and found peace through a relationship with Him. That has nothing to do with religion."

"Ok, I can tell this is something we'll have to disagree on then."

"I'm sorry it's so hard to understand. I didn't understand, until that one day and then it all started coming together."

"I guess as long as you're happy, that's the important thing."

"It doesn't really sound like you mean it, but thanks. I think what you're missing is the fact that I'm free."

"Free? Free from what? Thinking for yourself?"

"You know I think for myself. It seems to be a problem for you if someone doesn't think the same way you do though. You could use some freedom of thought. Maybe this wasn't such a good idea after all." She put her napkin down and stared out the window.

"I'm sorry. Yeah, you think for yourself. I just got caught up. You're a bit of a problem for me, that's all."

"That's encouraging."

"You know what I mean. You are making this whole thing hard on me with this religion..."

She looked back at him sharply.

He held up his hands. "I mean this whole Jesus thing. You're making it hard on me. Every move I make it's about what you can or can't do. It doesn't sound very free to me. I just don't know what to do with all of this."

"We just have different ideas of what people are supposed to be doing with their lives. That includes everything from dealing with their pain to how they treat other people."

"Yeah, I guess we do have some different ideas."

The waitress delivered the check. They both reached for it but he beat her to it.

"I've got it."

"I can pay my own. It's the least I can do," she shot back.

"Look, I don't have anything against you. I just don't understand you. You're pretty, smart, and don't back down, but I just don't get this other side of you yet. It doesn't mean I don't like you." He pulled the check back and took a look at it. He placed a twenty dollar bill on it and looked at her. "You ready?"

"I don't know. What are we going to do?"

"I'd still like to hang out tonight if you want. I tell you what. Why don't we get Parker and Ashley and let's go to a movie and get some dinner somewhere tonight. That way we can keep it light and I can have some time to think about all of this."

"Sure, that sounds good. We should be able to make it through dinner and a movie without making it too hard on you." She smiled and he shook his head. "Any you want to see?"

"I saw a poster at the airport for that new Matrix Reloaded movie. Want to see that?"

"Absolutely! I love the Matrix."

"Alright, let's get out of here so we can see if there are any flights tomorrow so we don't catch any flak for this diversion."

"Sounds great. I'm glad you still want to stay."

"I'm not sure where this will go, but now that I know what the rules of engagement are, I can plan for it at least." He gave her a quick smile as he got up from the table.

After they found a flight headed to Kuwait the next morning and informed SSG Hallis about the detour they feasted on some brats and beer at the pub for dinner. The theater was packed since the film had just opened the previous week. They were able to find some seats left of center near the middle of the theater. They settled in with some popcorn and soda. The pace of the film was steady with plenty of action. The story line and its innuendo of a chosen savior made Craig uncomfortable as he watched. He enjoyed the film anyway. The idea of a world that is not seen and reality not being what we think it is gnawed at him. He was immersed in the excitement of the fight scenes. He would re-emerge to be plagued by thoughts of dual realities and what the truth might really be. The lights came up as the credits rolled. The crowd made its way out talking about the cool actions scenes and animation.

"I liked it," Jessica thought aloud. "What did you think?"

"It was pretty cool. When I can stop bullets like that, I'll have it made." Craig leaned back and dodged the imaginary bullets headed his way.

"I think I'd rather be able to fly, myself." Jessica stated.

"Figures an Air Force chick would want to fly. If I could do that I think I'd head to the Bahamas for starters and go from beach to beach." Parker chimed in.

"A tropical island would be at the top of my list of destinations." Ashley hugged Parker's arm.

They talked through their favorite scenes on the short drive back to the apartment. Ashley and Parker excused themselves and took off for a walk when they got back.

Jessica and Craig walked up the stairs. Jessica pulled her keys out and talked as she unlocked the door. "I was thinking of a glass of wine. Would you like one?"

"I'd rather have another of those dark beers and a slice of leftover pizza."

"Coming up." She smiled at him over her shoulder.

"So which one are you?" He asked as he took a sip of his beer.

"What do you mean?"

"I'm thinking Trinity, but that's probably because I can't shake that outfit. But from the way you talk you're more like Morpheus."

"Is that so?"

"Yeah, Morpheus. A true believer. No matter what happens. Am I right?" He took another bite of his cold pizza and smiled.

"Maybe, but the real question is who are you? The commander?"

"Could be."

"Just remember the commander didn't get any of the girls with that heart of his."

"So, what are you saying? If I don't become a true believer then I don't get the girl?"

"I'm saying if you don't open your heart to the possibilities in life, then you'll miss out on the most important things. That's all."

The next morning Craig and Parker were in the air again. This flight to Kuwait was less exciting. The landing was normal without any drama. On the ground the place was full of activity. Kuwait was a springboard for the upcoming invasion for Iraq and the buildup was almost complete. They met the unit holding the crypto and hopped a flight back the same day. They sat in the bay of the C-17 trying to get comfortable for the long flight ahead.

"Man, I don't know about you, dude. We've had two trips to Germany and you're still on the couch."

"I know. This just keeps getting more complicated." Craig shook his head. "You have no idea."

36
BABY-SITTING

"What did you think of Kuwait?" SGT Ensly inquired as Craig and Parker walked into the commo area back at Bagram.

"That place is worse than this hole. They have less chicks there than we do. Only place I saw anything good was the flight line where the Air Force women were."

"Don't sweat it, you won't be headed back down there anytime soon. We'll probably let Steele here take those nice dry runs for a while. Speaking of having fun, Steele, you've got Haji duty tomorrow. Make sure you get plenty of sleep so you don't do anything stupid out there."

Craig's eyes narrowed as he glared at Ensly. He didn't say anything while he unpacked his computer. He handed it to the guys on shift to clear and put in the safe.

"I said you have a shift tomorrow, Steele. You got that, soldier?"

"Roger that." Craig turned and walked away.

Parker caught up with him as they entered the courtyard. "Ensly can be a jerk."

"You think?"

"Well, looks like you're on his radar now, huh?"

"I don't know what his deal is. I guess he was hoping I would get slapped with some UCMJ or something. I think he just likes to keep everyone in their place. Some sort of power trip thing."

"Looks like he took a special liking to you. You might want to lay low 'til he backs off."

"I'm just doing my job. If he has a problem then he can deal with it."

"Alright Craig, I'm just trying to warn you. He might come down hard on you, might want to be careful."

"I'll be fine."

"Roger that." Parker slapped Craig on the back. "Think I'll go check out the morale tent to see if there are any ladies there that can give my morale a boost. You game?"

"I've got duty tomorrow and I need my beauty sleep, remember?"

"Sleep when you're dead. There are ladies to be had."

"Words to live by, Parker, have fun."

The crisp early morning air nipped at Craig as he made his way to the front gate. The walk to the duty station was long. A dirty, dingy squad of soldiers was walking the opposite direction when one yelled out. "Craig!"

Craig couldn't make out who said it. Then he saw the guy break from the group and jog over.

"Kevin, what are you doing here?" he yelled in surprise.

"My squad just got back from a stroll through the neighborhood how about you?"

"Got a job baby-sitting Hajis that's going to take all day."

"You should've joined the infantry, dude. At least you wouldn't be pulling that kind of duty. Not that ours is so great, but at least we aren't babysitting Hajis."

"Not so great? I thought you guys would be kicking ass and taking names."

"Yeah, me too, but over here we haven't done much so far."

"Well don't you guys get out in the hills and hunt the bad guys?"

"Sure we do. Only problem is there's hardly ever any bad guys anymore. Looks like we missed a lot of the action. Only contact we make is with some goat herder or his kid when they take potshots at us from behind rocks somewhere."

"I had some of that driving to Kabul. Kinda funny so long as no one gets hurt."

"It'd be funny if it didn't suck so much. They shoot at us and we shoot back into the rocks. Then we go look to see if we can find a body or something but we never find a trace. Most of the time it's pretty boring, really. We just end up humping all through the mountains in the blazing heat or freezing cold, but that's it most of the time. I think they have it better down in Kandahar. There's a lot more action down there from what I hear."

"Doesn't sound like anyone is doing much of anything in this war right now except for the SF."

"Probably. I know we're not. We pull a lot of QRF duty, but that's like dealing with the goat herders in the mountains. Doesn't amount to much around here. We head outside the wire after a rocket attack or something, but don't ever find anybody. The locals that live nearby always say they don't know anything. Like they'd help us anyway." He shook his head in disgust.

"Wilson!" His team leader off in the distance called. "Let's go."

"Later, man. Gotta go clean weapons. Have fun with that baby-sitting gig."

"Yeah, see ya Kevin."

The same routine was taking place when he arrived for duty. He walked up and took a spot in line. It was like a spring dance. The Afghans were lined up on their side of the fence, the Americans on the other. Each eyed the other, entertaining different thoughts ranging from suspicion, to indifference, to flat-out distrust. Craig stood in line with a mixture of hate and distrust. He saw the contractor from his last duty and they made eye contact, but that was all. There was no fake smile or acknowledgment just a blank stare.

Craig was paired up with a different contractor this time. His new group was working on a building that was half constructed. Craig kept his distance and offered no conversation. He didn't want them to get the wrong impression. The day passed uneventfully. He rounded up the group and started the trek back to the gate. Craig trailed a few feet behind the group when they slowed down. They looked toward a building just left of the road and slowed to listen to a soldier yelling at someone. Craig looked and saw an old afghan man sitting in a metal chair. The soldier yelled at the old man while he closed the distance between them. Craig watched the scene unravel. His group paused in the road and stared at the exchange. Craig sped up his walk to make his way over to the soldier that was yelling.

Craig could feel his chest pounding. His eyes darted back and forth to take the scene in. He knew this wasn't good.

"What the hell are you doing, old man?" The soldier yelled at the Afghan. "You think you're on vacation or something? This look like a Haji lounge area to you?"

The old man offered a blank smile and a humble look. It was hard to say what that smile meant. It was somewhere between a goofy Gomer Pyle look and a veiled screw-you.

The sergeant grew more irritated with the old man. "Get out of my chair!" He raised his hand like he was going to hit him. The old man didn't flinch, he just kept smiling. The sergeant changed his mind and grabbed the chair. He picked it up with a jerk and threw the old man in to the dirt. The old man fell hard and face planted on the ground. A grunt came from the crumpled man on the ground. The other Afghan workers dropped what they were doing and started to move toward the soldier.

"Hey!" Craig yelled. The workers stopped in their tracks. "Lay off the old man!"

The Sergeant looked indignant at Craig.

"You talking to me?" He yelled at Craig in disbelief.

Craig wouldn't leave it alone. "What the hell are you doing?"

"You serious?" He looked at the old man. "He's a Haji. What do you care?"

Craig reached the old man who was starting to get up and helped him to his feet.

Craig slung his weapon over his back and started toward the Sergeant.

A soldier from another detail caught up and grabbed Craig. "Easy man, it's not worth it."

Craig snarled at the Sergeant. "You'll throw an old man around like a rag doll for a chair that doesn't even have a bottom?" The Sergeant's oversized rear dropped through as he sat down. "You're a smart one." The words dripped with sarcasm.

The Sergeant growled back. "He's a fucking Haji."

"He's like ninety or something. That old man's seen more combat than all three of us combined. Show a little respect."

"Who cares, he's still just a Haji."

"I guess it's a hard concept for a moron like you to understand."

"What unit are you in Specialist? Maybe we should go have a chat about this with your NCO."

"You would, you pansy. Come on by the commo shop in the big circus tent anytime, but you better leave the old man alone." Craig gritted his teeth and his knuckles grew white as he pointed at the SGT.

"Move on out, soldier. I'll swing by and have a chat with your NCO after I'm done here."

Craig and the other soldier left the SGT crammed into his chair.

"I actually know that guy," offered the other soldier. "He's been pulling Haji duty for months. He's not a bad guy. He's just tired of messing with these guys."

"So what, it's no reason to treat the old man like a dog. I'm sure I've seen worse than him. He needs an attitude adjustment."

"Maybe, but it won't be today."

"It could have been."

"Yeah, you can thank me later."

The soldier smiled and they parted ways to escort their groups back to the gate. His group was beginning to file into the cattle shoot to leave when the contractor he was working with walked up.

"Thank you for helping that man. The workers who saw you understand that you have bad men just like we do." He extended his hand.

"You're welcome." Craig took his hand and shook it. Craig noticed the other workers from his group watching and they nodded. He nodded back to them and watched as they made their way out of the cattle shoot and disappeared into the mass of workers. As he walked back to the tent he felt a little lighter. It had been a while since he felt good about being around the locals. So much had gone wrong lately. The wheels had just fallen off and it took a lot out of him. Things had just taken a downward spiral but they were starting to look up. He opened the flap to the tent and Parker greeted him.

"How was Mr.Haji's neighborhood today?"

37
SWEET GIG

Craig's step was lighter the next morning as he headed to the circus tent for work.

"Morning, Steele." Ensly puffed his chest out as Craig entered the commo shop and ignored him. Craig made his way back to the work area.

"Stop right there," Ensly interrupted. Craig was caught off guard by the intensity and the bewildered look on his face made it even more fun for Ensly. "That's right. I got a visit from SGT O'Hare last night."

"SGT who?"

"Read for yourself." Ensly slid a piece of paper across the table.

Craig recognized the counseling form. He bent over and began to read.

Ensly continued, "that's it. Keep it up, smart guy. I heard about your little side trip to Germany with Parker too. You just better sign this and maybe the side trip won't become an issue. If you don't sign here then I might just have to let SSG Hallis know about it." He put his hands behind his head and smiled. "It looks like you'll get some UCMJ after all."

"For what?" Craig laughed and shook his head.

"How's insubordination strike you?" Ensly leaned forward in his chair and sneered.

"You gotta be kidding me?" Craig replied as his tone changed.

"C'mon. Would I kid you? You'll probably get at least some extra duty and some loss of pay out of it." Ensly sat back in his chair pleased with himself.

"There's no way. You haven't even heard my side of the story."

"I don't need your side of the story. This isn't summer camp. This is the United States Army and an NCO has told me that you were insubordinate and that's good enough for me."

"I want to talk with SSG Hallis about this."

"I'm the senior NCO right now. SSG Hallis took off on emergency leave last night."

Craig felt like he just took a punch in the gut and looked up.

"That's right, his wife was in an accident, so we won't be seeing him for a while. Don't worry though. I'll take care of all the paperwork," he reassured him with a grin.

"Go ahead and sign the counseling form stating that you agree and you might be able to avoid some UCMJ. If you don't sign it, I'm not really sure what I can do for you." Ensly feigned concern as he thoroughly enjoyed the exchange.

Craig finished reading the statement on the form and stood there thinking about it.

"By the way, while I'm getting all this paperwork ready to submit, you go ahead and get back on Haji duty today. You're going to have some steady duty anyway so you might as well get used to it. So, you ready to sign?"

"I'll sign it SGT."

Ensly was more pleased than ever watching Craig sign the document. Craig checked the disagree box and slid the paper back.

"You want a showdown, Steele?" He fumed. "Well, you got one. Your life is about to get miserable. You better get to the gate. You're already running late for Haji duty. Move out, soldier." Ensly flashed his teeth as he barked the command.

Craig felt hot. A sweat broke across his forehead as he walked out of the tent. He complained to himself and cursed his luck. *Hallis wouldn't give that SGT's story a thought. I never thought Ensly would end up in charge of anything. It's a miracle that Ensly has made it so far in the Army already but this is unbelievable. Of all the Mickey Mouse bullshit. I'm going to be babysitting a bunch of Hajis because this paper pushing lifer without any imagination has it in for me.*

"You here for duty?" The duty Sergeant looked up as Craig walked in.

"You got it, Sergeant."

"Well, we're all booked up, but you can head out and see if any more crews show up. You never know. Go ahead and sign this sheet and head on over. If no one shows up, the rest of the day is yours."

"Roger that, Sergeant. That's the best news I've had today."

He made his way over to the corral and waited. A couple of soldiers from other units were there taking it easy. Sparking up cigarettes and sitting with their own thoughts, they relaxed in the shade.

"You believe this?" a soldier asked Craig as he walked up.

"What's that?"

"I've got this duty for a whole month."

"I hear you. I've got it for a while myself," Craig empathized as he took a seat nearby.

"Sweet gig, isn't it?"

"Come again?" Craig turned to him with a puzzled look.

"This is the best job I've had since I've been in the Army."

"How long have you been in?"

"Two years."

"And this is the best you've had it? What the heck do you do anyway?"

"I'm a cook."

"A cook? How'd you end up out here for a month?"

"I got caught with a female in my tent. They popped a surprise inspection on me. I think another girl of mine was jealous." He laughed. "How about you?"

"My NCO has it out for me, so I got stuck with this for a while."

"What'd you do?"

"Nothing, stopped some SGT from beating up an old dude."

"Hmm, I tell you what though, if I'm going to get in trouble, I want to get something out of it at least."

"I guess. So what do you like so much about this duty?"

"You kidding me man? This is cake. Especially days like this. You get here a little late at the end of the sign in time, and it's another day in paradise."

"So what are you going to do with your little piece of heaven?"

"Oh, my piece of heaven will be meeting me at my tent here in an hour, but for now I'm going to sit here and enjoy a smoke. I'll make my way back to my tent after I rest for a couple of minutes. When when my girl gets some free time, she's going to come on over."

"You trying to get kicked out of the Army?"

"Kicked out? Man, they ain't kicking me out. They can't get enough guys to do what I do. They have me working some crazy hours. I'm working ten hour days, sometimes more. I'll take this Haji gig any day."

"You joined the Army to be a cook?"

"I want to be a chef someday and it's the best way I could think of to get some real training."

"You cook back home?"

"Shoot fire! Did I cook back home? You name it. I would barbecue the best ribs you've ever had. But I want to learn how to cook those fancy foods that you see on those cable cooking shows. How about you, why'd you join?"

"Me? I've always wanted to be a soldier."

"Too much John Wayne and paint chips as a kid or something?"

Craig laughed. "I grew up around the military. My dad was in and my granddad had been in. It's like a rite of passage in my family."

"Like LT Dan in Forrest Gump?"

"Something like that, except we don't die."

"I see, you're the man of Steele, I'm Johnson."

"Yeah, good to meet you."

"So you just joined up because you thought you'd like it?"

"Pretty much. I did some college, but that didn't work for me. I don't like sitting around doing nothing."

"And so you joined the Army? You didn't know that most of the time all you do is sit around, huh? Hurry up and wait, now that should be the Army slogan. So now you're ticked about being here on Haji duty?"

"Yeah, I want to be doing something important."

"You need to broaden your horizons man. College is all about growth. This can be, too. Take me for example. I learned how to cook and now here I am deployed and I've got some ladies on the side. I've even got a little business that works just fine with the Army's timing. You can make this thing work, if you try. If you can't hack it, you may need to go join the infantry and run through the hills for a while. That might take it out of you."

"Why didn't you go to college, if you know so much?"

"College? Me? Man I've got two brothers and three sisters. No way I'm going to college unless I do it myself. Don't worry about me. Between the GI Bill and all I'm learning about business out here I'll be fine. I'll get a sweet setup when I get out. How about you, what are you going to do after the Army?"

"After the Army? I don't know. I'm not sure if there is an after the Army."

"A lifer? You don't strike me as a lifer. You don't have the patience for it. I can see it a mile away. If you're thinking about making the Army a permanent gig, you better get used to doing a lot of sitting around. Not to mention doing a whole lot of nothing. Should've picked up on that by now."

"This Haji duty may change my mind. We'll see. I've got some time on my hands to figure it all out."

"That you do, my friend. I think I'll catch a few Zs before I head out. It's been nice hanging with you but I have an appointment to keep after I bail. I need my beauty rest. Sounds like we can finish this tomorrow, or the next day, or the next. What'll you do after you leave here?"

"I can't go back to my tent. I'll check back in with that NCO that stuck me on this duty. If I don't he'll come by and I'll get roasted. Besides, like I said, I don't like sitting around doing nothing. It looks like we don't have any more crews coming anyway." Craig got to his feet to head back to the circus tent. "You better get a trip wire around your tent before you end up losing your business," Craig yelled over his shoulder.

"Not a bad idea. Later, bro." Johnson gave him a wave as he tipped his hat over his eyes.

Ensly was watching a movie on his laptop when Craig walked up and stood across the table.

"What are you doing here? You just trying to get some heavy UCMJ or what?"

"Nothing like that, Sergeant. I reported, but they already slotted all the work crews. They told me to wait a while to see if anymore showed up. Nobody showed so, here I am."

"Alright, Steele. You head back to the tent, because I don't want to see your face, but you'll pull Parker's tower guard tonight at 2200 hours. I'll see if I can round you up another to go with it. I'll send someone by to tell you when the second shift is. You'll have Haji duty again tomorrow so, don't worry, you've got plenty of time to pull it. Now get out of my sight."

"Roger that." Craig smiled at Ensly's frustration and headed back to the tent.

"You're back early from Haji duty. How was it?" Parker asked as he took a bite of a microwave meal.

"It was educational."

"Educational? What are you talking about?"

"Met a dude that is making his time here into some sort of side business. He was real happy to be getting Haji duty. Oh yeah, by the way, I also got your tower guard tonight with an option for another."

"Sweet! I don't have to pull duty tonight. Sorry about that, Craig. I told you to leave that Ensly alone."

"Not a problem. It'll give me some more time to think."

"There's nothing out here but time to think. You don't need any extra."

38
GO NATIVE

Craig began pulling Haji duty every day and tower guard every night or two. The days began to flow into a blur. It didn't seem like a big deal at first. A lot of sitting around doing nothing, but exhaustion started to kick in. The most unbearable part of the day was when he had to report to Ensly. Ensly ordered him to show up before and after Haji duty each day.

"I don't know how you put up with it." Charlie leaned back on his bunk with his DVD player and shook his head as he looked at Craig.

"What, baby-sitting Haji?" Craig sat down on his bunk after day eleven of Haji duty.

"No, having to deal with Ensly every day as he gloats about this whole thing. He's just toying with you and trying to get you to screw up again. He's like a cat and you're just his toy that he's smacking around."

"I'm not worried about him. Never have been really. I'm not sweating this duty either. The duty is the good part. It'd be worse if I had to look at him so smug behind that table all day. Not sure I could take that. I'll be done at some point and life will get back to normal. It's not like any of this stuff out here is hard anyway."

"I guess so, but I'd still want to jump across that table and take a shot at him."

"Sometimes I can't think of anything better than that either, but if there was ever anything not worth it, that would be it."

The days started to warm back up. It grew hotter by the day. Sixteen days later Haji duty had become the routine. The contractors and MPs became acquainted with him. He started to get the best crews since he showed up all the time. His crews worked inside, doing construction finishing off a site instead of sitting outside baking in the sun on a new project.

After some time he relaxed and decided to make the best of it. He started to chat with the contractors and ask what the word for this or that was to learn a little of the language. The workers would tell him their native language of Dari or Pashtu words for the object he asked about and he diligently wrote down the phonetic spelling. This encouraged the workers on his crews. It became a game of sorts to see who could offer a new word that wasn't in the book.

"This whole duty is getting way too easy." Johnson lit a cigarette as they sat in the shade by the cattle shoot.

"I didn't mean to miss the crews this morning. I wanted to practice the words I learned yesterday." Craig looked at the gate hoping for a crew to show.

"You're starting to worry me with all these friends you're making. You're becoming a local hero of sorts. Not to mention that thing with that old man. You becoming like that dude in "Dances with Wolves" or something? "

"Maybe. Maybe I'll sneak out one night and go native. Grow a beard, marry a woman with a burka and have little kids who'll hock old rifles and rocket propelled grenades to soldiers passing through."

"That'd be the life. Get you a little wife in every country you deploy to as long as they don't understand how the whole thing works."

"Maybe for you. Sounds like a scam you might run, but I think I'll pass. Say, I met a businessman like you up in Uzbekistan a little while back and he was looking for a partner that could provide him some products, food was something he was looking for. I told him I'd check around."

"Oh yeah? What did you have in mind?"

"I heard that sometimes food disappears, and sometimes when food expires you guys just burn it, that true?"

"True on both accounts. It's hard to keep that food locked down sometimes because there are so many businessmen around these days." He let out a smoke ring and smiled.

"Well, I need a person that is involved with those pallets up in K2."

"Sounds like you are starting to see the light, Craig. I know someone up there. Key question is what's in it for me?"

"I think you can work out those details with your contact up North. I can set up a meeting with my contact when you're ready. You co-ordinate with your guy for deliveries, if the terms work out for you."

"I'm surprised by you, Craig. I guess since you're going native I shouldn't be. He's a local, right?"

"Yep, he's a local guy who can pull the strings up there to make things happen. I've seen it myself."

"Might be a little trickier working with a local from way up there, but alright, I'll give my boy up there a call and we'll set it up. Glad to see you woke up to the opportunities out here."

"I'm just helping out a guy who needs it. Figured it might be useful down the road. You never know what might happen."

"You're a piece of work. You've got a moneymaking deal staring at you in the face and you pass it off?"

"Money comes and goes, Johnson. But it's always good to have friends."

"Not sure about you Craig, but you're on the right track at least. How much more time do you have?"

"No idea, I should be getting off this duty soon. I hope."

"I meant how many days 'til you rotate back?"

"I quit counting days, but it's getting close enough that I should, I guess. I think I've got about two months left, give or take."

"I've got about five, but I'll be heading home for some R&R soon enough."

"Let's get out of here."

"Alright." Johnson got up and they started the walk back. "You going to go see that SGT as usual?"

"Yep."

"You're crazy, but ok."

"You going to see that chick in your tent again?"

"You know it."

"You're the crazy one."

They made their way back to the main intersection and parted ways. Craig passed the MP's inspection to get onto the big circus tent compound and weaved his way through the officers to the commo shop.

"You off early again, Steele?"

"Yes, Sergeant."

"Regular schedule, duty at 2200 and 0300."

"Roger that, SGT."

Tower guard duty was becoming a habit. Check-in, head to the tower, stand around stare at nothing for a couple of hours then head back to the tent till the next duty. The sky was cloudless and the moon was full as he climbed the stairs and looked around. There was enough moonlight to see for a change. The village was dark except for the occasional light from a fire somewhere. Up the mountainside a fire dotted the landscape now and then. He entered the tower with a soldier from another section and they settled in. The buildings were washed in pale white. The moon was bright enough to cast shadows from the buildings and trees. The light made it look winter again.

They heard footsteps coming up the stairs to the tower half an hour into the duty. Once in a while an NCO in charge of duty would swing by to make sure they were awake. It kept them on their toes since they never knew when he might show up.

To their surprise a captain walked in. Two other people were on the landing next to the tower looking around.

"Evening, Sir." Craig didn't recognize the officer.

"Evening, boys." He made his way in as the others from the landing entered.

Craig's heart spiked. He almost stood at attention but caught himself. He stood up straighter just the same. The soldier from the other unit started to lock up at attention.

"At ease, Son." The general waved a hand quickly dismissing the formality.

"You boys see anything out there tonight?"

"Nothing out of the ordinary, Sir." Craig looked over his shoulder at the village then back at the general.

"You look familiar. Where do I know you from?"

"I work in the command tent, Sir. I'm in the commo section a few spots down."

"That's right. I remember seeing you around."

"How about you soldier? Things going alright for you out here?" The general turned his attention to the soldier with Craig.

"Yes, yes, Sir," he stammered.

"Fine, good to hear it." The general reached in his pocket then extended his hand to the soldier and shook it. The general turned to Steele and repeated the sequence. Steele shook the general's hand when he felt the heavy coin drop into his palm.

"You boys keep up the good work. I'll see you around."

"Yes, Sir."

The general turned and left with his entourage of officers.

Craig looked at the coin in his hand. The XVIII Airborne Corps logo was on one side with the general's two stars underneath. The other side showed the coalition flags surrounding the country of Afghanistan.

"I've never even had a coin. Now I get this one. This is awesome!" The soldier with Craig bounced the coin in his hand and beamed with pride.

"This is a nice one at that. Pretty cool thing to get pulling guard duty."

They looked at their coins in the soft light of the moon then tucked them away. The chatter about the coins died and they turned their attention back to the ruins in the distance to wait out their shift in the bright moonlight.

39

NVGS

Craig was on duty again at 0300 hours. It was harder to wake up this time. The grogginess of interrupted sleep was hard to overcome. He checked in and made his way back to the tower for his second shift of the night. The fog of sleep hung over him as he looked out into the night once again. He yawned spontaneously as he tried to shake off the accumulation of long days and nights.

"Hmmph," Craig let out as looked around. "This whole thing is getting too predictable."

"Tell me about it. Staring in the dark gets so old."

"You should try doing it a couple of times a night for a few weeks."

"Whatever dude, you taking a nap or can I?"

"Go for it. I'm awake now."

Craig thought the moonlight would make the night easier. More to see might make it more interesting. He was wrong. It was the same stillness except for the occasional rustle of grass in the slight breeze. It didn't take long for the scenery to become mundane even with the new found visibility. The endless days and nights had taken their toll. His body felt numb underneath his fatigues. His eyes grew heavier the longer he stared into the dark. His head dropped slowly. He caught himself and looked around startled.

Minutes passed and his head dropped again. His body swayed and his weapon squeaked as it pressed against the wood. He lost his balance then caught himself.

He looked down at the soldier sleeping on the floor. He thought about waking him then changed his mind. The shift was barely underway, but he was fading fast.

He started to move around the tower to get his blood flowing. He felt a little better. He was awake again and settled back on the sandbags to take up his watch. He rested the weapon on the bags. He shifted it to the left to get comfortable and leaned slightly into the wall on the sandbags. He watched the dark and his eyes grew heavy once again.

A twang broke the silence of the night air. It sounded like a scuffle had broken out somewhere. Craig's eyes sprung open. He wasn't dreaming. He heard another noise. It was off to his left.

Someone was on top of the hesco. Craig turned his weapon toward the figure. With his right foot he kicked back at the soldier sleeping.

"Huh? What?" The soldier was confused.

"There's something going on down the wire. Get on the radio ASAP. I'm about to shoot this joker."

"You serious?" The soldier slipped as he tried to get up in a hurry and his rifle clattered. The figure on the hesco paused and looked in the tower's direction then started to cross over. The other soldier stood, turned and grabbed the radio on the sandbag.

"Cherokee, this is tower five. We have someone on top of a hesco, we are about to engage over."

"Tower five, say again?"

"We have someone on top of a hesco, we are about to engage, over."

The figure on the hesco cleared the razor wire and threw something over the wire below then jumped on the lower hesco inside the compound. The figure rolled off onto the ground and jumped to its feet.

The figure looked left at the tower again and darted away from them heading toward the tents.

"Hold tower, let me get the lieutenant."

"I'm taking him down." Craig got the figure in his front sights and jerked the trigger. The distinct crack rang out in the night air. Dirt flew up a few feet to the left of the figure. "Watch the village," Craig ordered over his shoulder.

The figure looked back but kept running. Craig adjusted himself and breathed out. The slow exhale relaxed him as he sighted the figure again. He brought the target center mass into his sights. In the pause before his next breath, he squeezed the trigger gently.

The weapon jerked back as another crack rang out. He could smell the gun power as the round left the chamber toward its target. The figure dropped.

The other soldier took his position to look at the grass and buildings in front of him. His face revealed his confusion when the radio crackled. The soldier picked up the radio.

"What's going on? I heard shots fire, did you shoot?" the other end demanded.

"The intruder is down, I say again the intruder is down. We are scanning the area for others, over." He half shouted as the fear and excitement were evident.

The figured moved. His hand shot forward from his side. The explosion lit the night sky. The ground shook. The tower rattled as the energy wave passed through it.

Craig and the other soldier dropped down inside the tower. Dirt blew up then out over the compound. Metal ripped into the hesco walls. The sound of metal raced up the tower stairs and into the door.

Dust filled their mouths and noses. Craig opened his eyes then squinted. The dirt was like a cloud hanging over the area. It rained dirt down on the tower and the nearby tents.

Craig jumped to his feet and looked out toward the village. He scanned for any more activity, but it was calm.

"Tower five! What's going on out there?"

Craig grabbed the radio. "He had some kind of bomb on him or something," he stated disconnected from the adrenaline. "I shot him, he hit the ground, moved a little then he blew up."

"You guys okay? Anybody hurt?"

"No, I don't think so. He didn't get far enough."

"Ok, we're sending some guys over to check it out. You see anything else out there?"

"No, I'm looking, but I don't see anything."

"You guys hang tight. The QRF will roll out in a few but the LT wants to check on you guys in the meantime."

"Roger, tower five out."

Craig looked around then at the other soldier still on the floor. "You alright?"

"Yeah, I guess." He started patting himself down. "I'm ok. Wow, that dude had a bomb."

"Sure did. I wasn't expecting that. I thought he was going to pull a weapon out and start shooting or something. Glad we popped him when we did."

"No kidding. He could have killed a lot of people if he got to the tents. Wow."

The area was pitch dark once more as the cloud of dirt hung over the scene. The moonlight began to filter back into the area as the haze dissipated. The area began crawling with soldiers wanting to see what happened until the MPs secured the area and began to investigate the event. The LT checked on Craig and the other soldier then visited the scene below to see it for himself.

Craig watched in silence as he stared at the activity below. Once in a while he glanced out at the grass and ruins in front of the tower but his gaze drifted back to where the figure lay stretched out then disappeared. He could see the figure on top of the hesco again bouncing down to the ground before looking back and taking off. He stared in disbelief at the massive hole. The outward pattern from the hole was slowly disappearing as footsteps mashed the dirt back into the earth. It was like a dream now.

He couldn't begin to understand what would make someone want to do such a thing. *What would you get out of that? If that is their strategy to win a war how pathetically desperate is that idea?*

The investigation proceeded below. He watched and saw a soldier below point an MP to the tower. The MP walked to the tower and climbed the stair to the landing.

"One of you want to tell me what happened?" He held a clipboard and pulled out a pen as he entered the tower and looked at each of them.

"We were on watch, heard some movement over to the left. Then what sounded like some wire popping. Next thing you know I could make out a figure on the hescos so we called it in."

"So you didn't see the figure till it was on top of the hescos?" The MP turned and looked at the hesco wall below extending out into the distance.

"That's right."

"I can see the hescos pretty clear in this light. How come you didn't see him?" His lip curled up with a smirk. "You fellas sleeping on duty or something?

"Well, when you want to get us some NVGs or something then you can gripe about how we pull guard, till then we saw him when he was on top of the hesco."

The MP stared at them. He looked back at the hole behind him then at them again. "Alright, after you saw him what happened?"

"The guy dropped to the ground, looked back then started to run."

"So, you decided to shoot him?"

"Pretty much. There wasn't any time to interview him to find out what he was planning on doing. I thought at the least he could have a weapon or something so I should take him out."

"How about you? What's your story?" The MP pointed at the other soldier with his pen.

"It's like he said. He was on the left side so I couldn't see as much. I tried to call everything in, but it happened so fast we didn't have time to clear anything."

"How many shots were fired?"

"Two, the first missed," Craig interjected.

"But you didn't see him till he was on top of the hesco?"

"That's right." Craig's voice grew louder.

"I'm still not sure why you didn't see him till he was on top. I may have some more questions later." The MP finished writing some notes and looked at them for a moment. He walked down the stairs and returned to the scene below.

"Shoot, what was that all about?" The other soldier looked out of the tower door frame and looked at the MP and back at Craig.

"Sounds like he doesn't like how things turned out. I don't think it matters. The dude was a real threat and we took him out. Should we have gotten him sooner? I don't think they would have let us shoot him until he was inside anyway. Looks like it was for the best the way it worked out."

"I hope so. I don't want to get in any trouble or anything."

"What are they going to do? Send you to Afghanistan or something?"

40
THE GENERAL

The morning sun was already blazing as Craig walked his group to their building site. The spring weather brought an endless stream of building projects. Today his crew was installing windows in a newly finished building. He walked around to keep check on them as they worked scattered throughout the building in different areas. Lunch passed and he settled in a spot by the door downstairs. He closed his eyes for a moment to rest. He felt himself drifting into sleep.

A loud crash on the floor above him roared through the building. The figure next to the tower blew up and dirt was falling. He awoke instantly and was on his feet. He looked around and swung his weapon side to side looking for the enemy. His breath was quick and a light sweat broke out across his back. He saw the open room in front of him and remembered he was on duty inside a building. *Someone upstairs must have dropped something.* He laughed at himself. His nerves were starting to get to him.

His hands shook a little and he pressed his palm down his pant leg. He started his rounds throughout the building once more. Sleep was winning the battle with his weary body and it was starting to get dangerous. He was losing his grip on his own ability to tell how tired he really was. His mind was tricking him into falling asleep against his will.

"Steele!" He heard from the front of the building. "Steele!" A second call echoed through the open rooms.

The voice sounded familiar. He made his way to the front and saw Ensly standing with Charlie.

"Looks like I have your duty for a change." Charlie looked around the room.

"Huh?"

"You just seem to be in the middle of the action wherever you go, Steele." Ensly snorted as he escorted him out of the building. "The general wanted to meet the soldier who took out that suicide bomber last night. The colonel sent me to find you so you could do the meet and greet."

"Huh?"

"Heard about your big night. I swear, if I could I'd send you away. Excitement seems to find you no matter where you go."

"I guess that's one way of looking at it."

"The general will probably just want to hear what happened from you and shake your hand."

"Didn't he already get all that in the briefing?"

"Sure he did. He just likes to meet the guys who get the job done sometimes. Besides, the story is always best coming from the horse's mouth."

They made their way to the circus tent and back to the general's section. They were cleared to enter and waited for the general to finish speaking with an officer who sat across from him. The general sat back in his chair with his feet on the table in front of him. When the general noticed them he excused himself and stood up to meet them. The general's pressed uniform made Craig realize how wrinkled his own uniform was. He hadn't changed it in a couple of days either.

"Hey there SGT, is this the shooter that saved a bunch of soldiers' lives last night?" He smiled broadly and extended his hand to Craig.

"Yes, Sir." Ensly nodded and spit to his right. The general shot a sideways glance at Ensly then turned his attention to Craig once again.

"You look familiar. Have I spoken with you recently?" The general sifted his mind to connect the face.

"Yes, Sir. You visited the tower last night while I was on shift and gave me a challenge coin, Sir."

"Oh yeah, you're the soldier I keep seeing everywhere. You've had quite the deployment so far haven't you?"

"Yes, Sir."

"You look a little haggard. That event make it hard to sleep last night?"

"No, Sir. I don't get much sleep."

"Something seems a little off here. I saw you last night before all this happened and you were on shift then. How many shifts of duty are you pulling, Soldier?"

"Well, I..." Craig looked at Ensly with his eyebrows raised.

"Come on, Son, there's nothing here I can't find out," the general assured him confidently.

"I have a couple of night shifts topped off with a day shift, Sir."

"Is this true, Sergeant?" His tone became firm and he looked at Ensly with raised eyebrows.

"Uh, I, yes Sir." Ensly's voice cracked. "There have been some issues, Sir."

"Issues? Anything that I should be aware of?" the general demanded.

Ensly swallowed the tobacco juice in his mouth. "Uh, no Sir, I will check into it."

"Do that, Sergeant. I'd hate to find out we're endangering lives out here by doubling up on duties without good reason." The general turned his attention to Craig once more. "Sounds like you're staying busy, Steele. I'm glad you were on duty last night to make the right decision up there. Some people freeze up when it matters most. I'm glad you have what it takes to do what needs to be done."

"Yes, Sir."

"You promotable yet, Steele?"

"Yes, Sir." Craig relaxed finally. "I just passed my promotion board a few months back."

"You made any plans for your time in the Army?"

"Well, Sir,..." Craig shot another glance at Ensly. "I'm going to go to selection for Special Forces when I get back, if I can."

"Well, that's just fine, Steele. We could use good men like you. Have you sent in your paperwork yet?"

"No Sir, I just decided recently to go ahead and do it."

"Tom," the general called over his shoulder.

"Yes, Sir?" The major looked up from his computer.

"Tom, put a note down for me to call Mike back at Bragg so we can put in a word for Specialist Steele about an SF slot for him. We need these kinds of men and I don't want paperwork keeping this man from the training he deserves."

"Yes, Sir." The major nodded and looked back at his computer.

"Well, Steele I was going to give you a coin but looks like I already beat myself to it last night. Maybe getting you some help with you training would be better anyway."

"Yes, Sir." Craig smiled big as he looked over at Ensly.

"Well Son, I'm glad I got to meet you. Keep up the good work. I have another meeting here so you'll have to excuse me." He shook their hands and returned to his table.

"So you want to go SF, huh?" Ensly's voice shook a little as the words came out.

"I guess the general's call might just speed things along, huh?" Craig's voiced grew loud with excitement.

"One of the few ways to make something happen in the Army is to get one of those guys involved. So, about that extra duty stuff. The general will expect to hear it's resolved."

"He might at that, huh?" Steele enjoyed the moment as they walked back into the commo area.

"I think it will fade away. The paperwork will probably get lost in the shuffle. I don't think the general needs to be bothered with the details of those extra duties either. I'll just let him know its all been taken care of."

"Roger that SGT."

"Good, we should get your SF paperwork done and turned in ASAP. We need to have your stuff submitted when the general makes his call so it's in the pipeline and his people don't come asking questions," Ensly meekly instructed.

"Roger that, I'll do it after I get off duty."

"We'll let Charlie pull your duty today. Print out that paperwork and get it filled out so I can get it to the colonel." His face was pale. "I don't feel so good. Get that paperwork done." Ensly darted for the exit.

Craig enjoyed the moment. Ensly put his hand to his mouth and ran into an officer on his way out. The officer followed him wanting an explanation, but Ensly kept on without stopping.

The paperwork was simple. It was submitted the same day. Craig was back on the night shift and didn't hear anything for a month after he met with the general.

"Craig, get up."

A hand shook him awake and he looked up. "What?"

"C'mon, wake up."

Craig sat up and rubbed his face. "I have another crypto run to go on?"

SSG Hallis waited a minute for him to wake up. "No, but I thought you might like to see these."

"SSG Hallis, when did you get back?"

"Last night, but we got some orders in that you need to take care of."

Hallis held some papers out in front of him. Craig's heart sped up. He looked at the papers in front of him. The orders were to report to Fort Bragg for assessment in six weeks.

"Yes!" He jumped out of his bunk and punched the air.

"I thought that might be worth waking you up."

"Holy cow! I didn't really think it could happen that fast."

"A general can get things moving like God himself. If you want to take some leave when you get back you'll need to clear this post this week and hop a plane back."

"Roger that Sergeant, I'll clear in a couple of days. I have to get some training in. I have a lot of stuff to do."

"Don't worry about work, you're officially on the way home now. Do what you need to, but just remember the faster you're done here the faster you get home."

41

KING OF THE WILD

It was early when he arrived at the airport. Jessica met him hours before the sun came up. A thick fog hung low as they sat talking in the concourse. Each time they were together the conversations they shared left more questions than answers. It was good to be headed out to get some time to think it all through.

"I could try to call and go in late," she apologized.

"No, it's fine. This will give me time to get my focus before heading back."

"It was that rough?"

"Not sure what was harder, the deployment or our conversations."

"Well, soldier. I'm just trying to be honest with you. I hope you can handle it."

"Oh, I can handle it," he argued feeling the sting of the challenge.

"I hope so. I hope I hear from you."

"I'll be in touch. This thing isn't over yet. You've blown me away a few times so far, but I don't scare easy, so don't count me out."

"I have to get going. I'll be late..."

"So, can I at least get a hug or something?"

"Of course." She buried her head in his chest with an energetic hug. She held on for a moment.

"I don't want to get you in trouble, so you better get going. I'll give you a call after I get back."

"Okay, bye. I'll talk to you then." She looked up at him, squeezed him once more and let go.

She threw him a smile over her shoulder and he watched her walk back to her car and wave once more. He felt energized. He wasn't sure what was going to happen, but he knew he liked her. He had a lot to figure out in the meantime.

Craig stared at the phone. The airport was busy. The bustling energy of the soldiers ready to deploy or go home was electric. Travelers being paged echoed through the concourse. He knew he needed to call but had put it off with excuses while he was out-processing. He didn't make time at Jessica's place to call and now time was running out. He finally, decided he should call regardless of what his parents might think.

"Hey, Son, it's good to hear from you. You heading home soon?" His dad answered.

"I'm actually headed out of Germany today. I'll have to do some in-processing when I get back before I can take leave though."

"That's great to hear. It'll be good to see you."

"It'll be good to get home for a while before I go to training."

"Oh yeah? What training are you headed to this time?"

"Well, I met this guy who gave me some advice similar to yours. He told me to get out of the Army so I am."

"Getting out? How can you do that? You just got in."

"I'm taking a shot at the Special Forces. I leave for the assessment course six weeks after I get back."

"Special Forces? That's not quite what I had in mind, Son. I was hoping for something more like trading stocks and bonds or selling real estate. Go become a lawyer if you have to, but Special Forces?"

"It's pretty great, huh?"

"Not sure I'd say that. You sure you want to do this? I'm not sure how your mom's going to take this."

"Well, it's your fault, Dad."

"My fault? Come again?"

"Remember that talk we had on the back porch when I was home for R&R?"

"Sure, what about it?"

"You told me I could get killed in a car wreck at home just as easily as I could get shot in Afghanistan. That made a lot of sense. It helped me relax. When I was back on the job I worked with some SF guys and realized they get the best of both worlds. They get to mix with the locals and kill the bad guys. It couldn't get much better."

"Glad I could help," his dad let out half-hearted. "I tell you what. Why don't we talk about all this when you get back before you decide to do it."

"Too late, Dad. I already have orders."

"Orders can be changed. I'm sure we could talk with someone."

"I already did. I talked with a Special Forces captain that got me this slot to go to the assessment course. Not to mention the general that called in to get my orders moving. I can't skip out on this now. It wouldn't be good for my career to turn this down after strings that were pulled to get me this shot."

"Career? Son, you're moving pretty fast here, don't you think?"

"Not at all, Dad. This has been a long time in the making. I'll be fine. I'll be home in a week or so and we can talk all about it then, okay?"

"Okay, Son. I tell you what. I won't tell your mom so you can tell her."

Craig could see his dad's smile through the phone.

"Don't worry, Dad. I'll tell her."

"When you tell your mom, leave me out of the conversation, ok?"

Craig laughed out loud. "I have to give you credit, Dad. It was all your idea."

"No, you can really keep the credit for yourself on this one."

"Alright, I have to get going, but I just wanted to let you know. I knew it would be a surprise but that you'd understand."

"Not sure I do, but you need to make your own way, so that's worth something."

"Thanks, Dad. I'll see you soon." Craig hung up and heard his flight announced.

He grabbed his bag and headed to the gate. The bag was light on his shoulder. The sun broke through the clouds and lit up the runway. A dark gray C-5 awaited him on the tarmac. His heart skipped a beat as he saw the long body of the gray beast. New adventures awaited him and this ride would take him there.

The bottom was used for cargo headed back to the states so he found his seat on the second deck of the plane. It was packed with soldiers headed home. He settled into his seat for the long flight and pulled out his orders again. He couldn't believe what he read. He reached for the cross under his shirt and held it. Conner was right. He was headed out to become a combat soldier. He was headed to Fort Bragg for Special Forces Assessment. The dream he had since he was a kid was finally coming true. He was headed out to become a king of the wild.